Acclaim for *Tumulus* by

Andrew Murray Scott's first novel,
Tumulus, won the inaugural
Dundee Book Prize and was
published by Polygon in 2000.
Two of his non-fiction books have
been published by Polygon: a
biography of Alexander Trocchi,
The Making of the Monster, and
*Invisible Insurrection of a Million
Minds: A Trocchi Reader* which
he edited. He is presently working
on a collection of short stories.

Estuary Blue

Andrew Murray Scott

© Andrew Murray Scott, 2001

Polygon
An imprint of Edinburgh University Press Ltd
22 George Square, Edinburgh

Typeset in Sabon
by Hewer Text Ltd, Edinburgh, and
printed and bound in Great Britain by
Creative Print and Design, Ebbw Vale, Wales

A CIP record for this book is available
from the British Library.

ISBN 0 7486 6291 X (paperback)

For Frances

Contents

Acknowledgements

Big River by Johnny Cash © 1957, Knox Music Inc – All Rights Reserved – lyric reproduced by kind permission of Knox Music Ltd (Carlin) London NW1 8DB.

Cry Me A River, words & music by Arthur Hamilton © 1953 & 1955 Chappell & Co Inc, USA. Warner / Chappell Music Ltd, London W6 8BS. Reproduced by permission of International Music Publications Ltd. All Rights Reserved.

Lyrics from *You Don't Miss Your Water* © 1962 (Bell) by kind permission of Rondor Music International / Universal Music Publishing Ltd.

Estuary Blue

Part 1

Ebb-tide

1

It's deeply ambiguous. All these empty hours, an absence of water, warm sands stretching to infinity, drying under the sun. Lulled into complacency. Seals, sluggish dots on a hazy invisible waterline. But the waters are coming back. When you least expect it, the pent-up ocean is yards away, swirling over the submerged reef a mile a minute, a high white line of surf coming in upon me.

The shore and the forest is a mile away. During the quiet hours the water has been sidling innocently between sandbars, swelling 'the pool' between me and the shore. I run heavily across the darkening silt. The water glides perfectly, colourlessly, into my footsteps and catches me around the ankles . . . *leaving no footprints* . . . An oystercatcher *kervee-kervees* in alarm. There's sea on all sides.

Each time I think I'm not going to make it. Water, rough, salty, surges at my legs and thighs. Water swells, buoys me, water up to my armpits. But I keep my feet, aiming for the trees, finally skipping out of the playful shallows, collapsing into the low dunes, sand sticking to me, sand all over, breathing hard but breathing. I half-close my eyes and listen. My heartbeat. Bursts in the silence of war planes from RAF Leuchars. Like needles stitching ribbons together across a silk sky. Machine-gun fire stuttering from the military range at Barry Buddon. And nothing else but the sheer percussion of being alive. Being at a low ebb can never be a permanent condition. Life is change, always ambiguous, going both ways at once, having two faces.

3

Four weeks I've been here, illegally, in this beautiful place. Despite byelaw 13 – no tents, sheds, caravans or other structures for the purposes of camping – living in a bender in the woods. It's a National Nature Reserve; the green tiger beetle, the grass of parnassus, the coralroot orchid, the greyling butterfly – and me.

Alive. Walking in the shelter of the dunes round by the Point I see a white object reflecting the sun. Smooth away the sand around it, delve it out. It's not a stone, it's a warm seashell, light and hollow, full of echoing air. As large as my palm, its five whorls revolve anti-clockwise, unwinding into bloatedness. Silky yet chalky dry to the touch. The inner spirals glisten with an oily iridescence, a ghostly reminder of the soft-bodied mollusc. I hold the wide aperture of the empty vessel to my ear.

At first, I can't hear anything at all, then faint echoes. Of many stories, many voices, of ceaseless poundings in mountainous seas bulging and sucked upwards by the moon. I try to visualise the immensity of the weightless, soundless depths which it has scuttled or floated or been carried across . . . plucked lightly from a warm beach in the shade of palms . . . the Gulf Stream to the Azores, the North Atlantic. Passing through all the blue waters of the world and all the beaches. Yet here it is, intact, a perfect fossil. It blocks the sunlight and a warm glow spreads through the chitin. I place it reverently on the sand-scuffed log, and walk on, as if it was just something washed up and discarded at low tide in an estuary.

2

Daniel Morrow closed one eye and swivelled the high-powered telescope on its tripod seaward over the wide waters to gaze at a ship he could see coming in off Tayport. He let his eyeball rest for a few minutes upon it. A battered oil supply vessel with a powerful derrick crane mounted aft and coils of rusted iron hauser, creating a huge wake at her stern. The *Aretina*, a boat he'd noticed coming and going many times. Without taking his good eye from the glass, he reached in front of him to the windowsill with his left hand and his fingers found his drink. He took a sip of Pimm's through the plastic straw and let it cascade slowly down his throat. He could hear Kylie snivelling below in the walled patio. Stoned, at three in the afternoon! But he shouldn't have slapped her. She was just a lassie.

Impatiently, he moved the telescope around looking for something interesting to focus on. Perhaps some girls sunbathing on the raised gardens of Tayport, or yachts up on the stocks on the north quay. His eye was caught by something winking, sun on metal or glass, in the trees at Tentsmuir Point, and a thin line of smoke. Kids probably, playing at camping. It'd be nice out there now, in the heat, on the beach. Valuable land. Ideal for a top of the range private estate. Marina Drive, or Estuary Villas. A fortune to be made.

The mobile telephone exploded into its dizzy digital serenade on the oak desk behind him. Not wanting Kylie to hear, he withdrew into the pine-panelled bedroom at the top of the stairs that was his den and it was Steve of course. Just Steve.

5

'How's it goin, man?'

Wearing only his Calvin Kleins, Morrow slumped full-length on to the massive bed. He lolled luxuriously across the black silk duvet cover, enjoying the coolness on his body. 'Yeah?' he said, then laughed, 'yeah? Yir a mental cunt, ir yi no? Ir *name*? How dae eh wahnt t' ken that?'

The sunlight flooded like syrup into the warm-wooded room through dormer windows as he talked to his younger brother Steve in the penthouse in Knightsbridge that was one of their four homes. He had been banished there, to keep him out of trouble in Dundee. Steve was a wee bit retarded, somewhat slow on the uptake, not that it was ever mentioned in the family.

Daniel ran his fingers through the greying black hair which he kept short to draw attention from his receding hairline. In his late-forties, his physique had lost much of its youthful vigour, and had gained a swollen belly (too much beer and late-night curries at the Serang of Hoogly) which signified a slump into seal-like middle age. His broad face had a kind of swollen bluntness with a permanent suntan that comes from frequent expensive foreign holidays.

'Steve,' his voice went softer, in case Kylie had come into the house, 'Steve, eh wahnt yi t' dae sumhin fir iz, man. Aboot . . . aboot . . . ach, hang on a wee minute . . .'

He stood up, and slipping a casual hand inside his boxers to rearrange his genitals, slouched to the door and looked out of the porthole at the top of the staircase. He could see Kylie on the patio, in the recliner under the trees. He could see her bare legs, her top half was obscured by the sun umbrella. He stood watching, enjoying a cool breeze on his damp skin, feeling the twinges of desire.

'Steve, y'there? Yeah, look, speak t' thi lawyer . . . Barnet? Eh that's thi boy. Jermyn Street. Get um ti transfer a thi accoonts in thi name o Aretina Investments . . . yi listenin, eh? Fir fucksake, this is *important* man! Nothing on paper, mind . . . Yeah. Transfer ut ti Jersey, ken. Eh, owir thi next twa weeks. An mak shair ee laves thi accoonts open . . . yi got that, eh?'

He put down the phone and slouched across the room. Caught

6

sight of himself out of the corner of his eye in the drawing-table mirror. A strong oily, blunt face fastened with small ears. In one lobe hung a large gold earring. The thick lips crooked open to reveal a gap and some gold in the smile. Beneath the suntan, the smart, cropped dark hair, and the coal splinter eyes, was the Morrow swarthiness of his grandmother, a full-blooded Catalan. Gyppos they had been called at school, him, Steve, Kevin and Tracey. But he'd long since outgrown the pleasure of rubbing their noses in it and most of the old Peter, Paul and Mary's crowd were on the dole. He grinned at his reflection. It was the face of a man fully-grown into his forties who could afford to indulge the child in him. He roared when others whimpered, he blustered when others reasoned, yet despite his lack of education he'd had guile enough to listen when others blabbed their innermost secrets. He'd got on. Done better than his parents had dreamed possible. Bought them a quarter of a million pound villa at Balmerino in North Fife. *Eh. Me. Mehsel. Eh done that!* Daniel's eyes drifted downwards. Ah. He sucked his belly in. Must try to resume his exercises, maybe get a personal trainer. But the sight of his own body exposed in the mirror was unaccountably making him horny. For some reason he was already thinking of the student dancers Rachel, Sally and Kirsty and the rent-free flat he'd installed them in at Cunningham Street. The thought was acted on without delay. He picked up the mobile phone. After a few minutes, when a voice answered, he said:

'Zi Rachel? Aw – Kirsty? Yahriyt? Z' me, like. Yeah, Danny. Wha else? Ehm comin roond. Na – thi noo. Eh, yi lassies beh'ir git yir knickers aff!' Ten minutes ir that, yeah? So wut? Yi ken ehm a horny bastard.'

He pulled on chinos, a yellow cotton polo shirt and a pair of Gucci loafers and went out by the back door. He pinged the remote to unlock the red Ferrari Colibra and drove out underneath the still-opening electric gates, and at the road, turned towards the city centre. Kylie wouldn't know he was gone until he got back. By then she'd be over her sulk.

In the luxurious apartment at Lowndes Street in Knightsbridge, Steve Morrow crashed around, barging doors and raging loudly in incomplete sentences. 'Wut diz . . . wha dizee think . . . how dae eh hae ti . . . a thi bliddy time . . . ehm right fed-up wi ut an a!' A large blubbery child in man's clothing, he too had the dark Morrow cast, but a weaker strain, almost concealed by a puffy fleshiness that had softened the lines around the face and filled out the cheeks. He was sweating profusely around the oxters of his white polo shirt, which seemed too small for him and he wiped at his eyebrows with his sleeve.

He pulled a beer from the fridge, uncapped the bottle on the wall gadget and returned to the dim chocolate and cream living room. He slumped full length on to a brown leather sofa which could hold six with ease. It squealed on the wooden floor under his bulk. He hoisted the bottle to his lips. Now he had to see that bloody bent lawyer again, a man he hated, a posh toff who made him feel out of place in the modern, smoked-glass office. 'How kin Dan no dae ut hissel?' he complained to the empty room. 'Ee kens beh'ir than eh dae.'

He stared at the large television screen. Live tennis from Wimbledon. He watched without interest, barely recording the moments when the girls' skirts flirted up and showed their pants. He could feel the sweat at his palms at the thought of the responsibility which Dan had thrust on him. He had hoped to go back to doing the easy stuff like in the beginning, he didn't like all this financial wheeling-dealing. He hankered for the early days when all he had to do was give some guy a doing, or take bags of money and hide them. He liked it too even before that when they were just joiners, fitting up kitchens for old ladies in Balgillo or Perth Road. But Dan and Kevin laughed at him when he came out with this kind of talk. Called him a 'throwback', so he had to go along with it. Anyway, he didn't want to get the jail again. Six months was enough, and they said that one thug in the family was all that was needed.

Anyway, Serena was coming over later, so he could forget his worries till tomorrow. Even although she was an East-End scrubber, an escort girl, he'd grown attached to her. He knew she wouldn't rip him off; did what he asked without complaint and he paid her and she left. Not like that fat cow June who'd left him after going with the guys he used to call mates. June. Least he didn't have to worry about her anymore; she had dropped anchor and was safe forever and he didn't believe in ghosts, never had. Saved him a fortune in legal fees, not to mention costs of divorce. He was glad, glad, absolutely fucking ecstatic! And Dundee, little shit-heap of back-stabbers gossiping in a dialect no-one else could understand. Naebdees! He took a long slug of beer and belched. Better here, where he could be anybody he wanted.

The entrycom buzzed in the hall.

Cigarette smoke spiralled softly in the stagnant heat of the derelict jute factory which smelled of dry decay and crumbling plasterwork. Kevin Morrow, a shark of a man in jeans and a white T-shirt, leaned in a stray puddle of brilliant light on the concrete pier of a loading bay. He looked disinterestedly around him at the derelict remains of the former jute mill where vast fortunes had been made in the nineteenth century. For every hundred square feet of ground, he'd make a hundred grand clear, he reckoned. Four floors of flats. Half a million, maybe more. He flexed and unflexed the biceps and deltoids of his right arm, then his left. Throwing his muscles into tension up to the apex of his shoulders. His trapezius muscles stood out, accentuated by the suntan. He grinned to himself, his serrated teeth white against the tight tanned skin of his face and the crew-cut which was little more than a dark shadow across his hammer-headed skull. He was in better shape now than he'd ever been. To prove it to himself, he abruptly turned and launched his clenched fist against the wooden batten hanging by a wire flex from the smoke-blackened rafters. The batten twirled frantically, untwirled, slid to the ground, bringing with it a pile of dry rubble in a great crashing and smashing. A cloud of dust rose briefly then subsided in the stagnant light. Kevin flexed and unflexed his fist and looked at it. Not a scratch. He brushed down his shoulders and reached to the fag packet in his jeans back pocket, abstracted a Capstan full-strength and his gold lighter. He inhaled and exhaled slowly through his gills, his eyes alert. There was now no sound except the trickling of retreating rats in the fallen masonry, the flicker of subsiding dust motes – which his eyes detected at the extent of

9

their range – beyond the vast black pool of oil. But he was early. The sounds of cars at the junction of Caldwell Lane and Dundonald Street were muffled by the enclosed empty space of the old factory which he was going to convert to housing. He looked around and gloated. £45,000 each, on average, the bastards were going to pay him, and some a lot more. Built with large amounts of public money to subsidise the construction of low-cost housing for first-time buyers, it was impossible not to make a killing. He didn't need to put any of his own money in – except for a bank loan – but he took *everything* out. And in months the 'first-time buyers' would have quietly resold, as per arrangement, to new owners after a hefty price-hike. Easy money, and all he had to do was confirm the purchase price.

He heard shuffling sounds, and at the far end, a beam of light glanced around the empty space as a wooden door, previously relieved of its padlock, swung grudgingly inwards over tumbled plaster. He grinned. Molison, the Council's Chief Development Adviser, was going to get his shoes dusty!

'Ah, there you are, Mr Morrow!' he called fearfully, a long way off, picking his way over the rubble.

Kevin Morrow made no attempt to move towards him, leaning back with folded arms and a slight smile crooking his thick lips, waiting for Molison to reach him. Several times, the older man stumbled and exclaimed, then he stopped, wiped his forehead with a handkerchief, glanced nervously at Morrow, and said, 'Terrible mess?'

'Implying mibbe,' Morrow spoke quietly, 'we should hae oor meetins in yir office?' His small black eyes gleamed as he laughed and threw down his cigarette, which extinguished itself with a sputter in a small puddle of dust-coated oil. Imagine wearing a dark suit on a hot day like this? he was thinking. No wonder the cunt was sweating.

'Oh, no, not at all, here is okay, Mr Morrow – Kevin . . .' Molison said, summoning his energy to surmount the rubble that separated them.

'Glad ti hear ut – Jack . . .' Morrow said mockingly. He took out another cigarette and lit it. 'Noo yir here, Jack, kin yi tell iz when that application o mine iz comin up in front o thi posse o arse-bandits yi like ti creh thi Cooncul?'

'Eh, yes . . .' Molison undid his shirt top button and loosened his tie. 'It's going through the processes . . . my staff are dealing with it . . . it will come up at the August meeting . . . the 25th, that's . . .'

'Yeah,' Morrow interrupted him. 'Eh ken, thi second meetin o thi committee in August. Christ! How no thi first meetin? An August? Wut thi hell am eh gonna dae till August month? Eh?'

'I'm sorry but that's simply not my problem,' Molison said, wiping at his red face with a handkerchief.

'Bit ut's meh problem. Eh? Kin yi no hae ut moved up, takn sooner?'

'No, because the Council doesn't consider applications till August, so even if I could prioritise it, it would only be a matter of three weeks.'

'So ehm buggered, iz that thi story, eh? Wut aboot haein a word wi thi heid-bummer, ken, yir Provost boy?'

'Wouldn't help. Anyway, I'm wondering whether that might not cause waves . . . ?'

'Cause waves, oh *dear*?' Morrow sneered. 'Wi canna hae that!'

'But you could surely get a start on clearing this . . .'

'Yeah, yeah. Ut'll gae through ahriyt, eh?'

'Oh, yes. I'll – we'll – be recommending approval. The Council wants these inner areas improved. Even though the site will need to be redesignated from industrial use to residential . . . No problem though, but . . .'

Morrow looked up sharply, 'Bit?'

Molison looked uncomfortable. 'Oh nothing really to trouble you, but there will be conditions. The usual stuff, about the specifications, the numbers of flats, stipulations about not being resold within five years, the usual . . .'

'Aw eh, a coors thull be conditions,' Morrow said, grimacing, 'bit ehm peyin yiz fir t' see thi dinna gie iz grief.'

'Very kind of you,' Molison said, 'it's much appreciated . . .'

'Kind? Za lang bliddy time since abdee said eh wis "kind". No even meh ex-wife says eh wis "kind". Bit here's yir dosh.' He reached down and lifted the Tesco plastic bag which he had brought with him. 'Thirz twa grand here,' he said. 'Bit yud beh'ir mak damn shair yi earn ut, Mister Molison.'

Molison coughed and dabbed at his mouth as the smoke and stagnant dusty air got to him. His eyes were moist. 'I will, I will,' he croaked, as he grasped the plastic bag and began the tricky journey back to his car outside.

Morrow watched him go and finished his cigarette. Then he stood up on the concrete pier and stepping with the agile step of a man in peak physical condition, made his way across the sequence of narrow planks that he had placed end-to-end to surmount the rubble. He reached the small firedoor which opened to Caldrum Street. He liked to know what was going on. And he didn't like to lay out spends until he felt sure he would get the go-ahead to develop. Now, he could afford to wait until late August before confirming the land sale, a day or two before the Council rubber-stamped Molison's approval. Until then this site was a derelict property with development potential, costing its owners, CD Properties, property tax, council tax and God knows what else tax.

3

When Daniel came in there was an exotic aroma in the kitchen. Of course, it was the middle-aged bustling figure of Mrs Thompson who was in command, controlling switches, concocting plumes of steam. Kylie slumped at the breakfast bar with a tall, colourless drink, one hand propping up her head. She looked bored, as usual. Her hair seemed greasy in the glare of the striplighting.

'Mrs T,' he greeted respectfully. 'Somethin smells brah.'

'Ehm bored!' Kylie moaned. 'Kin we no gae oot thi niyt?'

He looked at her and distaste twisted his words. 'Yi no batherin t' dress noo, eh?'

'Eh am dressed,' she slurred.

'Eh, fir thi beach! Wut'll Mrs Thompson think seein yi hingin' oot lik that?'

Mrs Thompson studiously ignored them. A trim, active lady with piled-up hair who came in four afternoons a week to clean and to prepare the evening meal. She kept her opinions about their family life to herself. The job was well paid, cash on the nail. She never took sides although she pitied the young lass. It was a funny set-up: he much older than she. They didn't seem to get on. They'd only been married four months, including the month's honeymoon in Antigua.

'Git up thi stair an git proper claes on,' Daniel ordered, fingering his earring. 'An wutzat yir drinkin?'

'Soft drink,' she said, sulking. She slid off her high stool and left

13

the room, shaky on her feet. He suspected she'd been boozing it up all day, the lazy bitch!

'Wut hae yi got fir iz thi niyt, Mrs T?' he asked, with as much cheerfulness as he could summon.

'Lamb curry with various sauces. It's all in here, rice, poppadums, naan, and a green salad to go with it – that's in the fridge. I've opened a bottle of wine. Everything's ready. All Mrs Morrow has to do is serve it up.'

'Shull jist aboot manage that,' he said sourly, removing his jacket and folding it on the seat, on top of the attaché case.

'Well, I'm all done, so I'll leave you,' Mrs Thompson was saying, moving out into the hall. 'I'll see you on Monday.'

Daniel was thanking her when Kylie reappeared in the kitchen, stark naked.

'Ehv nothin ti wear,' she complained. Like a spoiled brat.

Mrs Thompson permitted herself to raise one eyebrow but she didn't let her lips curl fully into a smile till she was outside of the electronically controlled gates and walking back towards Fisher Street. She wondered if she had ever had such a perfect figure herself, such white clear-complexioned firmness, a sort of mermaid ripeness that glowed. But little Miss Rich Bitch was not happy and she should be; they had everything money could buy. The kitchen where, four days every week, she prepared their meals was kitted out with all the gadgets and luxuries technology could offer. It had been gutted and renovated at a cost of £36,000 on the wife's whim after their honeymoon, but she hadn't even learned to boil an egg. It was more sad than anything. At first, she'd tried to show her how to do basic cooking but she wasn't really interested. It bored her.

Back in the architect-designed opulence of The Fort, Daniel was on his second glass of wine. Kylie was in tears in the bathroom. The Indian meal, disregarded in the upper compartment of the oven, gave off faintly exotic aromas.

Daniel's mobile went off. He took the call in the study which overlooked the patio and the high wall beyond, and yachts tacking in the bay. A train emerged soundlessly from the steep-sided culvert at the bottom of the steep slope and ran along the foot of the garden, its roar completely muffled by the triple-glazing. Lights

14

were coming on across the water, streetlights, dots of orange and headlights, dashes of lemon yellow, the white of windowlights, and a vertical line of red; radio-mast on the hill.

When he returned to the kitchen he felt hungry. He helped himself to a plate of curry and rice and sat at the breakfast bar. Drank more wine. Presently, he heard movements elsewhere in the house, doors closing, opening. Kylie reappeared, looking chastened, in an emerald Emmanuel cocktail dress. She had dried her eyes, which looked red-rimmed and her lip had that characteristic pout that betrayed her mood.

'Thi food's brah,' he told her. 'Come an eat sumhin.'

Kylie nibbled a poppadum and put several spoonsful of curry on to a plate full of oven chips. She had chips with everything. She sat at the other end of the breakfast bar and pointed with the TV remote. Daniel poured himself a third glass of wine.

'Brah this, Australian.'

He went over to the cooking range and helped himself to more curry and rice and the selection of chutneys and sauces. He turned. 'Wahntin salad?' he asked. Kylie sullenly stared into her plate, forked a chip into her mouth and said nothing.

'Treh some a this,' he coaxed. 'Good fir yi. Mrs T says . . .'

'Eh dinna like ir,' Kylie said slyly. 'Eh dinna wahnt ir in meh hoose.'

'How no? She diz ir job. Shiz no a gossip an meh goad thirz loads t' gossip aboot uf she wahnted, wi you paradin in thi bufty.'

'Git rid o ir.'

'No way. Yi kin forgit ut.'

'She diznae like iz.'

'Dinna gie yirsel a showin up. Shiz only here t' clean an cook an she diz a brah joab. Michty, uf eh hud t' live aff wut yiz cooked . . . ehd . . . well, eh cudna . . . ehd sterve. Yi shid treh this, it's brah.' He sat down and watched the TV. Some programme about fashion, fronted by a blonde nyaff with flashing big teeth. Kylie stared at it and slowly forked chips on her plate without looking down. Her fork lazily scraped the plate. She was too young. Should never have married her. On the rebound from Suze. A big mistake, she never gave him any peace. Always wanted to be out on the razz.

She was turning to the drink in a big way too, now she was off the Peruvian nostril dust.

'Wull tak a wahnder doon t' Shoals later, uf yi fancy ut,' he said. 'Yi cud gie some a yir mates a bell, eh? Mak it fir aboot ten.'

'Okay,' Kylie said without enthusiasm.

He felt slightly annoyed. 'Yi dinna hae ti.'

She slumped upright and slipped off her stool. 'Eh'll phone Farrah an Shivonne,' she said, abandoning her plate.

Daniel clucked his annoyance. 'Shivonne! Eh canna bear that wee hoor. Eh dinna mind Farrah, an that wee . . . Elizabeth, iz ut? Bit that Shivonne's gonna git yi inta trouble. Thi erse shiz hingin aroon wi, wuts eez name . . . ? Barry . . . eh. Eez lang overdue free plastic surgery. Eez a lippy cunt. Stey awa fae um baith, Kylie, eh? Ehm telln yiz!' He glared at her. 'Ji hear wut ehm seyin, Kylie? Pey attention tae iz, eh?'

Kylie left the room.

Daniel flicked the remote switch to disconnect the TV, then began to pluck pieces of the coconut naan bread and poured himself the remainder of the bottle of wine. He was not looking forward to the evening ahead.

Shoals' nightclub, tucked into a secluded corner of the Seagate, had been profitable since the early 1980s when Derek Ivins made it into a club to cater for the over-thirties. Previously it had been a notorious dive, frequented by under-age scheme gangs. Often raided, it was the place to buy speed, e's, or participate in large-scale drink-fuelled battles to prove your manhood. After the brutal aftermath of one teenage riot, it had finally been closed and lay empty for six months. But Ivins had seen his chance and got it cheap off the owner. He started with a midnight licence only, then got it up to one, then two, by sending a teenage girl, a real stunner they said, round to an empty council house at the secluded back of Trottick once a month. A ground-floor flat opposite the trees and the pond. The Convenor of the Licences Board arrived there in a taxi from the Downfield Social Club, sometimes with his wee mate, the Convenor of Properties. And they got an extension, next time Ivins put in for a late licence. It was recommended for approval on the grounds of providing a useful social amenity. And when a bunch of ex-High School toffs tried to open a club along the Cowgate, he'd simply had to send two teenage girls, both stunners, to stay the night. As far as he knew half the Administration group had been up there that night. Not that he wanted to know, or at least that was his story. But Ivins had got too flash with his dosh, bought a big boat and first time out it hit a sandbank and got its arse ripped out. Soon he had cashflow problems. Kevin had got onto that at the start. He'd got a girl working at the place who told him Ivins was shagging a waitress. The waitress was a bit frightened of Kevin's smiling intensity and blabbed the lot to him after just two Bacardi and Cokes; where Ivins kept the genuine bar receipts, who his bent accountant was, all the strokes he was pulling. So Kevin put him a word to the wise and the brothers breezed in together just when they knew Ivins was desperate. Offered him a deal, which they ratted on after a month. Threatened him with the dud receipts, offered to help him with his problems with the taxman. Ivins was stuffed, but instead of having him done over they kept him on, as bar-manager, with Ged to oversee everything. It was much less hassle than having to get a new licence and, anyway, Ivins had the teenage sirens the Licences Board chief was keen on, so everything was kept quiet, but everyone said the Morrows made lots of improvements and Shoals became a big success. The over-thirties rarely caused trouble and had more money to spend. The only problem was stopping other club owners from moving into the over-thirties market. But that's another story.

See eh yased t' git Gary t' keep thi moh'ir runnin. Riyt ootside thi Ferry Port bar in Ferry Street, ken, in front o thi croods trehin ti get in. Then ehd step oot thi Roller, an dead casual like, eh up any dames in thi queue, then ehd push past thi bouncers an wahtch abiddy clear oot mi road. Thi barmaids, mibbe Linda, mibbe Sheree, ud pour meh cocktail in thi hehball gless an ehd hae a look aroon an see thit sumdy hud pit a wurd t' thi wehz ti thi cunts wha wir sittin at meh table under thi green striplights waur ye cud wahtch thi door fae t' see whas comin in. Like magic they cunts wir awa.

17

Ehd sit there sippin on meh cocktail wi a thi ithir cunts sloppin beer an pishin thirsels and trehn no ti look at iz. Then some lass wid lave ir mates a giggly an titter-titter, ken, an come up ti iz, then ut wid be free drinks a roond an ehd mak ut clear eh hud a Roller ootside an a michty big wad. Soon ehd git on thi mobile (an z' afore a'cunt hud mobiles) an ehd phone Kevin or Ged or Barry, an get thi gang a ready an mibbe they'd come doon t' thi Ferry Port ir meet iz at The Fort. An Suze wid hae t' git oot ir pit an let thi fuckers in.

Afore closin time, wud be aff, haeing a riyt giggle t' wirsels oot tae thi moh'ir ir taakin taxis ir that. They lasses kent wut t' expect cause wurd ud gaed roond, ken. Nae prick-teasers. Bit sometimes yid get some dumb bint wha didna ken thi score so yid ti pit um riyt. Ane niyt eh hud a French lassie, 'n exchange student-teachir ir some shit like that, comes up ti iz an shiz a riyt dolly ir that an ut a seemed ahriyt bit when eh got ir in thi Roller, fuckme, she sterted comin thi cunt, like, an widna gae doon on iz. Widna even git ir knickers aff. Wut thi fuck shiz thinkin o, eh dinna ken, ir mebbe ir heid wiz fuhll a mince . . . An a thi lads wir pishing thirsels at iz. So eh hud Gary drehvir oot t' thi middle o Angus an drap ur aff in fields. Pitch-fuckin-bleck. Yi wahnt ti play thi coo, eh tellt ir, y'kin eat gress a niyt! Teach thi cunt, eh. Anithir time some ald dame, forty if shiz a day, wiz giein iz rumpy in thi backseat an some bastard's rappin on thi back windae. Get t' fuck! An uts ir fuckin husband, ken, thi wee hoor wiz merriet! Tell thi cunt ti wait eez turn, Gary, eh sais. Tell um ee kin hae seconds! An Gary keeps thi locks on an thi cunt wiz going mental. Pure mental. Bit when eez sterted kickin thi chassis, man, that's when eh hud t' sort thi cunt oot. Brak eez fuckin neck, near. Fifty grand Roller! Cheeky cunt! Eh tellt um wut's wut.

'Daniel!'

'Eh, wut . . . ?'

'Wake up.'

'Wut . . . aw, ut's you,' he said, looking up at Kylie's sea-blue eyes and the blonde wisps that tumbled over her cheeks. 'Babes – eh wiz far awa. Wut izit? Wut ir yi wahntin?'

'Thirza fax come in fae Ged, sumhin aboot cash.'

'Aw, fuck, kin ut no wait . . . ? Ahriyt, eh'll be there in a

18

minute . . .' He swung his legs over the sides of the bed and rubbed at his temples. He blinked and tried to eradicate the previous night. His eyes had gritty, sand particles in the corners that scratched when he rubbed. He looked at his watch through watering eyes. Shite! It was nine, half past. He could see from the skylight that it was dark. He'd slept the day away. What the hell had he being doing . . . ? Ah, Kirsty . . . and Sally. Some night. No wonder he was shagged out. Kylie must have gone home by herself. No, he remembered. She'd been with Farrah and other mates of hers. Said they were going to the Casino.

'Git iz a gless a wattir, babes, eh?' His mouth was furred and slick with salt.

'Daniel,' she said, handing him the phone . . . 'Eh need t' speak t' yi.'

'Eh, okay, later, babes, eh.' He ran his hand over the stubby whiskers around his mouth. 'Ehm gaggin, gonna git iz thi wattir . . . ?'

4

With numerous houses and apartments in Dundee, London, New York, Cap d'Antibes and St John's, Antigua, the Morrow Brothers' empire was rumoured to exist in the convoluted financial accounts of dozens of companies which congealed on the taxman's desk like dead jellyfish. The Inland Revenue had tried in 1998 when Daniel's company BM Investments Ltd was prosecuted for minor health and safety infringements after a workman died on a building site at Cupar. The workman's family sued; Daniel offered £120,000 then declared himself bankrupt, selling the assets and the existing contracts to another of his companies. In court he claimed he was a paid employee of the companies and had no hand in running them. With one eye on the Sheriff and the other on the Bible, he said he was 'the typist and apprentice tea-boy'. Even the Sheriff was seen to guffaw at this. Daniel left the Sheriff Court with two fingers to the press in Bell Street. Climbed into the backseat of his Mercedes Benz and was driven away. It had all blown over. The law couldn't prove a thing. They were left loudly braying in an empty courtroom. Or at least, that's what Daniel was imagining when he sent a pound of carrots to the procurator fiscal's office by special delivery the next day.

But the taxman had made things more difficult. Although their money was spread worldwide, the source of it was local. The Morrows were big fish in a small pond. They felt uneasy away from the source of their wealth. In London or New York at some swank event, there was always the risk that they'd let fly a mouthful of pure Dundonian. They felt easier where they could lapse into the dialect of the streets – even though that often spoilt the effect of power. They were awash with public money, in the form of development grants. Millions had been siphoned from government agencies for grant-awarded renovation work in the schemes and for converting dozens of inner-city jute mills into blocks of rented flats. They had people on the inside of course; possible because it was a small city. If shrill voices were heard from time to time about public money being paid out to companies whose ownership was overseas, beyond Scottish legal jurisdiction, there was a strong lobby for work at any price. Many cheered to see the pace of redevelopment of the old and derelict industrial wasteland. If one or two of those who cheered the loudest did happen to have gone to school with one or other of the Morrow brothers, or were friends of Ron and Betty Morrow from Charleston Social Club, well – so what? Indeed there had been attempts to persuade Ron to stand for the Council in a safe seat but his health wasn't good enough these days.

'Thi stinkin tabloids jist need a photie o iz thigithir,' Daniel had said, when they secretly met up, more than two years ago, at the Loch Tay Hotel at Kenmore, sixty miles away. They'd driven there separately and parked at the back of the palatial building beneath some of the tallest trees in Perthshire. They drank cold beer in Daniel's suite on the first floor, eating salmon sandwiches. Daniel had brought along one of his lawyer friends from London, Derek Rutherford. 'An uf they kin jist git that one wee snap o iz thigithir at a meetin like this, then wir fucked. An thiv got wut they need fir t' kick aff a story. Ehm an undischarged bankrupt, yi'r stull director o thi companies an Steve iz director a maist a thi trusts.'

'Eh, bit ut's a legit noo . . .' Steve had complained, belching. 'Wut kin they dae aboot iz?'

'Ah, Stevie boy, listen, eh? We ken ut wid be difficult, even bliddy impossible fir um ti prove . . . bit wir no wahntin thi hassle o haen um crawlin' a owir iz. We wahnt ti keep wirsels low key.'

'Eh, well,' Steve had quickly changed tack. 'If that's thi story, ehd prefer ti stey doon in London. Ehm bliddy seek o this toon.'

Daniel ignored him. 'Wull keep oor meetins ti a minimum, an

21

nae cunt wull prove nothin. Thull be nae link, jist a bliddy paper-chase that leads nae-where. Thi taxman will be shafted.'

'Ehd love t' see that,' Steve grinned.

'Thi taxmen hae t' accept compromehzes,' Daniel continued. 'Z wut Charlie Mudie tellt iz. Ee yased t'be a tax inspector hissel, like. See, thir a public servants. Thir peyed beh results, ken. Z lang iz we pey mair tax thin we yased ti, thir happy. They ken wir at ut, bit they ken thuv nae time an money t' justify thi expense o trehin ti find oot whar uts a posed.'

'He's right,' said the young lawyer, Rutherford, quietly at the window, staring gloomily out at the rain-swept lawns and the well-cut privets. 'Happens with most companies. It's a kind of game.'

'We jist hae t' be careful. We kin meet when we hae ti, bit we need t' plan ahead an vary oor schedules. Wull hae mules fir t' cairry important messages between iz an wull yase fax machines fir oor reports. E-mail iz owir risky – material kin be intercepted an thi messages sit in electronic mailboxes fir owir lang. Naw – fax is best – an safest. Wull also lay false trails fae time t' time an ehm haen thi most dangerous hacks in thi area wahtchd. Thull git thi shit kicked oot o um uf they git owir close. Eh kin arrange that.'

'That yased t' be meh joab,' Steve grinned.

Daniel turned to look at his youngest brother. 'Bit noo yir owir important fir that kind o thing. Yull keep yirsel oot o trouble in London, savvy? An be available fir special projects.'

'Wut diz that mean?'

'Ut means trips abroad,' Kevin said. 'T' thi Bahamas, ti Miami, ti Jersey, t' mak contacts, t' confirm deals, that kind o thing. Yi kin slip awa easier than Daniel an me.'

'Eh?' Steve's grin broadened. 'That's brah.'

'Kevin, yull continue t' handle thi property an development an eh'll keep an eh on thi clubs an bars,' Daniel said. 'Ut's aboot a ehm able t' dae wi Mister sodding Trustee Kennedy sniffing up m' erse whenever eh lave thi hoose.'

'I thought his job was done,' Rutherford said. 'They should have called him off by now. The Crown Office report was completed ages ago.'

'True, bit Kennedy's got some kind o personal grudge. Dinna

worry. Eh've got um under control. Eez gonna come up smelling a shite.'

'That's sorted, eh, boys?' Steve grinned. 'Mair beer?'

'Help yirsel.'

Rutherford fiddled with his tie. 'I think you're right to cut down your meetings but won't it be tough on family life?' The brothers had fallen apart at this but Rutherford was being serious. The prat.

The building site, being near the top of a hill above Tayport, was clearly visible, but getting to it was another matter. It was Kevin's first visit to the development since the land had been acquired and he hadn't bothered to consult the site maps. He just assumed he'd find some kind of entry road via the Bett Bros' Tay View development. So he drove up Scotscraig Drive and found himself in a blind, in a Balmullo-chipped drive, looking into the blank windows of a two-bedroomed semi which he'd expected to be the show-house.

So he went out and back on to Scotscraig Drive and drove up the next right-hand turn and immediately saw the large sign he had somehow missed: JB DEVELOPMENT CONTRACTS. SHOW-HOUSE. It was beyond and above the Betts' site, behind the water tower, on the crest of the hill. The road to the site was unmade, a dusty track, deeply rutted by heavy machinery. The old farm lane. On either side were the uprooted corpses of substantial trees. They'd had to use cranes to get them out. Kevin parked the jag opposite the showhouse, which, he noted with disfavour, was closed, although there was a young couple in a car sitting outside it. Clearly waiting. He noticed signs of work in progress in the crescent of house structures but no sign of anyone. All the roof timbers were now on, and the felt, but no slates. They were more or less on schedule.

Kevin gathered up the files from the passenger seat. He got out and went over and tapped on the window of the other car. The girl wound it down.

'Waitin t' see thi showhoose?'

'That's right,' the girl agreed. 'We'd an appointment at eleven. Are you . . . ?' she hesitated, seeing his jeans and T-shirt.

'Naw. Ehm here fir a site meeting wi thi buhlders.

'Architect?'

Kevin shook his head and grinned. 'Director o thi company.' He was gratified by the girl's warm smile.

'Oh, so you're the boss?'

'Ehm thi boss,' he agreed, 'so eh'll treh ti find oot wa's in chairge o thi showhoose – an fire thi lazy b . . .'

She laughed. 'Thanks!'

Kevin strode off down the curving crescent of half-built houses looking for signs of activity. Nice people, first-time buyers. Girl was well worth it. Although there was equipment lying around he couldn't hear anything happening. In the sixth house, exactly halfway along, was a dumper truck and a stack of pallets. He heard voices inside the house and stepped into the foundations on to bare earth and saw stacks of plasterboard propped on battens. The men must have heard him but they weren't bothered. Football they were talking about.

'Looking for the showhouse, mate?' a chubby-cheeked ginger-haired youth in brown suit and loosened tie genially asked. He was pouring tea from a thermos into two mugs. The other man was older, in overalls, a flabby man, maybe late fifties. Kevin recognised him, a joiner. He glared at the youth.

'Naw, ehm no, you are, pahll!' he growled slowly, indicating the door with his thumb. 'Thirza couple oot thir wi an appintment fir eleeven. Ut's gone bliddy ten past.'

'I'm just going to open up. Soon's I finish my tea.'

'Yir no listenin. Noo. Open up noo. Git fuckin' movin, chum! An beh thi beh, wut's yir name?'

The youth slowly placed the thermos on to the stack of plasterboard. 'Eh? Who are you, when you're at home?' he demanded.

'Same iz wha eh am when ehm in meh oaffice,' Kevin snapped. 'Yir boss, that's wha, yi shitey wee cunt!'

The youth jumped to his feet, mouth open, breathing heavily. 'Oh. Oh, aye. Right, Mr Morrow.'

'Wut's yir name, sonny?'

'Johnstone. Fraser Johnstone.'

'Right. Eh'll mind ut.'

24

'I'm Stan Dawson,' the joiner said, apropos of nothing as he screwed down the flask stopper. He made no attempt to move and continued drinking his tea. 'You micht mind o iz fae ither sites. Eh kent yir dad.'

'Eh mind yi fine,' Kevin said, bending to remove some sticky paper from the sole of his shoe. 'This site looks fucken slack ti me.'

'It is a Settirday, yi ken. No mony lads in thi day.'

'How many, exactly?'

Dawson leaned back and screwed up his face. 'Ach – the young lad, me and anither jiner, Bill Edgar, aye, and twa laddies as labourers. But thir awa doon t' thi yaird t' fetch mair plesterboard.'

'That Johnstone's a cheeky wee toerag.'

'Eez no bad. Lads these days yi ken, thir a thi same. Dinna wahnt t' work at a. Different fae meh day.'

'Spare iz thi trip doon Memory Lane.'

'Eh wis jist seying . . .'

Kevin held up the flat of his hand. 'Eh ken, eh ken. Wut ir yi on thi day?'

'Feenishin thi straps fir t' tak thi plesterboard.'

'Aye, riyt. Okay, ehm awa t' meet thi site engineer.' His eyes narrowed as he squinted at the joiner. 'Ken thi boy, dae yi? Eh mean – t' see?'

'Gillanders? Eh. Eh ken um. Bit eh've no seen thi boy thi day. Eh doot ee'll no be in.'

'Riyt, well. See yi.'

'Eh, see yiz eftir. Mind me ti yir paw.'

'Eh'll dae that. Ehm seein um this denner.'

But it wasn't the site engineer Kevin was meeting. He'd seen Gillanders at the office earlier in the week and everything was in order, or as near as any building project was likely to be. It was Jack Molison he was waiting for, and the snooty bastard was late! He sat in the car watching the salesman chatting to the young couple in the showhouse. He could only see the upper half of the girl but she seemed well put together. The man was a tube. She was doing all the talking. Johnstone would probably lock up and have a wank when they left.

It was almost twenty to twelve before Molison put in an

25

appearance, driving cautiously, like an old woman, up the lane in his R-reg Toyota Celica. He parked carefully on the verge behind Kevin's Jag and got out.

Kevin greeted him without enthusiasm or remonstrance and they walked casually along the crescent of unfinished houses. He had wisely carried some files from the car as a blind but there was no-one watching. Kevin didn't like the air of natural superiority Molison exuded even when he was the paid minion.

'Thi last ane,' Kevin said gruffly. 'Abdy that sees iz wull think yir a contractors' site engineer or that.'

'Right,' Molison agreed, picking his way through the rolled hard-core in his expensive brown brogues.

'In here, ut's floored.'

They walked up a wooden ramp into the corner house, a detached villa, four bedrooms, top of the range, and stood in what was going to be a feature-window L-plan lounge. Their shoes rung hollow on the dusty bare floor. They stood at the windowless space which afforded a prime view of the sun winking on the estuary mudflats and the village of Tayport, the Lucky Beacon, and over to the north, the castle at Broughty Ferry across the water. Standing in proximity to the Chief Development Adviser, Kevin was unable to avoid the miasma of cologne that exuded from him. His nostrils wrinkled. 'Poof' was the word forming defensively in his mind. He could not conceal his dislike, which made brittle his conversation, honing his words into blades of enmity.

'Yi hae thi list fir iz, Molison?' he demanded hoarsely.

Molison coughed discreetly behind his hand and spoke hesitantly. 'I had a terrible job – oh, just terrible – but, yes, I did get you a list. I had to – of course – make out a case – because the development is so large, and, well, quite near, on our doorstep – so to speak – that, um, our Council was interested in it. I had to take their Chief Planning Officer out for a round at Rosemount and it cost me a hundred quid. A hundred.'

'Meh hert bleeds fir yi, Jack.'

'But then you're on your own,' Molison added, looking embarrassed, his soft hands coming up to pat his bouffant white hair. He shifted his feet, grinding plaster dust on the floor. 'I mean I can

26

reasonably only help with matters inside my own authority,' he said apologetically. 'I think that's fair.'

'Yeah, yeah, well . . . gies ut then.' Kevin gauged the urgency of his desire to smack those pink foppish hands, to tear the laundered lapels of that suit, to spoil, to rend . . . Even just to slap . . . once. He closed his eyes. No.

Molison slipped a hand inside the front of his smart grey suit and withdrew pages folded neatly, which he offered to Kevin without looking at him.

Kevin unfolded the pages and quickly scanned the lists of names and addresses. He reacted violently. '*Fuck*! Twa hunder an forty-three objectirs! That's owir thi score, man.' He waved the paper angrily within inches of Molison's startled face. '*Twa hunder an forty-three*! Thirz no that number livin within a mile of thi fucken site. Wha rattled thir cages?'

Molison strove to reassure him. 'Only thirty-eight actual objectors. The rest just signed their names to a letter of objection that was put up in the village shop.'

'Eh, bit thirty-eight z' bliddy lot objectirs fir a development wey oot in thi middle a naewaur.'

'It is. That's true,' Molison sympathised, playing with his hands. 'There's no disguising it. That was what I thought when I saw the list. Of course, quite a lot of them are only objecting to the removal of the trees. Not the development itself. Others are bothered only about the scale of the project.'

'*Trees?*' Kevin grimaced. 'Bit thirz no wey we kin keep thi trees. Snoh technically possible. Meh engineer sais thi roots extend well inta thi site. They hae t' come oot. They block thi view. That means lowir prices.'

'If it was coming up before my Council, I'd be looking to retain some at least of the existing trees,' Molison suggested. 'Even just to keep the locals on board.

'Fuck it, ehm plantin tree-screening riyt through thi development. Thull be mair trees when ut's feenished than wut thir iz noo.'

Molison patted at his lips with a monogrammed white handkerchief. Kevin stared at it with ill-disguised loathing, and felt his fists involuntarily clench.

The handkerchief was folded and replaced in Molison's breast pocket. Kevin watched every detail of its passage.

'Well, that's true of course,' Molison was saying, 'but these existing trees are several hundred years old and there is a sentimental attachment towards these old copses and woods.'

'Bit thir no under any kind o preservation ordir?'

'I believe not.'

'Naw. Thir no. Thir jist ald fuckin trees. And thir in thi bliddy wey. They dinna fit in wi thi concept o thi fuckin project. Imagine a new toon separated fae thi river beh a bliddy forest! Ut wid be fuckin laughabul! Eh mean – thirz a marina attached t' thi development so thir huz t' be parkin an access.'

'I understand. I do. I'm an engineer myself. But some of the planning committee, from what Paul Sheridan tells me, are practically obsessed with trees. There's a councillor, Jill Hogue, for example . . .'

'Aw – hur – shiz aff ir trolley. Social workir?'

'Yes.'

'Could yi no bliddy set up some kind o bliddy conference or that an git ir invited as guest speaker – eh dinna ken – some kind o social workirs' coafee moarnin ir sumhin fir thi day meh application comes up?'

Molison ignored the question by sneezing and rapidly applying his handkerchief to his nostrils. When he resumed equilibrium, he said: 'She's not the only one I understand. Most of the opposition councillors will back her just to make a stink.'

'Uh-huh,' Kevin scrutinised the names on the list. 'Z thi name o sumbdy fae Tayport. Unbelievubul! How dae eh ken this name, Marjorie Braid?'

'Oh yes. She objects to lots of developments throughout the area. In Dundee too, she's listed as an objector for the Caldwell Lane site if you remember. She's a teacher in Dundee. One of the founders of the action group.'

'Eh ken ir name fae sumplis.'

Broughty Castle reflected the sunlight which flashed from the windows near the sloping roof where, Kevin knew, there was a

28

viewing gallery. The Union flag hung limply. There was nothing further to be said.

'My advice about the project,' Molison said, 'if you're looking for advice of course . . . ?'

'Eh?' Kevin almost barked. 'Wut?'

Molison stepped backwards and one of his soft hands flew upwards as if to defend his mouth. He coughed and dabbed at his wet lips. 'Ah, um,' he said. 'The new town concept has gone off the boil a bit. Yes, Sheridan tells me there was too much opposition to it in general. So they've moved back to the idea of infill developments. A little bit here and there, peripheral to existing communities where these wouldn't strain existing services. It's the sheer scale . . .'

Kevin snorted. 'Z no wut thir bliddy seying t'me pahll. Z far iz ehv been tellt ut wiz thi easiest an less . . . controversial option. Thi ane likely t' loss um thi least votes. An thi site is bliddy perfect. Bugger ut – thi hale ehdea o scale cam fae thi damn Cooncul in thi first place. Ut wiz on thi original fuckin tendir. Ut's been in thi Area Plan fir years an bliddy years. Anyway, Molison, this is owir brah a project fir t' be stoapt beh arguments owir bliddy trees. Ehm stakin athin on ut. Eh'll git ut sorted, jist wahtch iz.'

'If there's nothing else . . . ?' Molison queried, wiping his lips with his handkerchief.

'Nut. Na, that's a fir thi noo.'

Kevin let Molison lead him back to the cars and followed some distance behind. He stopped outside the sixth house. The sounds of hammering. Stan was a worker alright. He remembered him well. He had given useful evidence – been loyal – at the Cupar Inquiry when Daniel nearly went down. He was right about the younger generation too. Workshy bastards the lot of them. The showroom was closed and he saw Johnstone sauntering along the main road to Tayport as if he hadn't a care in the world. The wee bastard was defying him! And those other bastards hadn't returned from the yard with the plaster-board. He'd mention it to the foreman and have them watched.

The snarling noise of the motorbikes woke me. I was drowsing then with my head just out of the flap of my little tent, and the rest of my body naked on top of my sleeping bag in the captive heat of the tent. A stray beam of sunlight opened up through the leafy screen above me and stood on end like a wonky striplight. I could see flies already busy in the warm air. The bikers were nearby but their noise came to me intermittently as they scrambled around the muddy tracks through the forest, between the tussocks and wooded mounds. Illegal, of course. There is a notice posted about it at the entrance to the forest, and a wooden barrier constructed to keep them out, which they ignore. You can see the deep ruts they've made around that particular obstacle.

So it must be Sunday. A day of bells, coming muffled to me in the forest from the parish church at Tayport. Sunday was the day they usually came, roaring out from somewhere else in Fife or from the city, on their high-powered racing bikes with the stuttering, tinny engines. Like modern highway robbers they'd come at you suddenly around a bend, the lower halves of their faces masked by white scarves, leaving behind a blue cocoon of petrol smoke to unwind loosely in the air above the track.

The worst thing about it was that their noise might attract the police – not that there was any real danger of my bender being discovered. In the weeks I've been here plenty of people have seen me, but they just assume I'm out for a walk. They wouldn't have a clue I've living here. Generally, people aren't that curious, and some are put off by my appearance. These clothes of mine are starting to deteriorate. The stitching's going and there are a few rents and tears. Luckily, there's several good charity shops in the village that have a good selection of second-hand clothes. I'll be making my weekly visit tomorrow. And my weekly visit to the new Leisure Centre for a swim. A luxury I look forward to. Always make sure the pool is empty or very nearly by going early in the morning before the schoolchildren arrive, and before pensioners' happy hour or whatever.

I interrupt these interesting musings to raise myself on my elbow and ferret into my plastic bag of provisions (which I keep suspended from the wooden spar that acts as the crossbar of my tent to deter ants) and locate the jar of coffee and a piece of camphor fuel tablet. And the matches in their tupperware cup, sealed to prevent moisture. In a minute or two I'll have water boiling for my coffee. The bikers must have gone down the other end. It's hot though. Given the position of the sun, I guess it's only mid-morning.

I pull myself out, feeling the stiffness in my lower back and at my hips and thighs. I do my exercises on the flat piece of soft pine needles between the two trees from which my tent is anchored. It's dry and dusty, a good exercise mat. As I stretch and limber up, I observe my fellow creatures, black ants, filing up the ridges in the rough bark of a fir tree. I'm more than happy to tolerate them since they tolerate me. The double plastic sheet under the sleeping bag works wonders. At first, I seemed to get a lot of bites. Doesn't bother me now. Suppose my hide is tougher.

I take my coffee over to the treestump which marks the entrance to the raised knoll of my campsite. I'm enjoying the warm breeze on my bare chest and legs. I can look from here down the coastal track back in the direction of the village and Lucky Scalp or east to the Point and Abertay Sands or north across the estuary to Barry, Monifieth and Carnoustie. There's only one person in view, a woman walking her dog. I've seen her before. I know she doesn't have a dog. Carries a lead though. Maybe it died. The tide is out and about a quarter of a mile away vast numbers of oystercatchers and gulls – some great black-backed – are feeding on invisible food at the water's edge. The sky is a little uncertain, piles of dramatic and very well-defined cumulonimbus clouds hang low over Angus and the North Sea, but there is a lot of blue too shifting behind the white gauze as if somebody is applying bandages to stop the world leaking. The blue means nothingness. It means that you can see twenty miles straight up, right into the atmosphere and right off the earth and, if your eyesight was miraculous, out to the stars and planets that litter the cosmos. You've a direct line of vision into deep space with nothing but a few layers of air molecules – nothing more substantial – to stop you falling off!

There's nothing like the kick of hot coffee in the open air at the beach when you've a day of pleasant contemplation planned. And nothing else. Even if the milk is slightly off. The bike noise has stopped. I suspect they've gone down to Kinshaldy beach. Wonder what disturbed them? Ah well. Yes, there! A bell, bells. Calling the faithful.

And I'm enlarging by one more day this quiet space I presently inhabit, this wonderful semester of silence. One more day when I can avoid the issue, remain uncommitted, keep my brain free from the clutter. If this was India, I'd be a sadhu, or a yogi. In Tibet, a lama, but here at my tent at Tentsmuir, I don't have that level of commitment, nothing in the way of faiths. We may deserve a life but what we get is existence. Tomorrow I go to the swimming pool and learn to live underwater for seconds even minutes at a time, a complete reversal of the scheme of evolution, not even breathing. I will buy clothes and that is affirmation enough. I will finish the bread and cheese, the sardines and the chocolate and clean my teeth with the soft twig like that Biafran, Jeff, whom I shared a flat with in London in the early days.

London. After ten years, coming back, the thought of having to register at the dole, of looking up relatives, friends – of starting again in my hometown – seemed too much effort. I was drawn up from the railway station to the river and stood there in strong sunshine at the taffrail to read the bronze inscription on the plinth about the opening of the bridge, 1966. The long, narrow bridge, windscreens of traffic winking all the way along it. Two and a quarter miles. Hadn't walked it since I was a boy. Why not walk it again? The beauty of the day led me along the road east to Tayport and from there out along the forest. It was a working day. I didn't meet a soul in the cool green shade inhabited by dancing midges. I sat down on a fallen treetrunk to watch a wren fidget in the crevice of a broken concrete pipe. Time was passing slowly. The tide was coming in then, pouring into the empty chasm between the populations of Angus and Fife melted alluvial ice, centuries old. It's a landscape that springs your imagination into the past. A mile over water, the fishing village of Broughty Ferry, the Lifeboat Shed, cannon turrets on the castle ramparts, yachts at Grassy Beach. In the west, the slump of the Sidlaw Hills, familiar as old school chums. Familiar too the city of my own past – my childhood. The politics of place, the meaning of location, us, here, now, came surging warmly into my mind. I wanted to think about my childhood there. And about the metropolis I had abandoned. To come to some conclusions. I was empty of feeling, a hollow man, drained and bloodless from living on nothing but dreams, deteriorating, laid up in the doldrums. I needed to feel the sun, the wind and rain, to make raw contact. This place seemed a suitable vantage point, a mirror for my emotions recollected in its tranquillity.

It's amazing how little money you need to get by. Tea-bags, the odd tin of beans. Luckily, there's a stream, and plenty of rabbits in the part of the wood two miles away where the men have been tree-felling. I snare them at the runs under fences and roast them in mud in a hole in the ground. I allow myself an occasional half-bottle of whisky. I'm living on less than a fiver a week. Cleaning my body out, all the shit of the London years. I've never felt fitter, or slept sounder. Rentfree, guiltfree, hasslefree. Well, almost. The midges can be a nuisance, and the clegs, but you get used to them. And even if the men who work in the forest were to come across my bender or smell my little fires, the worst that could happen would be that I'd be escorted out of my paradise. And I could always come back.

5

'**C** 'mon,' Kylie said to the girls. 'Let's awa up. Mibbe some nice laddies wull chat iz up.' She didn't care if he heard or not.

'An wut wid yir hubbie say?' Elizabeth put in, the wee sook.

'Awa an pish,' said Kylie to herself as she pushed her way through the crowded bar. Most of the guys had clocked them when they came in. Elizabeth's strawberry tattoo on her shoulder and silver nose stud, white wrap-around top and a micro-skirt. Farrah the bottle blonde with thick overhanging Jennifer Aniston hair, cropped pink top and belly-button ring. Shivonne's ample proportions crammed into a black velvet bustier.

'Thirz a hunk owir thir,' she was saying, pointing with her cigarette. 'Thi laddie in thi black jeans. Git a swatch o eez erse!'

'Eh, snoh bahd,' the girls agreed.

'Ee thinks eez Erchie, though, diz ee no,' said Elizabeth. 'An eez got awfy big lugs.'

'Aw – yi kid pit a seck owir eez haid,' Shivonne said. 'Wha's bathered aboot eez ears?'

'Ehm no half bliddy needin a shag!' Farrah confided. 'Eh've no hud a laddie fir bliddy weeks.'

'Me an ah. Ehm on thi puhll thi niyt!' Shivonne thrust out her front and downed her Bacardi Breezer in a gulp.

'C'mon,' Kylie said. 'Eh like this ane.'

'Ahriyt. Eftir you.'

The girls exploded on to the dance floor. Conscious but un-

34

heeding of the looks they were getting. Kylie, in her emerald silk dress moving rhythmically, in a trance, fingers popping, moving with a kind of intuitive synergy in the dark-slashed light. It was what had attracted Daniel first, her dancing. Even though he was a married man. She was a kind of peasant, a pampered, teenage siren enslaved by the voodoo. When she was dancing was maybe the only time she was outside herself enough not to be melancholy. She was not conscious that she raised the temperature, upped the beat, increased the pressure. Made things interesting for the men who flapped helplessly in front of her, making urgent movements which she failed to see, doomed, like dying goldfish.

The floor raved with the pulse of house music, *Ibiza Anthems 99*. Kylie and a hundred others jammed together close, flailed and screamed at the air, letting it all go. They danced as an entity, a hydra-headed monster, now touching each other, now pushing each other apart. Hers was a performance in as much as it could be seen and separated from the pulsing mêlée by the roving spotlights.

When there came a break in the relentless beats, Kylie returned to herself, and opened her eyes, bathing the floor in light. The men looked away, desiring her but unwilling to meet her eyes. Most felt more alone for having seen a glimpse of something which only offered confirmation that it was beyond reach. And the girl walking from the floor with her friends was breathtakingly ordinary.

They stood at the bar. Shivonne pushed through to them.

'This is Alan,' she mouthed, tugging the forearm of the boy in black jeans they had been admiring earlier.

'Nice erse,' Elizabeth remarked, making a big show of putting her hands on him. The boy grinned. He had short dark hair, well cut, and neat sideburns, and a physique – obvious through his V-neck black vest – that came from the gym; broad freckly shoulders and the bearing of an athlete.

'Mariah Carey's new ane!' Shivonne shouted, grabbing the boy away from the bar.

'That's thi last wull see o ir thi niyt,' Elizabeth said. 'Eh need a drink.'

'Bet she gits a shag – an we dinna! Thi lucky cow!' Farrah exclaimed.

'Wut's she got that we dinna?'

'Mair brass neck, that's wut. Shiz a riyt brazen wee hoor.'

'Let's phone thi bar,' Farrah suggested, 'an git that nice Colin t' bring wir drinks owir. Eh canna be arsed standin at thi bar.'

'Brah ehdea! Go fir ut.'

The girls clustered around the payphone in the foyer, giggling and pulling at each other to get to speak to Colin.

'I'll get the drinks in,' offered a posh-looking bloke called Gordon.

Elizabeth was annoyed at his interrupting her chat to a guy called Brady or Brody. 'Na, dinna bathir. Colin wull bring um owir. Eh'll hae a Morgan's spiced.'

'Pineapple Bacardi Breezer fir me,' Farrah said.

'Hooch for me,' Gordon said. 'An my mate will have . . .'

'What about me? I'll have a pint of Stella.'

'Wha thi fuck ir you?' Elizabeth shouted. 'Ugly pus.'

'He's my mate,' said Gordon. 'Sam. He was born that way.'

'Eh, well, git yir hand affa meh erse, riyt!'

'I'm not!'

'He's cool, it's okay . . .'

'So, wut d'yiz dae?'

'Well, sumbdy hud eez hand on meh erse . . .'

'I'm a student,' Sam said, running his fingers through his cropped orange hair. 'At Abertay. Fancy dancing?'

'Eh, wha'r yi askin?' Farrah and Elizabeth asked simultaneously and burst out laughing.

Gordon was chatting Kylie up but Elizabeth's arm hooked around his waist.

'C'mon, big lad,' she said. 'Eh need a man . . .'

Kylie looked up and across the foyer on the landing beyond the chrome rails saw her husband drinking with his mates. She also saw a boy she knew who would have some gear in his car and began pushing her way over to him. She barely felt the pressure of bodies all around her, the elbows, feet, shoulders that stuck out at her. The crowded stale air was rising in plumes of smoke, the persistent heavy beats drove the floor, but all she was aware of was the single thought that with her friends on the dance floor no-one was watching her; now was the time to score.

Balmerino, quaint settlement of a few dozen homes on the south bank of the river. A few dusty lanes along the shore and around the ruins of a sandstone abbey and the magnificent Spanish chestnut planted by Mary, Queen of Scots. The troubled city is in the future, sliding seaward down the estuary somewhere east beneath bridges. Walking down from the abbey and along the shore as the young queen must have done, you come upon the water, corroded by a narrow scar of shingle upon which the stainless tides barely impinge except at evening. Looking northwards, towards Invergowrie Bay, or east to the western half of the city, or west to the treed spire of Errolbank, the water is at its maximum; thirty-five shining square miles of sandbanks barely covered, of labyrinths of water courses invisible except from above. At a distant, almost imperceptible point, the reed beds emerge gently to become the fertility of the Carse, backed by distant blue hills and crags of the Sidlaws. If the air is clear, the Grampians hang upside down in the changing northern skies. Small planes take off and land at Riverside, merging with houses and trees, their engine noise like distant gnats, an irritant briefly and then dissolving into the air.

Sometimes, mist plumes low on the water, occluding the lower estuary and making it mysterious. Oystercatchers, dressed for dinner, scream out of the haar and squadrons of geese flying intently in tight formation splash down noisily, forming vast rafts of birds that can be heard distantly at Kingoodie. A good view can be had from the bay windows and glass doors of such a house as this, newly built out of the hillside on the rise above the shore. Its triple-glazed conservatory is the ideal location to observe the natural drama. Designer-planned, extensive gardens of buddleia, azalea and rhododendron slope down to a high wall and, reached by a locked gate, the beach. From a small terrace, on the wrought-iron chairs and benches one can gaze north, east or west and the view is majestic, even on rain-blurred days. There is tranquillity in such a place – as if the clocks have stopped – as if history itself is suspended.

But today the view is considered only by plastic garden gnomes. It held little interest for them and one gnome showed his shining pink bottom to the invisible city across the river. Several pvc water nymphs held up birdbaths and chatted over their shoulders to the seated fairy who sat fishing disconsolately at an odd angle on the rim of the brick wishing well. The stale lump of superglue he was sitting on was giving him piles. Several cast-concrete tortoises, rabbits and a donkey stood mutely nearby in a pool of pink gravel. Brain-dead, according to the gnomes. The cane furniture inside the conservatory was unused. Indeed, it still had the price tags on the legs. It was the fantasy of the fairy, who'd heard about it from several blue-tits who regularly perched on the brick wall, that he might one day be taken inside to sit on a cushion beside the overstuffed plush velvet bear who grinned inanely out at all the birds on the patio from one season's end to the next.

There was no sign of human life except for red lights winking in the dashboard of the expensive car parked on the raised tarmac drive at the top of the garden. Entering the house from the conservatory, passing into a rear hall and walking its length, led into a front hall, which the inhabitants, who were innured in the modernised kitchen, off to the left, called 'thi loabby'. The kitchen was the dimmest and meanest room in the house whose single window stared straight out on the whitewashed wall of the garage and the cornfield over the rise. Cluttered with gadgets and nick-nacks, with corn-dollies and fridge magnets, it acted also as a dining room, although there was one of those elsewhere. Some-how, they felt more comfortable in this small room. They had spent the thirty-five years of their marriage in a council semi. The designer-built house intimidated them a little. It was beyond their wildest dreams and also perhaps a little beyond their capacity to enjoy. The silence for them was too absolute and so they remained indoors, prisoners of opulence, shutting it out with TV, radio, video.

The man's bulk, in his string vest, dominated the kitchen table. White hairs stood out among the dark hairs on his upper chest and shoulders. Bruised blue tattoos straddled forearms holding the red-top newspaper, whose garish headlines he was slowly scanning. A cigarette drooped ash on to the bulge of his belly. His lips were flattened, obtruse, and the cigarette smoke rising in front of the flabby, exhausted but suntanned face drifted on over the bald dome of the skull among stray flattened hairs of indeterminate grey and a few prominent moles and freckles.

'It says here, mother,' he read, screwing up his eyes against the smoke, 'it says here that Carol Smillie's goin to be openin thi Homes and Gairdins exhibition thi moarnz moarn.'

His wife, a small, busty woman in a green housecoat tied in the middle, was frying bacon at the range. 'She's a riyt bonny lassie.'

'We'll mibbe get the chance to speak to her. Eh wonder uf shull be wearin that broon leather miniskirt?'

'Yi like ir in that, Ron.'

'Shiz a wee cracker,' the man said. After some reflection, he added gloomily, 'Eh'd give ir one, if eh wiz younger, eh wid.'

His wife scraped fried food out of the frying pan.

'Eh wid,' the man repeated, exhaling cigarette smoke.

'Well, mibbe things wull be beh'ir eftir thi operation, love,' she said, placing his plate in front of him. 'Mind, ut's hoat.'

'Cudnae git worse,' Ron replied. 'Waur's thi tomatter sass?'

'Here. Watna cuppa tea thi noo?'

'Na. Jist a gless a wattir. Need t'tak these bliddy pills.'

Betty ran the water and filled a crystal goblet to overflowing. One of a set the boys had given her on her sixtieth birthday. She handed him the small tray which contained his various medicines. Same routine every morning.

'Yull hear iz rattle soon, wummin,' he grumbled.

'Eh'll pit thi telly on fir yi while eh git dressed. Here's thi remote thingy. Eh'll get yir tea in a meenut. Jist gies a shout, eh'll be ben.'

Betty heard the creak of her husband's wooden chair as he set to his breakfast, watching the Sports Channel. She walked down the hall past the porthole window which gave on to the trees surrounding the abbey ruins and entered the large guest bedroom which had been used by Daniel and Suze, poor Suze, and would perhaps soon

39

be used by his present wife, Kylie, whom she hoped to meet. But it was difficult, with his business and that.

The pink-plush-carpeted room had a floor-to-ceiling built-in wardrobe which extended the entire length of the room and was finished in mirrored smoked glass. The four-poster bed, draped in pink and cream, and the leather chaise longue with its pink heart-shaped cushions were the only other furnishings in the room.

She slid open the wardrobe and felt her pulse quicken at the magnificent garments. She liked to admire herself in them even if her only audience was the mirror and her own imagination. The dresses had accumulated over many chauffeur-driven shopping expeditions to the shops in Edinburgh and Glasgow and further afield. Daniel had provided her with a driver of her own, a nice young man, and one of those cars where the driver sat behind glass and the part where you sat was a living room on wheels, with drinks cabinet, a seat you could lie out on and a pull-down padded rest for your feet. The limousine couldn't quite negotiate the narrow lane down to the house. It was too steep, too narrow, too hemmed-in by brambles, so it wasn't quite door-to-door.

Betty pulled off her housecoat and stripped down to her under-wear. Six years ago, she'd been a school cleaner, now she was wearing Janet Reger. The wife of a jannie, although Ron had been on the sick for his last two years at the local school. And that'd been their life. Now, she was going to wear Elizabeth David, a wine-red tulle ballgown. She held it up in front of herself in the mirror and felt a twinge of pleasure that, at sixty-two, she was holding up well. All that bending and cleaning over twenty years in school toilets had kept her trim. And she had the appetite of a mouse. Didn't go for fancy foods. She'd never smoked either. It helped that she was small and slender, although big-busted. They were sagging heavily, needed a firm support brassiere. Best of all was she'd always kept out of the sun and avoided that mottled freckly skin that some older women get. Her hair looked nice, dyed of course and the small operation on her neck and chin had defeated gravity for the moment. Yes. She could pass for ten years younger. Of course, she couldn't let the world see the tops of her thighs, which were getting puffy and veins were appearing rather too close to the surface, but stockings concealed that, and their shape was good. Her legs and her bust had always attracted the boys when she was at school and later, at the dancing in the Star Ballroom and the Palais and the Barracuda.

Betty discarded the ballgown and zipped herself into an evening blue velvet and black lace cocktail dress. Very fetching! A snip at just under a thousand. Prada at Frasers in Glasgow. Of course, she would never wear it, but the sheer sensual pleasure of having these beautiful garments next to her skin was enough. Even just pretending to be Lady Muck gave her a thrill. Ron didn't understand, complained that she was wasting money, but it was a tiny drop in the ocean when you had access to millions. And the boys had always been willing to splash out, though Daniel pointed out some of it was investment, that 'portable goods' retained value. Whether he'd said that to make her and Ron feel better about living in luxury she didn't know.

And if she stood side-on like this, her legs together . . . well, she could imagine the men looking. And the fine gold ankle chain. Not that Ron paid much attention. He was no longer able for that anymore. But love him as she did – and Betty did – it had crossed her mind more than once how good it would be to have a man's eyes on her, a real man wanting her. A younger man wanting her. Even if it was only for her money.

A quick twirl and Betty smiled at herself. What other reason would a younger man have for wanting her, other than her money? You did read about it sometimes in magazines. What would it be like, she wondered, to be an unfaithful woman? She'd never had these thoughts until Ron had had his last attack. Now she felt less guilty about them. Hail Mary, she said to herself, full of grace. These are my sins. Impure and impious thoughts.

She suddenly remembered Ron in the kitchen. He'd want his tea. She'd been in another world, posing and fancying herself no end. She stripped off the ballgown and pulled on her pale-green velour tracksuit and jogging pants and a cream-coloured cardigan. She visited the bathroom to put on her face and heard the taped applause of thousands of spectators at some sporting event in some sunny part of the world. Ron liked his sport.

41

Betty returned to the kitchen gloom and saw that her husband was asleep, his head supported on the table by his folded arms near to his plate and a small pile of bacon rind and congealed grease. A cigarette had smouldered itself out in a line of tapering ash in the Tennent's Lager ashtray brought from the Balgowan Arms, his former local. 'Stolen yi mean,' she'd accused him. 'Owir heckit t' beh an ashtray . . .' He'd just laughed at her. 'Z' only money, wummin, thi rich hae erseholes jist like iz. An ashtray's jist a blamin ashtray.'

Betty sighed and rolled up her sleeves to do the washing-up. Outside, seen only by the stroppy plastic garden gnomes, the pvc nymphs and the itching fairy with the bent fishing rod, the haar was coming unglued from the surface of the river, trailing north over the Angus hills, leaving the clear shining mudflats to the seals, the mallards, eiders and oystercatchers.

6

Pull the Chain after Use

Moray Neill started his new career the moment he saw Tracey Morrow, done up to the nines, waving a mobile phone for all to admire in the High Street. Such a sight really offended him. Moray was the lugubrious type, easily irritated by vulgar ostentation of the lesser ranks. It made his bluish lantern jaws quiver with righteous anger. Besides, he had been unemployed for some time and he had to emerge somehow from his squalid niche and extend himself a little, latch on to any passing opportunity. Tracey Morrow was it. He knew something of her background through his years – albeit cruelly curtailed – as a trainee with the local paper. The kind of jobs he'd been given; taking police briefings and attending interminable sessions at the Sheriff Court, the journalistic equivalent of potty-training, had given him the lowdown, the gen, the goss and the sp on grubbers like her. She needed taking down a peg or three. He was just the kind of languid galoot to do it. For some weeks he'd had a suspicion about a mobile phone number advertising 'Escort Services' in the personal services column of the otherwise respectable, if embarrassingly Unionist newspaper, *The Hootsmon*. He ducked into a phone booth, inserted fifty pence, rang the number, clamped the receiver to his elongated, saturnine face and watched Morrow stop to answer her mobile. Bingo! Yes, there was a local girl who could fulfill all his needs. Yes, there was a place he could visit.

43

'Bit eh canna gie yi thi address until eh ken when yi wahnt ti meet. When dae yi wahnt ti meet? S' efternane. Aboot fowir? Eh well, yull need t' ring iz back. Eh canna discuss that noo. Yull hae t' ring iz back at fowir on this number.'

Moray knew there is only one sense in which a person can be a grubber. It means someone of low class or no class, but it's not political. Nor is it sociological. It's a matter of attitude, an absolute lack of moral fibre, a complete absence of responsibility. A grubber is someone who does not care who they hurt or what anyone thinks of them. It's an endemic meanness. They don't give a toss about amenity or community, neighbourliness or decency, questions of right or wrong. Grubbers only care about themselves, about what they can get and how they can get away with it, while the getting is good. Always at the expense of others. Grubbers are the ugliest pond-life of society, lower even than minks, for being a mink is to do with given social status and appearance, which can be altered. Grubber-hood is for life. To say Tracey Morrow is a grubber is to define her in possibly the only way that means anything. She first swam into view at SS Peter, Paul and Mary's when she was caught attempting to steal exam answers from a teacher's desk but left school at sixteen without any O-grades, hers or anyone else's. And a reputation for swearing and fighting. She was something of a bully and most of the boys avoided her. She had the sallow skin of the Morrows, rather oily, her thick black hair streaked with grey from her early teens. Her breasts remained defiantly small and her teeth were wayward and yellowish. She was no beauty, but that wasn't her fault. Her most common descriptor was 'nae brenns'. She disappeared from view for several years then re-emerged employed as a kind of secretary to her brothers' burgeoning joinery business. They were doing renovations, flat conversions and prop-erty lettings from a small office in the ground floor of a tenement in Arklay Street. She was already picking up punters in the sawdust-floored Maritime Bar at the corner of Commercial Street and Exchange Street, outside the Sailors' Home on Dock Street and in several bars on the Hilltown. She'd been seen touting for trade at the dark junction of Middle Street and Constable Street. She became well known. To the wifies of Dundee she was 'no better

44

than she should be'. By the time she was in her early twenties, she was already being described as 'mumsy'. From the rear, in the dark, she looked almost sexy in her short leather skirt, black stockings, high heels and heavy shoulder-length black hair. But the face spoiled the impression. Those wayward, yellowish and tobacco-stained teeth, the oily pitted skin, the double chin and the flabby neck. The assistance of scientifically-designed lingerie to thrust her charms into public view simply made the sucked thinness of her breasts more obvious. Most of her customers were elderly, or short-sighted – and much of her trade was discount.

The local addresses she'd given him were in Baxter Park Terrace, Isla Street near Dens Park and the Seagate. Now all Moray needed was pictures.

He arranged to meet her in the city centre, at the junction of Seagate and Gellatly Street. He parked in the 24-hour carpark and stowed his wallet in the glove compartment, and left the camera in the boot.

She arrived half an hour late, with attaché case, mobile phone and big bunch of keys. She was brisk and businesslike.

'Hi,' she said. 'I'm Brenda. Got yir money?'

He followed her around the corner into the dark and smelly close behind the Atlas snackbar. She unlocked a battered wooden door and led him into a dark, smelly stairwell.

'Top floor,' she said, jangling the keys.

'Would be,' he mumbled.

On the first floor, the stairwell opened out and they came on to a plettie or stone balcony and continued up the stairs. Most of the flats looked derelict.

The close on the fourth floor had a green outer door secured by a horizontal iron bar and heavy padlock. He was reassured. That meant no heavies inside. Might as well have a look, he reasoned. More detail for the story.

It was a dank, airless slum – he could see through open doors to empty rooms. The room he was shown into had dingy net curtains and was oppressed by the closeness of the grimy buildings oppo-site. The single bed was covered with a rumpled primrose nylon sheet, disgustingly stained.

Morrow came into the room and put down her bag. She took off her jacket and hung it on a wire coathanger supported by a nail. He noticed the patches of sweat around the armpits of her white T-shirt.

'Well, Jack, wut d' yi wahnt iz t' dae?' she asked.

'I don't know your prices,' he said.

She sighed and pulled the cap off her mobile phone and pressed redial. He could hear the ringing tone. She grimaced at him. 'Hand relief's fufteen, French iz twin'ay an fuhll service iz thir'ay. Eh dinna dae unprotected.'

'Full service?' he queried, acting like a rube from the sticks.

She glanced from the phone to his face. 'Eh, face-to-face.'

'Yeah, but . . . how long . . . do I get?'

Morrow snorted disbelievingly, as she clipped the phone shut. 'Eh? How lang dae yi need? Pen's wut yir wahntin.'

The mobile phone buzzed. 'Eh? Wha iz this? Aw, eh,' Morrow said. 'When ji wahnt t'see iz like? Eh, yull hae t'phone iz back, ehm wi a customer at the minute, ken.'

Then Moray put his hand into his jeans back-pocket to make the discovery that his wallet was missing.

'Must have left it in the car.'

She glared at him. 'That's jist fuckin brah!'

'Sorry.'

'Eh, y' wull be an a. Yir owin iz fir mi time. How d'yi no check yir money doon thi stair?'

'Well, there's nothing I can do about it now.'

'Yir takin thi piss oot o iz!' she shouted. 'Wutz yir gemme, eh? Yid beh'ir no touch iz . . . Ehm warnin yi, pahll . . .'

As Moray made for the door, she grabbed his wrist.

'Wutziz? Z' a Timex. Series 12. Much that cost yi?'

'About fifty quid a few years ago.'

'It ull dae. Gies ut. Yi kin hae a feel a meh tits.' She pulled him towards her. He caught a close-up glimpse of her lips and teeth and smelt her nicotine breath. He wrenched himself away.

'You're disgusting. The place stinks.'

He moved fast. Evaded her swinging fist with its heavy bunch of keys. Got into the hall, down the stairs.

'Yi . . . fuckin . . . bastardin . . . shiteyhole! '*Rape!*'

He fled headlong, legs springing him down three stairs at a time. When he got down on to the Seagate all was normal. The air was fresh and it wafted away the putrid aroma of the slum he had been in. By the time he'd retrieved the camera, there was no trace of Mumsy Morrow. He felt that he had the greasy stink of the place about him for the rest of the afternoon and had to have several beers in the dense smokiness of the Phoenix before he felt better.

Now Wash Your Hands

Several days after that incident, Moray Neill was brushing his back teeth when there was a knock at the door of his flat. A smart young man, in a leather jacket, yellow shirt and pink tie, introduced himself as a reporter from the *Noise of the Worms*.

'I'm Niall Barr,' he said, offering his hand. 'Believe you've got a story for us?'

'Yeah, come on in.'

The reporter was sharp and arrogant, full of business. He had thick cultivated sideburns, his black hair slicked back, he smelt of male perfume and he had a number of irritated red plukes on his forehead and cheeks. He sat on the sofa and deftly juggled with the cup of coffee Moray had offered him and with cigarettes, lighter, notebook and biro. Moray wasn't chuffed about the cigarette smoke but went to find a saucer that could be used as an ashtray.

'So who's this tart?' he wanted to know. 'And how did you meet her?'

'No, no', Moray told him patiently. 'That's not the way this is going down. As I said on the phone this is my story and I want a byline. I'm not *in* the story and I want a firm arrangement about the money. Got that, chum?'

'Of course, chief, goes without saying. But how do we know there is a story anyway? Could be a load of balls.'

'Oh there is a story. You wouldn't be here otherwise.'

'Ah steady, Brian. It's true I'm a freelance but all the *Nudes of the Wolds* stories in Scotland are done through me. They won't take a

Scottish story unless it comes from me. That's why I'm here, to check it out, see if it stands up.'

'It'll stand up. I've got all the facts. I wrote the story and I faxed it down to them. You've got it with you, have you?'

Barr shook his head. 'No chief. I've not seen what you wrote. It doesn't work like that. All I was given was your address and something about a shagging story. So it'll do no harm to go over it again. It's your story but we'll work together. There'll be good pay if it stands up. I'll see you right; don't worry. Trust me.'

So Moray gave Niall Barr the contact details and over several cups of coffee ran over the tale again. While he was telling him about his visit to the Seagate flat, there was a knock on the door. A tough-looking guy with long thick hair receding at the front, and a thick droopy moustache, stood outside in a sleeveless combat jacket festooned with heavy cameras and lenses.

'It's Sharkey!' the reporter exclaimed, from the depths of the sofa where he was lounging with his feet up on an armchair. 'Let the mad motherfucker in!'

'I heard that!' the photographer said, barging in past Moray. 'Any coffee on the go? And choccy biccys? Magic. Two sugars for me.'

'This is the snapper who'll shoot your tart,' Barr said. 'Back, front and up the skirt.'

The photographer disrobed himself of the camera equipment and sat down in Moray's seat and began to roll himself a cigarette.

'Yeah, we'll soon find out if she's got anything to declare!'

Days went by, a week, and it was nearly a fortnight later that Moray spotted the story on the front page of the *News of the Screws*, continued inside. They had pictures: Morrow, rear view, kissing a middle-aged businessman client, whose head and shoulders were all that could be seen; Morrow and another girl, very busty, in which both girls were shot from low down to make their legs look longer and their skirts look shorter. There were snaps of the 'seedy flats' in Isla Street and the Seagate. It was his story alright but his name wasn't on it. His story but they'd added to it. Some rubbish about home-visiting massage and some punter called Derek (32) 'a regular client' who said that he had used her

48

services for about a year and that she frequently suggested 'kinky services' were on offer. She had told him that 'business was good and that she ran three other girls.' But the red headline scorched its way across the front page: SHAME OF SECRETARY IN SLEAZY SEX-TRADE: 'Kinky Lusts Dictated by Typist of Sin.' The headline was on every hoarding in the city centre. He felt a momentary sense of pity for Morrow, who was quoted in the story saying 'I don't want to speak about it; my daughter is ill.' Then he felt a sense of anger that his name was not on the story. Later, this changed to relief. It was a dirty business, why get himself besmirched? The Morrows were powerful and might come after him. This way he was safe, obscure.

Several weeks later, a cheque for £200 arrived in the mail and with it a brief note from Niall Barr. 'Sorry about the byline. The Editor wouldn't wear it. Thanks for your help, Niall.' His '*help*'? It was his story. Two hundred quid and no byline. He could be sure Barr had made a lot more. He wouldn't be so green next time.

7

Conveniences for the Use of the Public

'Surrogate motherhood,' roared the voice, 'now there's a career! Easy money, cause it's based on desperately needy people, see, childless couples. Anybody that desperate will pay and pay. They're so desperate they'll put up with almost anything. Well, hell-llo! It's just a perfect opportunity for your average grubber to exploit.'

'It's three in the bloody morning,' Moray complained. 'Who the hell is this?'

'It's Niall, Niall Barr, of the fucking *Nudes of the Pseuds* mate.'

'Barr? You owe me money – *mate*!'

'Not get the dosh I sent?'

'You ripped me off. It was my story.'

'I think you'll find the story had my byline on it, chum. Ancient history now, anyway, whatever it was. "Sleazy Secretary in Sex Trade"? was that it? Or . . . well, anyway, I owe nobody, pal. Anyway, the *Lewds of the Pseuds* never sleeps. It's a 24-hour job. Maybe not for lazy bastards like you who need their beddy-byes. Anyway, in case you are interested, this is a new story – about surrogacy – see. I just done the story, right. It's in tomorrow's. Hear it here first and weep. Reason I phoned you? Guess who's in the story?'

'What are you havering about, Barr? I'm in bed for godsake, yi chancer!'

50

'It's your tart, Mumsy bloody Morrow. Got your attention now, have I?'

'What's she done now?'

'Farted a bloody big hole through the surrogacy legislation, that's what. The Surrogacy Arrangements Act 1985, to be precise. Prevents payments except for expenses. But the Act doesn't limit the expenses and there's no way of checking. The agency fixes a rough amount that they think the surrogate mother will claim but there's no way of enforcing it and the thing that they, the agency and the agencies' clients, are terrified of is publicity, so you have them over a barrel, chum. Mum's the word. Easy money.'

'Eh?'

'Wake up, ye tosser. This is the story we done. And don't interrupt. See, what the surrogates are really selling is their time and, as every grubber knows, time is money. The baby comes free as part of the package.'

'If you say so.'

'Oh, I do, mate, I do. See, so many women offered themselves as surrogates that none of the agencies could do any vetting. The women were just names to them, names on lists. The grubbers were quids-in.'

'How does this affect Mumsy Morrow?'

'Your pal was on one of the lists and one fine day got a letter, see, inquiring whether she could help a childless couple in their late twenties from Hertfordshire. At first, everything went well. Mumsy travelled to London, to a Harley Street clinic to be artificially incinerated and that, and it all went ahead okay on the day.'

'Good for her. Three fucking cheers!'

'Yeah. Except that, on the train home, she popped the 'morning after' pill with a cup of coffee. Nice one, eh? That was just the first part of her crafty little scheme. Then she became the pregnant mother and began to demand this and that, and within two months she'd had more than six grand from the couple. They began to smell a rat and got on to the agency. Anyway, some checking was done and the agency soon discovered her slimy past. Not that they had any intention of letting their clients know. That might have been bloody tricky. The finger could be pointed at them for not checking earlier. So they became party to Mumsy's little scam, only they assumed she was actually up the duff. And she was, but not quite as preggers as everyone thought. It was barely showing, see, a very minor bump but of course neither the agency nor their clients could see it. Are you following all this?'

'I'm still awake if that's what you mean? Just.'

'Good. Well, phase two went into operation when the couple believed that the pregnancy was in its seventh month. Telephone calls, letters: Ehv decided to keep the baby . . . Only to tearfully relent after the promise of more money. Much more money. Receipts so far now totalling – would you believe – an incredible fifteen grand? Then just when the couple thought everything was sorted, all contact ceased. Telephone number disconnected. New number not listed. Mail returned undelivered. The agency got busy. The Hertfordshire clients were threatening to sue for breach of contract. The surrogate mother had promised the agency, but the clients had a contract. Their contract was enforceable, the arrangement with the surrogate was voluntary, impossible to enforce.'

'That's it? She did a bunk?'

'Not! What kind of story is that? No. Contact was restored. Even more tearfully, you know who, dear old Mumsy, agreeing to fulfil the deal after more money is promised. But had to agree to a DNA test before it was sent. In vain, our Mumsy protested but was told point-blank that the money could only be collected at the Harley Street clinic after the test was done. Back she travelled to London and was tested, and, shock, horror, surprise, surprise, the DNA test proved that Hertfordshire husband was not the baby's father. You know who went into seizures at this, wailing and howling . . .'

'Yeah, I'll bet . . .' Moray said, grimly.

Barr continued '. . . with one eye on the clock so she wouldn't miss her train. Oh how can this be? she asked plaintively. What kind of a mistake have we here? The test must be wrong, for as you can see, gentlemen, I am up the spout, with a large bun in the oven and I have spent nine months in such a condition (well seven if truth be told) but I have to head home now, so I'll see yiz later. Keep sending the cheques.'

'And that's it? That's your story?'

52

'More or less, yeah, give or take . . . Of course not, you arse! Later, she is delivered of a boy. The Hertfordshire couple decide that they will still honour the deal if she will hand over the baby. At first this seems likely. But because of the DNA test and the baby not being the natural child of Hertfordshire man, the surrogate, you know who, demurs with a straight face, and always with the best interests of the child at heart of course.'

'Glad to hear it, Barr. Standards being kept up. Jolly good show, what-what!'

'Sarky bastard! Yeah, the long and short of it is, yes, the baby is finally handed over at a secret rendezvous in a carpark in London, after no less than ten grand is handed over in a brown paper envelope. The couple both in tears because they've had to resort to such grubby methods of so obviously buying a baby for cash.'

'As one would be in the circs.'

'True. But this is the killer. Final par. A week later, they're in shock when two policemen arrive, shortly after the postman has delivered a lawyer's letter, bearing a Court seal of Dundee Sheriff Court, giving a Parental Order under section 30 of the 1990 Human Fertilisation and Embryology Act, over the little child to her real parents, you know who and her husband. Oh yes.'

'No kidding?'

'Hey – great pun! I could've worked that in somehow. Anyway, the private hearings went ahead but the Hertfordshire couple had no chance against positive DNA tests. They had no proof of any payments of the surrogate arrangement and even if they had it would have been illegal. Great!'

'So? What you're saying is . . . ?'

'Yup. The Hertfordshire couple had subsidised you know who's own pregnancy to the tune of twenty-five grand. Whoopdedoo-dledoo! Hey, did I get you out of bed? Aw, shame. Nice story though, eh? All credit to me. I'll get a grand at least for it, no worries. So, thanks for putting me on to such a great source, I'll be sure to send you a tenner . . .'

'You patronising cunt!' Moray raged. Don't ever phone me again!' But the line was dead. *Something had to be done . . .*

In the Sewage System

Standing in the shadow of the large trees at the back of Trottick is certainly not Moray Neill's idea of fun. It's a Tuesday, just after 9 p.m., the third blinking Tuesday evening he's spent here, fruitlessly lurking in the shadows like some child-molesting pervert.

All because of a tip-off from someone at best congenitally unreliable. Of all likely snouts, Frankie, the overweight DJ of the Fizzing Duck Disco in the Claverhouse Arms, was the worst, most probably showing off, but, as usual, adamant.

He pushed his long, greasy, dark hair out of his face with a bandaged hand in the High Street. 'Seen it with my own eyes,' he said, 'every Tuesday, regular as clockwork, the dirty devils.'

It seemed a bit unlikely but if it was going on, it was a front pager for sure. Maybe even TV. A shagging story of top quality worth a really decent bung. Of course, there was the possibility that Frankie was acting out of hate. The lardy-arsed Labourite had many enemies and Frankie was one of them. Johnny Two-seats had natural ability to rub people up wrongly. When election time came around he didn't bother to write an election leaflet, he distributed menus for four years of troughing-it. Those not invited often took offence. Frankie was unlikely to be anyone's dining companion. His teeth belonged to someone else.

So Moray had obtained the loan of camera equipment and set himself up as a freelance. He was spotted in the High Street by Mr Summers, his former history teacher. Old sarky suede shoes.

'And in what field,' sarky began, 'are your present endeavours confined?'

Moray boasted of the long-range potential of his lenses. Old sarky was unimpressed. The retired teacher was now white-haired but looked alarmingly bohemian in his spindly-legged jeans and his belted sand-coloured safari jacket. He had not changed, his tongue was ascerbic, sharpened on the whetstone of bitter experience.

'We have descended to the sub-literary I see,' he mused. 'How very sad. You were once the possessor of a fertile imagination, but now fertiliser seems to be more your concern. The so-called news-paper you mention should be sold in rolls to ease the disorders of the copious fundaments of the masses.'

Typical old sarky, Moray winced. Six words where one would do.

Anyway, here he was, again.

He hoisted the 'long tom' 330mm telescopic lens on to the monopod he'd stuck in the earth and gazed through fading light at the glass entrance of the nearest of a line of 4-in-a block tenement flats. Nothing at all was happening, a few dim lights in windows, the distant sound of car tyres at the roundabout. There was a light in the flat and he knew that it had been switched on by the girl who had arrived half an hour ago in the taxi. His keen sense of anticipation was dimmed only somewhat by the knowledge that it had all not happened before. And the light was fading. The bloody light was going to fade.

He heard a car and tensed, crouching behind the bush. No. Gone past. He'd been disturbed twice by dog walkers. It'd be typical if he was spotted and some bright spark called the police. That'd be the perfect end to a wonderful evening. Matter of fact, he didn't trust Frankie not to call the police himself to get a fiver tip-off fee. He thought about old sarky's copious fundaments of the masses. Copious fundaments . . . fundamental copy . . . coin of the realm and the fun that meant . . .

When they came – if they came – they couldn't get in the front entrance. He'd checked as soon as he arrived that it was locked. And the girl herself had come in by the rear entrance, through the open courtyard. There were a few cars parked, but none obscured his view of the main entrance. That's where the taxi would arrive bringing the lardybutt Convenor of Licences and his baldy wee toad of a mate, the Convenor of Properties. Both were married. Doubtless it was wee Welks who had arranged the vacant flat for the randy rendezvous.

Moray sees a car, its lights on, coming down the Old Glamis Road. He notices that the bloody light is fading. The streetlights have chosen just that moment to come on. It's a taxi. A Handicabs white Sierra. Stopping. It's bloody stopping and there's two passengers. Moray is inwardly exulting as he struggles with his equipment. 'Ah, now, this heavy bloody lens . . .' he fumbles . . . 'get it . . . no, no . . . shit! *Shit*! Aargh!'

8

Today has been a great day for walkers. Great troops of them, a school outing I think, nature trail or something. Always stopping to look at things. I considered moving my bender; it's kids I worry about, they're the ones most likely to leave the path. Apathy ruled the day though and I left it where it was. It's well hidden, in its little dip at the top of a grassed-over mound where the forest is thickest. To find it, you'd have to climb up a steep little cliff into a flat hollow. There's no other way in. My bender is well-camouflaged with ferns and twigs. Invisible unless you can get up into this knoll and into the flat hollow, and the knoll itself is difficult to find because of the thickness of the trees and brambles. It's a craw's nest, a vantage point to watch the movement of waters.

I was ten before I grasped the mind-boggling concept that all waters are one. A newspaper story about a Galapagos turtle washed ashore on Iona. The earth was two-thirds water and all seas and oceans were one big drink. Hard to imagine the cold, iron waters of Tay fretting upon the warm pink coral of the Antipodes, the sandy shores of the Aegean, or slapping against pack-ice in the Bering Straits.

The father of a schoolfriend of mine, Duncan Law, was skipper of one of the 'Fifies', the steamers that plied the river before the road bridge. During the war, he'd been in submarines. He died, aged sixty, when we were in our early teens. I remember him as a short, squat man with turtle-neck sweaters and a broad, Slavonic face. His real name was Luwkovicz: Polish. He wore a peaked black cap and always had a cigarette dangling athwart his lips. People called him 'skipper' and Duncan's mother had a picture of him in full dress uniform on the mantlepiece. They'd met at the fruit-picking, the 'berries', in Tealing near where the Luwkovicz grandparents had lived since their arrival in Scotland, fleeing the Tsarist pogroms. The berryfields' gaffer wasn't much good at spelling and didn't even try with foreign names. The real surname's on the wedding certificate of course, with 'known as Law' added.

Many times we dodged school to stand beside him at the rail from Newport to the ramp by Paladini's garage on Riverside where the 'Fifies' used to dock. He always seemed very old to me then, though he was probably only in his late fifties. Sometimes he'd let us operate the foghorn. It sounded like a sea-monster moaning out in the haar, powerfully nasal, lovelorn.

Our early years were coloured with the glamour of imperial wars. The German navy scuttling itself at Scapa Flow, the retreat from Burma, jungle war in Malaya and Borneo. We swapped the illustrated war picture books produced in the redbrick edifice in the centre of our own town. And the maritime tales of whalers, of whaling ships lost in the Arctic pack-ice. Captain Scott and Oates and the others frozen to death in their tent, the *Terra Nova*, *Discovery*, the *Balaena*. Later, many of our classmates joined the Merchant Navy and saw a lot of the world themselves. They got to know the joined-up, distant blue seas of the globe. Duncan signed up at eighteen after a year as an apprentice electrician with Lockhart and Maxwell, which he didn't take seriously. I remember postcards from Venezuela, Galveston and Johannesburg. I only saw him a couple of times after that. Some of his photos show him dressed in white shorts, dress tunic and peaked cap, and always with his arm around some dusky lovelies in a bazaar. I remember his stories of fourteen-year-old whores in South America who cost less than a bottle of rum and stories about punch-ups in Hong-Kong and opium-smoking, coral reefs and sharks.

'We went t' this roadhouse bar, ken, near Houston,' he told me. 'Thir wiz a hale mob o iz an, in thi bar, thirz a these, like, coohands wi big stetsons. Bill, thi radio operator on oor boat – ee wiz fae

Middlesbrough – ee taks it inta eez heid t' hae a decko. Bit ee dizna see nae dames at a, so ee gaes, ken, dehd loud, ken: "Texas is fuhll a steers an queers bit eh dinna see nae steers!"

'Thi place fell apert! A brah punch-up. Dehd brilliant – bit we wir lucky t' git oot a thir alehv, ken, coz thir wiz nae Feds – nae polis – t' stop thi lads wreckin thi place. An that bastard, Bill, wiz thi oanly wan o iz thit ended up wi'oot a scratch. Eh, wid yi credit it? Man, we wir bliddy lucky t' git oot alehv.'

When you're counting the years to adulthood, time passes excruciatingly slowly but something seemed to overtake our dreams and Duncan was a sparky and I was walking down Reform Street in a pin-stripe suit (£3.50 from Oxfam) a bri-nylon pink shirt and a brown tie, going to my first job as a clerical assistant in the office of Cummings, Ritchie and Gilruth. All I had to do was make tea, deliver letters and fantasise about one of the secretaries, Miss June Chalmers, a demure beauty of twenty-two, with long straight black hair and a body whose intimate movements I knew almost better than she did. I stuck the job for two months then got a job at Cairds in the Menswear Department.

In our final year at school, when the others were swotting for O-grades, we used to plunk off down by the Camperdown dock for a mug of tea at Rosa's Portakabin. We'd have a smoke along by the sheds and warehouses, throwing our butts into the oily water, syphilitic with floating debris.

'Meh maw says ehm no tae jine thi Merch,' Duncan said one day, as we stood watching fitters greasing a marine engine. He spat into the water, trying to land his spittle on a dead pigeon that drifted near to the dock gates. He was better than me at heching and hit it on his third go.

'Yull hae t' git yir knob oot t' hae a chans,' he jeered.

'Okay, yi win Gochler O Thi Year. Big deal. What's the time?'

'Ach, snoh hauf twelve yit.'

The river pilot was veering towards the dock from mid-river, from the rusty orange stern of the *Paramanathan III*, which was returning to Karachi.

'Headin t' ir berth. Tehs up owir thir, ken.' Duncan pointed to the far wall where a battered and dented tug rode at anchor.

'Funny to think of that wee motorboat pulling the likes of they tankers.'

'Na, ut dizna puhll um, jist guides um in a wee bit.' That was Duncan. Everything literal. The literal truth.

Close-to, the pilot boat was sturdy and workman-like, its hull covered in blistering tar, with an outboard at the stern. The pilot and the harbourmaster were leaning back against the gunwhales smoking cigarettes. Although it was a boiling-hot day, both were wrapped in donkey jackets and had their bunnets on. The wash began to arrive at the gates and we ran to the other side to see how high up it would come. The pilot half-turned, having recognised Skipper Law's son. Duncan just stood hands in pockets, watching closely.

'Maybe your maw will change her mind,' I said, because I knew it was bothering him.

He spat into the water. 'Na. Shiz no wahntin iz t' gie up meh 'prenticeship.'

'But your brother John's in the Merch.'

'Eh, eez different, she says. Eh canna mak ir oot. Eh'll gie it a year then ehm aff wuther she likes it ir no.' He turned to me. 'You cud come an a'. Thi baith o iz cud jine thigithir.'

'Maybe.' But I had never fancied it in reality. Stay or go, advance or retreat. It was the only decision that was yours to make; move or stop. Except it wasn't possible to stop – everything is in flux. To stop was to regress, turn back the pages of history, write yourself out, to subside, die. I ebbed on the familiar shore, Duncan sailed with the flood tide. And here I am like jetsam or flotsam, or both.

Part 2

Backwash

9

S he'd been startled by his sudden appearance from nowhere on to the track in front of her. She stopped, apprehensive, gripping the stick she'd picked up earlier.

'I'm sorry to startle you,' he tried to say, grimacing. Except his tongue was firmly stuck inside his mouth and nothing came out but a sort of moist squeak. Eventually . . . 'Sorry . . .' came out. And, 'I mean I . . . haven't spoken to anyone . . . for days . . .'

'I see,' she said firmly, walking past him and looking down at her feet, fist still clenched around the coiled dog lead.

'I'm in a kind of limbo,' he blurted out.

Limbo? Is that what he'd said? 'Oh well, you've got a good day for it,' she replied, over her shoulder and partly to herself, from further up the track.

Further up, where the track passes the information board at Tentsmuir Point and joins a maze of other tracks heading south to Kinshaldy Beach, the woman, Marjorie Braid, felt her breathing return to normal. She could be sure he wasn't following her. Had given her a start jumping out like that. Her dominant feeling was sympathy. Poor chap, not quite right, obviously. This must be the man sleeping rough in the woods that village rumour had suggested. Beneath the grime, he was younger than he looked, younger than the stories had suggested. Well, she wasn't about to enlighten the village gossips in the Spar. She'd never hear the end of it. And he'd looked as if he'd die of embarrassment too. What on earth was that about 'limbo'? She began to feel a smile warm its way across her face. He was harmless really; she was sure of it. She wondered if he knew she had no dog. Or rather that her dog was mythical, a device to allow her to go stravaiging off by herself in the woods. An excuse to leave the flat in Butter Wynd with its view over the red roofs and the Gospel Hall to the estuary. She had seen the man in the village, too, surely, going into the charity shop in Rose Street. Yes. Like her, someone with time on his hands. Perhaps they should get together and form a society: Friends of Limbo, or Tayport Limbo Dancers, or something of the sort.

It had been a fine morning. She had turned into Tay Street and down School Wynd heading for Harbour Road. All new houses. At the corner, the sudden vista of the mudflats, the old wooden beacon on stilts directly in line with Broughty Castle across the firth. She had walked along beside the low wall which swerved around the bay. Over to the right the small boating pond in the park was empty as usual, except for squabbling seagulls. Two Scots pines shaded the public toilets near the caravan park. Marjorie walked on the narrow road between the lines of permanently-settled mobile homes, whose wheels had been replaced by concrete blocks. Each had a small fenced-off area with folding chairs, cosy nooks and little rockeries and most had a name plaque, some couthy: Hame o Mine, Bide-a-Wee, Dunmoanin, some pretentious. Outside the caravan site, two boys practised golf shots on a strip of grass under a sign reading 'No Golf Practice'. A line of stunted pines fronted the edge of a small council housing estate and the Foodmek factory. Cars were parked on rough grass at the end of the tarmac road which became a track, crossing a bridge over a burn and heading around the bay into the woods.

She came off the track and deviated up into a narrower track that rode along the top of the bank and afforded a view of the shoreline and the vast open sandbank. She sniffed the air, burning, woodsmoke. Was there anything as gorgeous as woodsmoke and the tangle of the sea? For the millionth time she asked herself what was she doing here, on the fringes of the urban landscape, when she had promised herself that she would learn Gaelic and take off for a new life on one of the magical Hebridean islands. A sort of Shirley

McValentine. It had all come to nothing, when Derek died six years ago. It had been their dream but after the funeral it seemed she no longer had the drive to do it alone. So unfair. All the hills, mountain-peaks, long excursions and sailing trips were no longer accessible to a single woman. What did she have instead? A life of drudgery as an education enforcer, trying to instil some aesthetic appreciation of literature into a new generation obsessed with brash, noisy trivia, whose attention-span was conditioned by point-and-click technology to micro-seconds. What did they want of Shakespeare, Stevenson, even Irvine Welsh? 'Just read us the naughty bits, Miss.'

More Problems of Plumbing

After the cock-up in Trottick, Moray Neill did not have the nerve to try any more snapping. His knee still hurt and the lens he'd borrowed had almost been damaged beyond repair. No-one was going to lend him any more gear after that either, so he effected a liaison with Sharkey, an experienced snapper. Sharkey was the guy who'd done the pics of Mumsy Morrow for Niall rip-off Barr of the *News of the Screws*, but Moray had got himself well in with the editor of the ever-more-popular redtop, the soakaway *Scottish Source,* a former colleague on the local paper, and was keen to give it a go. He had to do something.

  Barry Munday, a grizzled local freelance, warned him about the line of work he'd be required to do. 'Muck-raking. Shagging stories, beastings, lots of stakeouts, stories about druggies dying in tenement flats, about poofs doing . . . well . . . anything at all. Better get yourself some broon corduroy troosers, m'boy. The *Source,* or the sore-erse as us cynical hacks love to call it, craps on the punters from a great height. The more crap you provide, and the smellier it is, the more pay you get. True. More stink is more printer's ink is more chink chink in your pooches, ken. That's how the redtops work, and the sore-erse is the best payer, or used to be. Ma wife now, she hates that kind of work. One night, we're having our tea and the front windae goes in. This pig's heid has been thrown right through it. Somebody pissed off about a story I done.

Wife's really cracking up. "Silence, wummin, I say. Get into the kitchen. We'll make soup with it." '

Moray phoned Sharkey about an eviction party up in Drumgeith. He'd been told by Candy Rue at a bus stop: 'Ken those neighbours fae hell the papers have been goin on aboot? They're finally bein evicted on Monday so she's invited abiddy to an eviction perty in the hoose. Eh'm telt she's plannin an indoor barbeque!'

Sharkey was impressed. 'Sounds good. But when is it happening?'

'Dunno. Some time this evening.'

'Ach, the light'll be impossible. Can you not get them to have the barbeque earlier, say early afternoon?'

'You're jokin? This is a woman who's threatened to torch any reporters she finds in the area, especially reporters from the *Source*.'

Sharkey parked the car several streets away from the house, which was on a busy corner, not far from a small outpost of battered shops and a chipper. They were aware that they stuck out like a sore thumb. Most of the other cars were Ladas or joyriders' specials. They sat in silence broken only by the husky breathing of Marilyn Monroe . . . *river of no return* . . . Sharkey switched the radio off. 'God, that's depressing,' he said.

'What? The song?'

'Na. That Marilyn's deid. I love that woman. Good singer too.'

'Uh-huh.'

'So tell me again about this family?' Sharkey asked, as they sat behind the thickening condensation, his fingers busily rolling a cigarette in licorice paper.

'The usual neighbours from hell scenario,' Moray told him. 'Bunch of wild kids shoplifting. Terrorised one of the local shopkeepers into early retirement. But the youngest boy – the *youngest*, mind you – robbed a bank in the town with his sister. In the High Street.'

'I remember. How old was he?'

'Twelve and she was nine. He distracted the teller's attention and

66

the wee girl snatched a bag of money from under the perspex security cover.'

'Right wee entrepreneurs. How much they get?'

'Five grand. Cool as cucumbers they hailed a taxi. Imagine, kids that age and they were off. But they gave the taxi-driver a twenty and said to keep the change. That made him suspicious. When the police arrived the boy was fighting his sister in the street. She was for keeping the lot. She'd only given him five quid and he wasn't happy. He thought the job was worth at least a tenner. Of course, they were caught on video camera and the police knew them very well. They broke a policewoman's nose when they were arrested.'

'Jeez. Some family.'

'Yeah, but they were only the *novices*. The older kids were a *real* nightmare. One of them had a gun when he was arrested. The mother is a gang boss, because it's not just one family, there's all their friends and mates. It's a crime-gang, several dozen strong. The father's in prison.'

'Fuck me, mate, we'd better watch our step. Trouble is, these cameras of mine are a dead giveaway in the schemes.'

'Crapping out?'

Sharkey stroked his receding hairline. 'No. No. No me, pal. Fuck it, I've snapped bottle fights in the Garngad and riots on the terracings at Ibrox. Cheeky cunt.' He sucked on his rolly-up. 'And after I've taught you everything you know!'

'Look, I'll go for a scout around, see what's doing.'

'Aye, you do that, buggerlugs.'

Moray strolled along and back, lots of people hanging around on the corner and some of them looked unpleasant but nothing doing. An hour later, he tried again. Nothing, and the light was going.

Sharkey called up McLean, the day's editor at the *Scottish Source*. 'We're blown here, boss. The light's gone and nothing's happened. I'm off. Anything does go down, your man will fax copy. Yeah? We're on for a dayshift fee. Both? Yeah.'

So Moray went home and gave it several hours, had something to eat and cycled back. It took him half an hour. He slowly circumnavigated the streets. Dead quiet. No-one. Then he almost fell off the bicycle. People, loads of people were sitting out on their pletties, in the dark, silently, waiting, watching.

He spoke to a man leaning out of a darkened first-floor window. 'Anything happening?'

'Not yet.'

He cycled into Ballindarroch Avenue. The silence was ominous. It was a different story when he turned into Baldriech Street. Noise was coming from the house in question, whose front door spilled yellow light on to the wrecked cars that lay around the small piece of wasteground that had once been a playpark. There were a couple of arguments going on and someone was revving an engine. A bystander told him the polis had been around a couple of times and lifted someone for thumping his wife. The usual. Not a story he could sell to the *Source*. His hopes faded.

A girl he knew was coming towards him. He recognised Jill Feeney, the local Councillor. Born here in Drumgeith, she knew everyone. She wasn't your average councillor, for a start she was only twenty-one, she was drop-your-drawers pretty and she was not any kind of party hack. Typical, she'd been invited to the eviction party.

Moray cycled around the block several times, then went home.

Sharkey phoned him later. 'Nothing doing?'

'Got clocked by the local councillor, she'd been invited to the party and wanted me to go in with her. In fact, she tried to pull me in, would you believe? She's a good laugh.'

Sharkey sounded annoyed. 'Wait – you got invited inside . . . and you didn't go?

'No, course not.'

'Why, had you forgotten your lighter?'

'Eh?'

'Well, If it was me chum, I'd have lobbed a good few lit cigarettes doon the back o the sofa. After all, we was promised a barbecue. Sometimes, man, you have to make things happen.'

'You weren't there. I'd have been done in before I got near the door.'

68

'Ach, you have to take a risk now and then. So. No story? I assume you've checked with the polis?'

'Yes. Nothing. Few arrests for drunkenness, minor vandalism. Two trees pulled down. One of them stole a car.'

'Better luck next time.'

10

Working Beneath the Drains

It was the simplest of jobs. They knew where he lived, they had the tip-off, the story was in the bag. All they needed was an image of the cunt himself.

Sharkey picked him up in the Volvo estate. He had his lenses and camera bodies in the boot and a metal cool box full of high-speed film. If snappers had their own regiment, he'd be the heavy artillery.

Sharkey barely glanced at Moray as he opened the door and sat in the front passenger seat. 'Off, are we?' he grunted. He was listening to the tape and thrumming his fingers on the wheel to Johnny Cash's nasal baritone and the monotonous clank-clank of rhythm guitar . . . *then ah heard ma dream went back downstream cavortin in Davenport* . . . There was something of the shitkicker in Sharkey, the sideburns, the cowboy boots, the leather waistcoats, the casual attitude, brazenly uncool, a man out of time, but Moray didn't intend to raise any of these points with him. They drove along the Kingsway and the Forfar Road to the big roundabout, heading for Fintry. *She loves you big river more than me . . . bong bong bong bong bong b-bong* the song ended as if gurgling down a drain.

'What school is it?' Sharkey asked and was told. Apart from that they didn't talk. The tape went into rewind. The narrator clutched the bit of paper which had the name of a school and the school jannie.

'Ages since I've been in this neck,' Sharkey said, steering the Volvo into a quiet street of terraced council houses whose lower walls were clad in dark wood panels. 'Upwardly mobile – look, some of the doors have been painted.'

'Number four,' Moray told him, pointing with a biro.

'Bingo,' Sharkey said. 'Here's the s.p.: bring the guy to the door. I'll do the rest.' He grinned, his broken teeth showing nicotine stains. 'Make sure you keep well back so he has to come forward – yeah – that's the trick.'

And Moray was out of the nice warm car on to the hostile street, trying to look nonchalant. Hands in pockets. He went up the path to number 6, read the name, Lennox, went back down. Walked up number 4. Snatched a quick look back at the car. Sharkey had the window down and sat there like the Russian mafia, his long lens resting on some kind of cloth. He gave the thumbs up. The front door was opening.

The man who pulled the door half-open did not evince signs of panic or great irritation. An ordinary wee man in dark trousers, tied at the waist with rope, an open white shirt and an unshaven, dishevelled appearance.

'Aye?' he inquired patiently, leaning forward and the narrator caught a strong whiff of stale sweat.

'Mr Lennox?' Moray inquired, stepping smartly backwards.

A look of comprehension swept across the man's face. Or was it relief? And he came forward, out of the lee of the door on to the path to indicate the neighbouring door. Moray continued to step backwards and forced himself not to look at the car. Surely the idiot must have clocked it? No. He seemed quite happy to talk.

'And you're Brady,' he suddenly asked, whipping out his dicta-phone, 'yeah? The jannie that's been done for molesting a school-boy?'

The change in subject was too rapid for the wee man. 'Eh?' he quavered. 'Yi wut?' His face darkened and in that instant, he saw it all, the dictaphone thrust at him, the camera pointing at him from the car, and moved with astonishing alacrity back into the house.

Sharkey was jubilant. 'Got the fucker!' he crowed. 'No bother.' He started the engine. 'He say anything?'

71

'Nothing.'

'Didn't apologise for being a pervy wee shite, no?'

'He didn't.'

'Shockin!'

On the way back, more Country 'n' Western.

'Ah, sing it, Jerry, man,' Sharkey went, eyes half-closed, thrumming the steering column . . . *ya don't miss your water* . . . *till the well runs dry* . . .

So the picture and two pars went in and the wee man was 'beasted'. Next to shagging stories, beastings are the fodder of tabloids like the *Source*. The punters want to see the faces, the looks on the faces of the 'beasts' when they get snapped. Want them splattered all over page three conveniently next to the teenage tits to gawp at over their cornflakes. Disgrace, outrage, shame. To give their lives some sense of progress, that right is advancing, that things are getting better, that no-one's ever going to find out their own dirty little secrets, when the truth is all that's not pendulous is at least circular, goes grinding round and round, year after year, the same, as before, routine mediocre unimaginative sins. Three weeks later, in a small par on page thirty-six; the jannie admonished in court for slapping a schoolboy who'd set a fire in the gymnasium that burned down most of the school. But by then, Moray was hard at work on his next sensational scoop for the *Source*.

Mrs Thompson saw the police car parked on the main road. Two uniformed constables were questioning Daniel Morrow in the living room, in front of the floor-to-ceiling tinted windows which overlooked the estuary. From his rumpled, shirt-sleeves and unshaven face, she could tell he'd had a bad night.

'Mi wife's missin,' he said, by way of explanation. 'Naebdy's seen ir since Frehday. Shiz no seyed nothin ti yirsel?'

'And this is . . . ?' one of the policemen inquired, rising to his feet.

'Mrs Thompson, wir home help,' Daniel said. 'Shi wiz workin here on Frehday bit no owir thi weekend.'

'No, Mr Morrow, your wife never said anything to me when I saw her on Friday. She wouldn't confide in me.'

'Eh didna think so.' Daniel rummaged over his face with his hands. 'Eh dinna think shiz . . . like . . . missin. Bit eh jist canna find ir. Eh dinna ken waur shiz.'

The policemen looked at each other. They were young, mid to late twenties, clean-shaven, lanky. They could have been twins, except one had thick bushy black eyebrows and a heavy growth and the other was almost callow, unhealthily pale. It was eyebrows who was asking the questions. 'You don't think this has anything to do with your business affairs?'

'It's known, Mr Morrow, that you have many enemies,' said the sallow constable.

'Naw, cudna be . . . Eh mean, wha wid . . . ?' He leaned back to consider. 'Fir god's sake, ur yi seyin she miyt hae been . . . kidnapped?'

'Always a possibility, sir, only a suggestion. Is there anyone with a strong grudge, in particular?'

Daniel's broad face assumed a guarded expression. 'Fuck-eh, thirz loads a jealous cunts in this wee toon. Maist widna git in mi wey . . . bit eh kid think o a few bams that widna mind haein a go.'

'Business rivals?'

'Eh'll mak a wee list.'

'In the meantime, Mr Morrow it's only been 36 hours, so we must not jump to conclusions,' said eyebrows. 'Still by far the most likely scenario is that she's staying with a friend.'

When the police left, Mrs Thompson attempted to carry on as normal. Only he, Daniel, couldn't see that the lass was with someone else. Plainly she hadn't been happy.

'I really think, Mr Morrow, that she's gone somewhere of her own accord. You know how . . .' she hesitated, selecting just the right word . . . 'how wilful she can be, if you don't mind me saying.'

Daniel, slumped on the sofa, cradled his mobile phone, almost desperately hoping it would ring.

'Aw eh, yir no wrang . . .'

Mrs Thompson was preoccupied as went about her routine

73

cleaning tasks. You'd think he would be glad she'd gone! A momentary thought struck her. This wasn't all a deception? She'd heard some of the stories about him, but surely, he looked too distraught? It was a fact that his second wife, Suze, had taken her own life. A friend of her husband's, who had been in the CID, told a story that it was because of an affair Daniel was having. The wife had confronted him in the crowded Ferry Port Bar and given him a very public ultimatum. 'It's either her or me,' she was supposed to have said. According to the friend from the CID, he'd given her a sour look and replied, 'Aw eh? Riyt – in that case it's her.' Suze had driven straight home in her BMW, closed the garage doors and opened the car windows. Twelve hours later, the engine was still running. It later emerged that she hadn't planned to die, she'd expected him to come home and find her and be struck by remorse, in a big reconciliation scene. His enemies said that he deliberately hadn't gone home because he suspected what she was going to do. It came out in court that he always went home and this was the first time that he had stayed away all night. That was a long time before he'd met Kylie of course. So they said. She wasn't the girl in the story.

Mrs Thompson could see him slumped in the sofa, more than halfway through a bottle of Glenfiddich. No, Kylie'd gone off and was letting him sweat. The young generation; married one day, divorced the next, easy come easy go, wet behind the ears. Each as bad as the other.

11

Letting the Matter Drop

It was a time when public outrage over moneylenders was at its
height. Moray Neill thought he could make an easy score. He knew
there was a lot of it going on locally. All he needed was a face, a
shot – preferably a smudged shot – of something dodgy at a street
corner, money changing hands, allegations backed up by state-
ments, addresses, tales of beatings-up for non-payment. If he could
get these, the story would stand up.

Sharkey was strangely pessimistic. 'Okay, we'll suck it and
see,' he said, reluctantly. 'But anything heavy and you're on
your own.'

Moray had some names and began to ask around. One name
turned out to be the Mr Big of local loansharking. Of the three
punters he spoke to in the Balena Bar, two thought the guy should
be recommended for citizen of the year, the third just wanted him
to get an OBE.

'Eez daein a public service, Jim. Lots a fowk cudna git beh wi'oot
thi moneylendirs.'

'Wut?' exclaimed another sozzled punter. 'Yi wahnt iz t' name
thi boay? Jing, crivvens, help ma boab! Yi must be aff yir chump!'

It wasn't going to be easy but rent was due at the end of the
month and he had nothing else in the offing. McLean at the *Source*
advocated caution. Moray decided to recce the area under cover of
darkness.

75

'You sure you've got the right address?' Sharkey asked as they drove to the north-west of the city.

'We'll just take a look,' Moray insisted. 'We don't want to arouse suspicion. Anyway, the action takes place outside the post office in Balgowan Avenue during the day.

Sharkey turned on to the dual carriageway at the Downfield roundabout. They drove parallel to the housing estate on the hill, which seemed almost inviting with its twinkling blue and white lights. Like a constellation of stars. The nether regions of Kirkton. Narrow roads. Claustrophobic. They felt like alien invaders. The windows were uncurtained, there was a blue TV reflection in each.

Sharkey wound down the window. 'You need ti get the smell of a place,' he said. They could hear shouting in the middle distance. Aimless violence was the main sport of the area, dependency the style of its culture. He turned into Derwent Avenue then Dunmore Street, where a few of the houses had been extracted from council ownership by the prolonged efforts of solicitors. Parked cars lined both sides of the narrow street. Sharkey changed down to second. They had reached a junction of three streets, blocked by a badly-parked ice-cream van.

'What a mugwump!' Sharkey said, and added under his breath, 'Lock your door.'

But the small queue of adults and children queuing at the van paid them no heed. The van moved on. 'It's an old trick,' Sharkey said: 'They grab stuff out of your car, when you're stopped. Your wallet, briefcase, mobile phone, wife, girlfriend or daughter . . .'

There was a lack of streetsigns. 'That's to disorientate the visitor and the polis,' Sharkey said. 'It's deliberate.'

They turned the corner and saw a streetsign in impeccable nick, except that the letter 'H' had been daubed on the front of 'Ashlaw Place'. It was a dead-end, a cul-de-sac.

'Typical,' said Sharkey. 'The only effing street that doesn't need a sign. Who'd want to come here?'

Most of the houses were empty, boarded up. There were few cars. The front gardens, whose fencing had long since been removed, were dumps of rubbish, the blackened contents of one house, open to the sky. The place was deserted.

'What number do you have?' Sharkey asked, parking behind the burnt-out remains of a Ford Cortina which lacked wheels. Its axles rested on bricks. 'Here is where old cars come to die,' he added. 'The joyriders' terminus.'

'Looks quiet enough,' Moray said. 'It's the end one.'

There were six blocks of flats on each side of the street with four flats in each and while most were darkened and boarded up, the end two houses were blazing with light.

'I'll wait here,' Sharkey said. When Moray looked sharply at him, he took out his rolly-ups. 'Fuck it, just a recce you said. Haven't even got my cameras.'

Feeling like a lap dancer at the Assembly of the Church of Scotland, Moray edged up the street. He noticed that the two end houses had, by some renovation or other, been joined together – there was only one front door. He saw that it was freshly painted, had a large expensive brass knocker, solid-brass letterbox. To the side where the bin storage area should be, he saw a Victorian-style conservatory and flickering colours of a massive flat-screen TV reflecting on the glass. Finally, he slid around the gable end to look in the front windows, casting a giant shadow of himself down the street.

He stood gaping into Aladdin's cave. The room gleamed with treasures and luxury items stacked as if on show. It was like Harrod's shop-window, or an Argos catalogue display. Rows of hi-fi's in unscratched matt black, videos still in their boxes, TVs galore piled on top of each other, punch-balls, exercise equipment, attaché cases, computers, lap-tops, golf-bags, air-rifles, rails of suits and dresses, stacked snooker tables, rows of brass lamps and chandeliers on the floor, camcorders, electric guitars . . . and each item seemed to gleam particularly invitingly in the bright light, winking and flashing at him. His spine crawled. He stepped backwards, began to back away. Saw someone watching him from an unlighted window on the upper floor. The face of the money-lender, strangely smiling benignly – and that was the scariest thing of all. He hurried back to the car.

'Go!' he said urgently. 'Get me out of here!'

Sharkey knew the smell of fear and the Volvo shot down the

street with a squeal of tyres and took the corner in third and avoided hitting any of the cars and was away out of the estate.

It was several days before Moray summoned the nerve to work on the story again. It was a tricky job, calling for perfect positioning of the car so that they had both a good view and could make a quick getaway if things went pear-shaped.

The perfect position was tucked in behind a dusty battered old caravanette, just twenty feet from the chipshop and a further fifteen from the sub-post office.

'Nine now,' he said. 'Look they're taking off the metal shutters and the grilles and the iron bars.'

'Like Beirut here,' Sharkey grunted. 'The walls are held together by the weight of the graffiti. Look – there's a guy sniffin glue at the bus stop. Must be waitin for the number 13. On his way to the Job Centre. Hmn, bit too early for signin on though: he must be staff.'

A small queue had formed outside the post office but there seemed to be some sort of hold-up. No-one was getting in.

'There he is,' Sharkey said quietly. 'The boy in the leather jacket. See, he's just gone over to the queue. See him, now, yes, he's handing out the family credit books. Aw, look – the old man's no getting one . . . what a shame. That's discrimination that is. Wait – he's getting . . . yes, here's your pension book . . .'

'I wouldn't have believed it if I hadn't seen it with my own eyes,' Moray commented.

'Aye, and there's the bag man waiting, see, in the red Lada. He'll be collecting the books in again, with the dosh of course, once the punters have done the business at the counter. You've got to hand it to them, it's a slick operation.'

Moray and Sharkey watched the operation for almost an hour. They had had no idea loansharking was so widespread. Scores of people had had dealings with the two men outside the post office. Young and old, family credit books for single parents, pension books for the old and signing-on cards for everyone else.

There was a moderate tap at the window on the narrator's side. A balding fit-looking middle-aged man in a brown leather jacket, jeans and trainers indicated that he should wind down the window. Moray did so.

The man leaned in, resting his elbows on the window. 'Mornin lads,' he said affably. 'Noo – wuv got yir licence number an yir names. We ken wut yir trehin t' dae an wha yir trehin t' dae ut fir, an we ken whar yiz baith live. Eh've been tellt ti gie yiz a wee message that uf anythin appears in thi *Scottish Source* ir any ither pippir, then . . . wull, then . . . Ji ken wut ehm saying . . . ?' He was very calm, and that was the most frightening thing. There was a long shocked silence in the car.

'Oh yes, sure, no problem, sir,' Sharkey said. 'We won't give you no bother. We're off now. Look – I'm starting the car. You won't see us here again. Right, okay? Bye bye.'

Moray angrily hurled recriminations of cowardice at Sharkey's head all the way back to the city centre. Sharkey glowered until he could bear it no more.

'Fuck me, man,' he said. 'You don't argue when the cunts have shooters. You couldn't see it. The boys in the van behind us had a fuckin sawn-off shotgun.'

'Van behind us? Well – why didn't you tell me?' Moray demanded.

Sharkey scowled. 'You were too busy pissing yourself. Look at the bloody mess you've made of my seat!'

12

The engine turned over, weakly, and gave out with a tinny whine. Exasperated, Gavin Cathro looked at his wristwatch, then removed the keys. He swung his legs out of the ancient red Astra, on to the weed-fringed path and returned indoors via the porch.

Carly, in her white dressing gown, barely looked up as he came in. The windows of the bright, cluttered cottage kitchen were steamed with condensation. The children sat at the table, little Kenny swinging his legs and waving his plastic spoon. Gavin slung his denim jacket on the back of the chair.

'Again?' Carly asked, pouring out cornflakes for Susan, who was neatly dressed in her grey school uniform. Gavin sat down at his place at the table, pushed his long dark hair out of his eyes and poured himself another cup of coffee.

'Daddy, is the car broken again?' Susan inquired, looking worried.

'Uh-huh, sweet thang,' Gavin told her. 'She's an old car, she has days when she just doesn't feel like driving.'

'Daddy is silly,' Susan confided to her mother.

'He is,' Carly agreed, sitting down and pulling the lapels of her dressing gown together. 'Are you going by bus?'

'Looks like I'll have to.'

'Daddy on bus!' Kenny shouted delightedly, banging his mela-ware spoon on the table.

'Kenny, put it down!' Carly ordered, removing the spoon. 'Maybe you can get a lift off Mr Lanelly if you're quick?'

'He's already gone, babe. Saw his car at the junction. It's only a Philosophy seminar I'll be missing. Professor Cobb, Descartes. He's daft as a brush anyway. I'll get the handouts off my mates. I could get the bus at eleven.'

Carly snorted. 'Well, you can walk Susan to school then.'

'Aye, okay. I'll just finish my coffee first.'

'I'll get my bag, Daddy.'

Gavin took Susan's hand. 'Come on, trouble.'

'Oh, I forgot something.'

Gavin was glad at the prospect of a morning at home. He had reached the stage of life when he hated to spend time away from the house, the garden, his books and the novel he was trying to write. He liked being a family man and adored Carly, absolutely, utterly and without reservation, studious Susan and chuckle-headed wee Kenny, and living at Inchmartins, a detached cottage, whose front windows looked up at the houses of Errolbank and the church with its four-spired hat. Whose back garden had a view of the wide open flat plains stretching eastwards and south to the trees and the river beyond. Life was peaceful and clean and uncluttered. The garden was not large and not small, just big enough to grow a reasonable quantity of vegetables, herbs and fruits. After six years they felt they had it just the way they wanted it. It captured the sun nearly all day. They had many friends in the area. They belonged. After years in cities Gavin felt that he had finally come home. Oh yes, he loved Inchmartins. This was, after all, the area which his uncle and his grandfather had once farmed. Cathro was an old Pictish name. There had been Cathros in Errolbank since the Battle of Pitalpin. Probably there were Cathros he hadn't met still sleeping off that fierce conflict with the Scots. Gavin liked the idea of continuity, albeit impossible to prove with any certainty.

Of course, they didn't own their cottage. They were liable to the whim of the factor of the Hay Estates, but the rent was reasonable. Which was just as well because they existed on a precarious level of income. Carly's part-time earnings as shop assistant at the village Spar shop and his own student loan money, which would have to be repaid, if he ever got a full-time job. Gavin enjoyed the mental effort his university course demanded, but did not expect it to lead anywhere. He would pass his exams and graduate in two years' time but what then? An arts degree was next to useless unless you wanted to be a teacher. And who would? There were no other jobs unless he moved away and he didn't want to do that. Also, at thirty-two, he wasn't about to drastically change his image, cut his long, thick hair and become a ruthless, thrusting, dynamic career-grabber. He hated that kind of Thatcherite bullshit. What he wanted he mostly already had: the love of a good woman, a happy family life, a peaceful time in the country where he could watch the seasons come and go in his own garden, smoke a little dope and drink a lot of homebrew, have an uncomplicated friendly social life with a wide group of mates and other couples and time to reflect, space to think. A good laugh, that was all he wanted. Nothing heavier than that. He enjoyed some of his classes at university, especially Philosophy and Literature, liked to test his mind, encounter new theories – and it was good for his own writing – but really he was marking time.

'Daddy, I'm ready,' Susan called, from the doorway.

He went into the kitchen and kissed Carly on the back of the neck between her beaded braids. 'I'll try and get Jed to look at the car this morning,' he said.

'Well, see you at tea-time, honeybun,' Carly said grouchily, turning back to the dishes in the sink. It was her time of the month and she was a martyr to it. Kenny slithered out of his high chair and was trying to come after him.

'Daddy!' he shouted gleefully, bobbing forward to grab hold of Gavin's leg.

Gavin lifted him high to kiss him. 'See you later, wee wee man!'

'Come *on*, Daddy, I don't want to be late!' Susan called from the hallway.

'I'll catch the wee rascal,' Carly said, cornering the giggling Kenny under the table.

Gavin smiled complacently as he followed Susan down the weed-fringed path to the garden gate and across the cracked, potholed tarmac road that led a hundred yards south to New Farm. There was no hedge or wall and they walked across the stubble field to the ditch between two willow trees where Gavin had created a simple bridge with four thick planks.

'Come on, Suse,' he said, holding out his hand to help her over. The field sloped upwards to the village and led to the main road. The track struggled between hedges of bright-yellow gorse and pink rosa rugosa. There was little traffic between the isolated cottages along the winding road between Kingoodie and Errolbank. He waited for Susan to catch up – she was wearing enormous clumpy black shoes. The continuity of drystone dykes ran to New Farm, and beyond that, a hundred yards further, to the trees which protected the slow water, idling by, sifting through reedbeds.

'Gorgeous day,' he said, 'eh, sugar?'

Now she was in front and pulled him strongly by the hand. 'Come on, Daddy, I don't want to be late. I hate to miss the lines.'

Susan was, at eight, a most diligent pupil, according to her immaculate report cards, though rather prone to solitary pursuits, not keen on sports and games. Very like her mother. Carly had been more studious, more ambitious than he. When they first met she already had a BA degree in Art from Edinburgh. With her friend, Lou Rawnsley, Carly had had several joint exhibitions and both had sold stuff. Lou went to London. Carly had been restless for a while, planned an exhibition at the Cottage Gallery in Newtyle which didn't come off. Gavin had worried about holding her back although she always denied it. Then Susan came along and somehow she never got back to the painting and got a part-time job and then Kenny had been expected and they'd bumped along quite happily, and Carly gave up painting. Now she was a shop assistant. Her art stuff occupied two plastic bags in the attic. There were no jobs around that he could get hold of. He'd tried. He'd gone after many jobs over the years, in Dundee, Forfar, Glamis, Perth, even St Andrews, but something about his laid-back, almost comatose style, his obvious lack of ambition always seemed to scupper his chances. Being a mature student was a four-year career-break from signing-on.

The pavement started from the semi-detached cottages. In the rear garden of the end cottage, he saw Jed's neighbour hanging out washing. Mrs McGreevey waved, mouth full of plastic pegs. On the front step of the adjacent cottage, Jed was tinkering with the innards of his Kawasaki motorbike, in black T-shirt and black jeans with a colourful bandanna tied around his long greasy blond hair.

'Jed, man, how's it going?' he called.

'Aye, mate,' Jed said, swooping to his feet and coming over in loosely-fastened black cowboy boots. His grin revealed the teeth missing in his jaw. 'Nae gaun t' thi Coallege thi day?' Spotting Susan up ahead, he called, 'Hiya princhesh!'

'Daddy, I'll be late!'

'Jed – back in five minutes, man. Get the coffee on.'

He caught up with Susan. They walked side by side along the main road, under overhanging trees at the garden walls of substantial houses, across the gravel entrance to the coachworks adjacent to the first of the prefab classrooms behind the fence. There were four blue-painted huts, in one of which his daughter would spend the best part of her day. The school building appeared around trees. Several parents stood outside at the railings. It was an attractively symmetrical stone building. A modest spire astride the identical halves of the façade punctured a weathervane in the form of a fish.

Susan gave him an anxious peck on the cheek when he leant forward and she rushed off through the school gates just as the bell went. He observed her among the grey-clad pupils, waving from the little group of her friends when they filed inside. He turned away. *She was loved.*

When he reached the cul-de-sac of Gowrie Place, Gavin stopped to consider the panorama of the Sidlaws, those benign slivers of rock which had slipped from the marching glaciers to form the banks of the wide and watery Carse. Under water, all this, he remembered, until the eighteenth century, this wide, fertile strath then like an inland sea, thirty miles long and ten miles wide. Which of course, Gavin knew, was why it was now so fertile. Too much water then, but now, the big danger was silting-up. They'd sold off the dredgers. It was the serenity of the Carse that attracted him. You could see it for miles. A plume of smoke here, a tractor reversing in a field there, and, to the south, the continual deep running of the water. The permanency and assurance of the water was what had given rise to his notions of Pictishness, centuries of continuous history, fantasies of Cathros sleeping in unmarked graves, a kind of obscure pseudo-religion which Gavin believed in when he felt elated or mystical. In his 'poetic moments', a quiet blissful certitude, an intense feeling of karma or perfect 'being-ness', of feeling absolutely right.

And above was the soaring sky, vast and unfathomable. It was going to be a hot day. A matter of keeping your head down against such an overwhelmingly wonderful landscape. The Carse was of one piece, a double-stitched tapestry of fields, trees, dykes and homes, complete, perfect.

Yet it was down there, Gavin knew, tasting reflux of saliva which caused him to swallow hard, down there – that planners wanted to build an entire new town. Large-scale housing, hun-dreds, maybe two thousand houses stuck together like Lego. New roads, a new school, thousands of new people who knew nothing of each other or the area. To the planners it was a convenient site, a disused military airfield in the middle of nowhere. There weren't even people and existing homes to clear. They missed the point. Why had it been a military airfield? Because the level landscape of the Carse and the river basin could hide aircraft and the low buildings of the airfield. They merged into the distance, dissolved into the perspective. Two thousand houses could certainly be built, but it wouldn't ever be a town. 'Town' suggested a community, with neighbours and friendliness and amenities. This would be Legoland-on-Tay. Errolbank village had evolved over centuries, set up for a purpose by people who wanted to live in proximity. It was an organic community which operated for its own reasons and was not a slave to anyone's whim, no-one ruled it, no-one controlled it, except the villagers themselves. For seventy-five million quid in the pockets of less than half-a-dozen individuals, for a few hundred jobs for a year or eighteen months at most, the planners would destroy forever the community spirit – and its connection to history – of the Carse by creating this blot on the landscape, this commuter suburb of nowhere, with no spirit or ethos of its own. No tradition, no social fabric, nothing but security lights, lap-larch fencing, satellite dishes. Two thousand families promised 'a country life-style without the inconveniences of rural living.'

Of course, some of the locals would think it was a great idea. Jed would mock his fears. 'Z' dehd brilliant man! Mair hooses means mair young babes gaen aboot . . . mair cunt!' The dismantled Kawasaki engine dripped oil on the step. The front door was propped open with a heavy wrench.

'Jed?' he called, moving through the lobby into the kitchen. Familiar noises of Jimi Hendrix came from the dormer bedroom above, a cacophony of churning lead guitar and the muttered refrain of voices: *you got me floating* . . .

'Jed!' he shouted up the stairs. There was a stirring of feet on the floor of the attic bedroom.

'Right, mate! Eh'm comin doon.'

Jed lumbered down the wooden stairs in his heavy boots. 'Fancy a blast, Gavin, m' man? Eh'v got some braw Leb. Rerr stuff.'

'Oh aye. I'm getting the bus at eleven though.'

'Eh'll run y' in man, yeah, soon's eh git thi bike fixed. How's about rollin-up fir iz? Thi stuff's on thi mantelpiece, man. Meh mitts is a ile.'

'First, how about a coffee?'

'Please yirsel, eh'll jist yase this rag ti wipe meh hauns.'

While Gavin went into the kitchen, Jed lowered himself into the heavy chintz settee and started to roll a joint on the cover of Simon and Garfunkel's *Bridge Over Troubled Water*.

'Any danger you could hae a look at my Astra this morning?'

'Eh, mibbe, wut's a wrang wi it?'

'Nae idea. The alternator. Battery trouble again, I think.'

'That Astra, man! Yi ought tae git rid. A the bathir it gies yi, eh? Git yirsel a real motor. How no come wi iz next time eh tak a trip ti thi auctions at Forfar? Eh'll get yi a brah wee runner an eh'll dae it up chaip fir yi an a.'

'Great,' said Gavin without much enthusiasm. Jed had been making the same promise for two years. 'Two sugars you take?'

'Yeah, right.'

But Jed had fixed up other people's cars, that was true. He loved guddling about in oily bits of machinery more than he liked to put them all back together. He could recite from memory the serial numbers of interesting engine parts he'd worked on, and cars, motorbikes, tractors, bicycles, lawnmowers held great attractions for him. As soon as he saw them he wanted to take them apart to make them go better. He was an intuitive mechanic even before his five years as an apprentice at Soutar's Garage, where he now worked four days a week.

Jed held the long, twisted joint up to the daylight streaming into the living room from a side window festooned with sprawling spider plants and scarlet geraniums. The light tinged the surfaces in the room with gold dust. 'A thing of joy, eh?' he said.

'You've got it arse-aboot,' Gavin said. 'A thing of beauty,' he corrected, 'is a joy forever.'

'Yeah, man? Well near enough to boogie, eh?' He flicked the cap off his brass lighter and ignited the crimped end of the joint.

'Ah well, just a wee toot,' Gavin said. 'To blaw oot the cobwebs. Then we'll go and look at the motor?'

'Eh, wull hae a wee look,' Jed agreed.

Gavin relaxed on the other end of the sofa, eyes closed as he inwardly observed the trail of smoke through the vesicles of his lungs, interfacing with red blood cells at the molecular level.

'Let's dig some sounds, man,' Jed said, kneeling by the hi-fi. He selected from the record collection stacked edgeways on the floor, which stretched across the room from wall to wall held in place by a large brass bong. At last count, about five thousand. He removed the vinyl and placed it on the turntable. Not for Jed the technological improvements of CD, mini-disk or MP3. 'All pish, man, it's the bands playin' that matters, no the anorak geeks in the factory.' Jed had never been the same since the Perthshire rock festival where some DJ had started scratching Led Zeppelin tracks in a hip-hop mix. 'Pure fuckin sacrilege, man!' he'd stormed. 'If eh coulda got near thi stage, eh'd hae panned his pus fir um. See, thuv got nothin new, so they jist rob a thi brah stuff o bands that can play. Ach, man . . . yi ken yirsel . . .'

Jed sat down and after a jarring scratching, the familiar sound of Californian surf on sand, the lengthy pacific intro, then, *da-duuuh . . . riders on the storm . . .* Dope smoke lazily ascending to the low ceiling, sunlight haze, rippling melody of piano on the first track. Jed rolled another joint. Gavin contemplated his life: so sure, so solid that maybe nothing could change it. Early days anyway. Blots on the landscape? Try to forget it.

13

Blockage at the Treatment Plant

McLean was coming to town, to find out what was impeding the smooth flow of good stories to the *Scottish Source* from their end.

Moray Neill met him outside the station kiosk on the upper level. He'd been told that his bark was worse than his bite but the man looked like a sea lion. Frizzy greying hairs stuck out sideways from the back of his head. His forehead was bald but most noticeable was the rosiness of the lips of his small mincing mouth. He looked rumpled and paunchy yet stepped delicately on his toes in sharp-pointed black suede shoes. He had bad catarrh and availed himself of the pavement at the taxi-rank. The narrator offered him a handshake but he seemed not to see the proffered appendage.

'You're giving me stuff I couldn't wipe my arse with,' he complained. 'Forget the big investigations, just feed me snappy picture stories. Set them up if you have to. Fucksake, there's a circulation war on and the *Recorder*,' he spat on to the pavement, 'is getting one or two scoops from these parts. Fucksake, just last week the bastards had a front pager about someone in the Council offices running up a £225 bill for calls to a chatline. Half a fucking page. Great story.' He spat again. 'Arseholes. Fucksake, you guys are letting the side down. How did you not get to it? Fucksake, a month now you've been on a retainer and what have you gave me? Eh? Fuckall and that's it.' He glanced around. 'The Shark joinin us in the boozer, is he?'

The Anchor Bar in Union Street is a traditional boozer which hasn't altered in decades. The narrator hadn't been there before but soon found McLean had an encyclopaedic knowledge of all the pubs in Dundee.

'Didn't use to let skirt in here,' he mused over the frothy top of a brace of pints of golden brown Caledonian Extra. 'The good old days.'

'Never used to wear one myself,' Moray mumbled behind his hand, 'so I wouldn't know.'

'Eh? Say something?' McLean quizzed. 'Didn't catch . . . Look here, mate, things is desperate,' he said, leaning back. 'I've had to chop the expenses of some of our top boys. The editor-in-chief's in Glasgow for a week just looking for an excuse to close down the whole Scottish operation. The big boss, Sir Philip de Cundy himself, no less.'

'No? But you're within ten thousand of the *Recorder*'s circulation figures. That'd be madness.'

'Yeah, he thinks he could close us down, put a kilt on the London edition and still be in contention . . .'

Sharkey swaggered in through the swing doors, in jeans and cowboy boots, long wire-coloured hair sweeping the lapels of his black silk bomber jacket.

'Howdy,' he grunted, clocking the pints. 'My round?'

'Of course, the Shark's case is a little different,' McLean said loudly. He began to gargle with the sputum in his throat and wiped it on to a paper tissue which appeared just in time. 'Yeah, he's on a retainer too, of course, but his allows him to do work for other rags. Except the *Recorder*, of course, that so, Sharks?'

'Aye, abiddy except the *Recorder*. Mind, I've done stuff fir them in the past. Pay better 'n this lot.'

'Rebellious talk, Sharks,' McLean said, hoisting the fresh pint. Apart from the three of them there was nobody in the darkened dusty bar except Phinn, the lanky half-asleep barman slowly sluicing glasses in a sink below the bar. Moray fancied he saw him begin to lean as if he was going to topple into sleep.

'How come,' McLean grunted, rubbing the back of his neck to

90

create a dandruff storm, 'how come you weren't at the official launch of the Summer Festival where that councillor's skirt went over her head and gave everyone a look at her M&S knicks? Eh, Sharks? That's the kind of snaps we want.'

'I was on a job at Dens when that story blew up,' Sharkey grinned. 'Anyway, it was blown out of all proportion. She's a dog. Now if it was Nicole Kidman . . .'

'In Dundee? More likely to be Nora Batty,' Moray muttered.

'You're missing the point, Sharks. If it'd been me I'd have asked for an action replay. Fucksake, these politicians like to be in the papers. Helps them get elected.'

'Maybe they should sew party logos on their knickers just in case,' said Moray sarcastically.

'Fucksake . . .' McLean continued to struggle with a pro-tracted blockage in his tubes before he was able to snarl it out into a handkerchief. 'Fucksake, what have you got for this week?'

Sharkey looked at Moray who looked at the shiny floor. Dim dusty light floated in from the street through the high stained-glass windows.

Moray coughed. 'Eh, uh, story about a dodgy landlord who's always perving about with his student tenants.'

McLean nodded. 'Uh? Good shagging story, but can you make it stand up?'

His mouth contracted to a mean pout. 'I mean, fucksake, you've got blown out on loads of other stories. What you need to do is think how you can get the story easiest. There's always a way. Like, get one of the lassies to give you the details. Make it up if you need to but make it juicy. Get her to pose in her scanties . . . that kind of thing. It's easy.'

Moray realised McLean was taking the idea seriously. 'But what's in it for her? I mean, the guy is highly respected in the town. Drinks with councillors. He's on the Committee at the Sailing Club. He's a heavy bloke, knows lots of bad guys. It'll be her word against his.'

'This is what you do,' McLean said, shaking his head sorrowfully. 'Fucksake, I've put fucking *amateurs* on a retainer . . . Say you'll see her alright. Promise her a ton, maybe even more.'

'Really? Will you stand for a ton?'

McLean's pintpot hit the table. Sweat was running down the dome of the forehead. 'Don't you fucking dare, mate! Fucksake, what? Jesus! With Sir Philip here? No, you *promise* the bird a ton. Say it'll be sent as a cheque. Not your fault if it never arrives, and by that time the story'll be long dead. Make sure you don't sign nothing, and promise as little as possible. It's amazing how punters think papers will pay them thousands for shit. Fucksake, most guys try not to let the punter even know which paper it's going to be in. Only use your real name if you have to. Never ever ever give them your address. We get loads of punters harassing us for money, but they've got no evidence to support their claim. Just the word of some guy they talked to. Fucksake. I shouldn't have to be telling you all this. Wise up quick, or you're no bloody use to us. Sharkey knows the score, eh? Listen to him on stories.'

He stood up. Wiped his lips with his sleeve. 'Get this pervy rachman to me by Wednesday, boys, or your retainers are gone. Kaput! Lots of pics, as many girls as you like, nice tits, legs, lingerie. Do what you have to and keep 'em coming, a story a week is not too much to expect from this dump. Now, I'm off to Tannadice, cab rank still in the High Street?'

And McLean was gone. Leaving behind a sodden tissue in the ashtray and two empty pintpots.

'Bad sinuses, the cunt,' Sharkey said by way of explanation. 'Dodgy landlord story, eh? You just make that up?'

'Not a bit of it, I know just the geezer,' said Moray. 'He's long overdue a bit of publicity. Years ago, see, a girlfriend and her mate were staying in one of his flats in Broughty Ferry. He kept suddenly appearing in the flat at midnight just as one of them was coming out of the shower, or getting ready to go to bed. Usually drunk, and he tried it on, you know, "how's about a rentfree week if one of you girls is nice to me . . ." Believe me, he's had a lot of slaps in the pus. He's had it coming for a long time.'

'Married is he?'

'Oh yeah, and he's a big nob in rotary circles.'

Sharkey grinned. 'Big knob . . . you should use that. When do we bust him?'

Moray pulled out his wallet. 'Soon. Soon. Another pint?'

When Gavin woke, he found he could remember most of the dream and the sense of anxiety that coloured the fabric of it. He lay on his side staring into the grey early light shimmering around the floating curtains. He had known that there would be no stopping them . . . *they had breached the Nettlebed Woods, now little more than a few straggly bushes on either side of a deeply rutted swamp of heavy tyre-tracks. The whole west side was a steaming tarmac playpark. And they had swarmed on, breasting the rise, coveting the four-acre fruit farm, oddly unfamiliar, where Gavin's uncle had worked as a teenager, where his grandfather had farmed. They had rumbled along the farmtrack to the mill stream (now culverted under a concrete bridge spanned by a roundabout and four new roads), and over the stream halfway up to the old stone circle. Even Woodbridge House and grounds hadn't halted the flood tide of progress. The old couple had died childless and in those orchards where previous generations of town boys would make a long autumn pilgrimage to steal plums, the bulldozers stood waiting for legal confirmation of the deeds of sale. The Council had executed a compulsory purchase order and there were no living relatives to lie down in the face of the devastation the machines would wreak in that paradise that had been two lives' work, so lovingly tended in partnership, an outward symbol of the couple's lifelong bond, never a cross word. Now ringing to the foreman's cursing of day labourers hired from some urban slum, the muddy ground beneath their boots littered with cigarette stubs and torn fragments of sepia photographs of previous generations squinting under heavy hats and formal stiff collars. Already the gable end was bashed in by two mighty sideways sweeps of a JCB. The smell of dust, plaster and concrete hung over everything and lingered in the nostrils.*

And the neat and nasty semi's squatted in their harled squadrons, looking blankly down on the fields, which had a vulnerable and disused look, already much used by the dogs that the new residents – the semi-beings – had brought with them. And the hedgerows had already gone after complaints about vermin and rabbits and the noisy dawn chorus affecting the sleeping of night-shift workers. In its place a row of concrete lamp-posts, plexi-glass bus shelter (vandal-proof, but heavily-vandalised), electric board metal box protected by an iron fence, a tarmac path leading nowhere. Inside their compounds, the new residents, aliens drawn from all the planets of the solar system, turned up the gas on their BBQ sets and poked a desultory zinc fork into the row of pink low-budget cholesterol-rich sausages, and heartily wished all the building work completed. That all the estates, all the neat and nasty little semi's were adjoined, lap larch fence to lap larch fence, from John O'Groat's to Land's End, for then, then, there would be no more dust, concrete, plaster, no more interruptions, no more unplanned interventions of scary, freakish nature. The whole bastard wild green savagery of bugs and flying things that bite and noisy things that cheep and sing and slimy things that eat each other would be gone and nothing could halt the onward progress the unlimited miles of TV aerials of people like us.

There would be no stopping them now. They were already in situ and the brick setts of their drives were already laid and their lawns were covered in visqueen and layers of pink gravel. Beside their tin alloy BBQ sets the controlled water features bubbled out of large green pebbles bought from a garden centre and a few plastic gnomes stood ready to kill with wheelbarrow, fishing rod and shovel. The ground oozes rapid weedkiller and deadly sybol and paraquat to keep away any little things crawling or oozing that might dare to make it across the patio to the sacred pansies.

And an economy-sized dog hops about, newly castrated, ex-ercising its ire on what's permitted to grow, and the only living thing in the 'garden' that's unplanned, a tiny raspberry plant thrusting up in the dark corner, the only thing that's a bit wild, is saturated and discoloured with cat's pee, being on a junction of feline territories. These hulking sadists, overfed on oily processed catnosh still find it necessary to trap and kill the few blue-tits, finches, siskins which still occasionally visit these suburban deserts with windows attracted by the recommended wooden bird tables bought at the garden centres on the advice of the TV garden experts.

But the diligent Council, mindful of the lack of green in all these miles of new concrete and stone, has decided to set up a wildlife theme park on the edge of Woodbridge House, although they know that 'pressures' will lead to its being 'released' for development before the park is put into effect. But they must allay the fears of the environmental lobby somehow. And one day the fences will go up to keep the wildlife in. Crates of ducks will be bussed in for weekenders to gawp at and throw bread to and one or two will occasionally find its way out as someone's Christmas dinner. And the place will be a great silent wilderness, litter-strewn, 'managed', whose wildlife left long ago. But at least it will present no logistical difficulties for the bulldozers when the day finally comes and Woodbridge Park Estate foundations are laid in rivers of wet concrete.

And down come the trees down with a mighty crash, except the sound is off, so these murderous acts are silent and largely unseen. Thirty, forty, eighty, perhaps two hundred years old. Ah, who cares? Ancient trees, bloody old things, half rotten anyway, look, you can snap the branches off easy. Not that all the trees go all at once. Some are left as 'fig-leafs' of the planning process but keep getting in the way of the bulldozers, so 'accidentally' disappear, a little judicious pruning and lopping today, felling tomorrow, on a public holiday when there's some absolutely crucial English 3rd Division football match or televised bingo, or an EastEnders Omnibus on, so nobody will be around to notice. But don't worry, the press are told, we'll replant with tree 'screen' if it bothers you. As if trees are a decorative feature to help sell houses. And a few straggly bushes go up in plastic sleeves which kids hack to pieces and climb into and break up for sticks to beat rival gangs in the suburban estates' wars.

And the hills flatten out, the woods rename streets, the fresh air is claimed by the loop of streetlights. And still you see the occasional wild visitor: a cute hedgehog maybe, yes, face-down, flat on the side of the road . . .

Gavin's dream had lost its visual quality inside his head and gained the coherence of anger. As he consciously reached back into the dream, he found that he was already controlling it. Ideas were

95

taking the place of images. But still his anger wrote sentences in his mind, imprinting itself across his mind's eye.

. . . these new estates levitate above the hill like flying saucers. Lines and lines of white and blue shimmering lights. No signs of human life, a great silent sterility when night falls, everyone locked into their little cube, all mod cons, sentry lights on the outer walls in case, heaven forbid, anyone should approach uninvited, garages' security cameras ready defensively winking red to capture anything that might approach, the tiniest moth that seeks to invade the paid-for space. But there never is . . . there is nothing to approach. For no-one lives here except those with mortgages. Who are these people? Where do they come from? How do we communicate with them? Take me to your leader. I am a tree . . .

Gavin sat up, visualising the gnarled friendly texture of bark, and opened his eyes to see the profile of Carly's face next to him in the bed in the cottage in the world he knew, undeveloped, un-ravaged, still beautiful despite its age, billions of billennia older than time. He sighed gently, freed by his sense of relief. A sort of controlled nightmare.

'You awake?' he whispered.

Carly barely stirred. 'Shush, it's too early. Go back to sleep.'

'I think I'll get up.' He sat up and waited for her to say something.

'Well, go on then . . . if you're going.'

'Okay, I will,'

'You were kicking again,' she said accusingly.

He looked briefly at her, tucked in and neat, and pulled on his jeans and moved from the dark bedroom into the hall. He went out into the garden and sat on the front-door step. The sun was just starting to glow behind the Fife hills, daylight emerging from the east. It was marvellously cool, the watery morning air lapped at his throat, his mouth, nostrils and eyes. He went back into the kitchen and poured himself a glass of water. Indoors was stuffy after the coolness of the garden. He returned outside, barefoot. It had been a while since he had been alone like this with the waned moon and the river and the silent landscape. Funny how visible the moving clouds could be at night in the sky. It was not yet morning but night

96

was almost gone; it was a sort of limbo, in abeyance, in waiting – like him. For what? For the tide to turn, for the onrush of an idea? He thought of Carly sleeping lightly in their bed upstairs and in the attic room, little Kenneth, on his side, snoring quietly in that way he had of utter abandonment and Susan sleeping calmly surrounded by soft bears and bagpusses and fluffy mice and rabbits, face concentrating, barely breathing. His family. A welling-up sob of emotion broke through him and left him intensely glad. And yet he enjoyed this feeling of being outside them – of separation – of looking in from above or beyond. A quiet moment of definite truth, reality with the skin scraped off, where he was at and wanted to be. You couldn't beat this! And leaving the door open, he went for a stroll with his glass of water across the garden and on to the dyke and sat there, observing the shimmering lights of the road bridge, five clear miles away. He could make out the headlights of cars crossing.

The dream had been horribly real even if the landscape was fictional. Nettlebed Woods? That wasn't anywhere he knew. Funny how the dreaming mind creates variations of reality.

He heard faint sounds of a car engine and looking east picked up the flicker of distant headlights. It was a long way off, and the noise came to him intermittently, taking the tight bends at Grange before the long straight to the junction. He watched it appear on the main road heading up the curving bend to the village. The car erupted past the road end, seconds later, a Mini, going too fast. He saw on the kitchen clock that it was 4.15 a.m. The engine noise, shattering the silence of the countryside, could be heard for miles, and across the silent blackness of the river. At that speed, rabbits better look out.

He wondered if he was in the mood for poetry and fetched down his notebook, sitting in the soft armchair in the living room, switched on the sidelight, read a few of the scribbled pages but his eyes began to blink and the effort of reading was too great, and the notebook slipped to the floor and he was asleep in the cool breeze entering the house from the open front door, which also admitted the waif moon, orphaned and alone and the sound of the great silent river running through all his dreams.

97

14

For Marjorie Braid, Sunday meant getting up about nine thirty, casting back the curtains and, this Sunday being no exception, taking a long look out over the estuary and the shingle island of Lucky Scalp. Not a bad day, moist, fresh, with a hint of warm sunshine to come. She opened the window and let the cool breeze stir the Venetian blinds. Already she could hear the distant rattle of machine-gun fire and the faintly throbbing engines of a boat at the harbour. On a quiet Sunday, sounds travelled especially well over water.

She brushed her hair in front of the bathroom mirror, trying to untangle kinks in her strawberry-fair fringe, then pushed the hair behind her neck and fastened it in a loose plait with a butterfly clasp. She washed, pulled on a cerise sweatshirt, jogging bottoms and trainers, stretched rashers of bacon on the grill at a medium heat, flicked the kettle switch and, leaving the door ajar, skipped out to the shop for a newspaper and rolls. Up the street, round the corner and along a little bit and there it was. Then she was sitting at the pine table in the golden glow of the window alcove, with a coffee, bacon rolls and the papers. She always read the papers thoroughly, except for the financial section and the sports section and the kiddies section and the employment section and the motoring section and the travel section and the holiday section and the games sections – she read almost everything else.

She became absorbed in a news-feature investigation of surrogacy agencies. When finally she sipped her coffee, it was cold. She

98

turned back to the article and again the familiar name leaped out at her: Tracey Morrow of Dundee. Tracey Morrow . . . well, well! That was a name she had not heard for some time. Two years since the last court case, and the article referred to another tabloid story about her . . . some dreadful case of extortion.

She looked at the clock. Nearly eleven. She didn't have to be at Carly's till two thirty. She changed into her faded jeans and a white cotton rolltop sweater, put on socks and walking boots and took down her green fleecy. On the inside of the front door hung Barney's lead. She looked at it. She looked at it again. No.

The breeze was in her face as she walked along Harbour Road, listening to the church bells, doing her face exercises when there was no-one to see, enjoying the soothing play of cool air into the crevices of her eye sockets. On days like these she could forget about teaching, about her failures, about lonely widowhood – and be glad just to be. A seal close to shore was following her along the path, thirty yards off, raising his head right out to have a good look at her. Probably a common seal, the grey ones are more wary, she thought. It was male attention of a sort. Somehow she felt that it *was* male. She could see hundreds of wading birds, redshanks, turnstones in their mottled summer plumage, mallards in pairs, a shelduck further out and cormorants flying diagonally low over the water, thin necks stretched in front of them. If she had her binoculars, she would identify purple sandpipers, dunlin, ring-necked plovers, golden plovers. Further out she saw two vertically-diving terns. Probably sandwich terns. Difficult to tell. All of the birds were patrolling the narrow strip of shingle, intersecting, fluttering, jibing at each other. She noticed a couple of black-backed gulls, and, on the wall further along, two herring-gulls surveying the scene with murderous intent. Marjorie had a theory that gulls were killing other birds more often, as fish became scarcer perhaps. She shooed them away but they merely turned to stare ironically at her with a baleful eye. The nearest fluttered his wings a little and let the two halves of the curved yellow beak fall open and release a prolonged jeering screech. Its beak was tipped with fresh blood.

Marjorie reached the little bridge leading walkers on to the forest paths skirting the shoreline. She preferred the undulating beach path that turned along the shingle and the dunes. From there to a particular felled log just off the path in the gap between two dunes was a good twenty-minute walk. The log provided a useful seat for Marjorie where she often sat for a few moments before turning for home. It was about halfway to the wide scrubland of the Point with a good view of the estuary.

She was so used to being alone there that she didn't notice, until she had left the path and was halfway across a flat area of marram grass that the log was occupied. It was the tramp – and he had seen her. She made as if to pass by but there was nowhere else to go except the shingle, which at that point was almost impassable. Nothing for it. She sat down abruptly on the far end of the log.

'Buenos días, señora,' I said.

She gave me a funny look.

'Gorgeous day,' I said because I could sense that the silence was awkward. She was sitting within three feet of me, impossible to ignore.

'Uh-huh,' she said, rather hesitatingly.

'No dog today?' I smiled or tried to smile. Funny how you need to practise smiling, it doesn't form on your face naturally. It's an adjunct to talking, and so if you don't talk, I suppose you don't smile.

'No dog, period,' she said. 'He died.'

'Sorry to hear that. What species was it?'

'Sorry? Species?'

'Oh, type, what kind of dog?'

'Fox terrier. Wire-haired fox terrier. A wee scamp.' She smiled and seemed to relax as if she had decided it was safe to speak to me. 'I've seen you here before, haven't I?'

'Yes, don't tell everybody, but I'm living here. The rent is reasonable.'

She smiled again and I noticed for the first time that her eyes were seaweed-green and moist. I had no idea how old she might be. 'I did suspect it,' she said. 'There's a bit of a rumour in the village about someone sleeping rough. It must be very difficult . . . You don't seem the type somehow. A tramp I mean. You're younger than . . . than might have been expected.'

There was another silence. I didn't know what to say. I felt that she wanted to talk but I didn't want to surrender my independence. The woman would be sure to gossip and the next thing there would be others, policemen maybe. But maybe it *was* time to move on? Six weeks is a long time to be by yourself. Maybe I'd no right to expect to have any more. I knew it couldn't last more than a few weeks. Up to now I'd been lucky.

'I didn't mean to be personal,' she said. 'I hope you don't mind me asking but how do you manage it?'

'It's easy enough,' I told her. 'Basic survival skills. I have some money if I get stuck.'

'Yes, I think I've seen you in the shops.'

'I'm not a real tramp, you know,' I found myself saying. 'Not entirely *bona fide*. Playing at it really. I've been living in London for ten years, working, and it all got a bit much, so I decided to come home. And when I arrived, I found I didn't really want to be there I suppose. It was a beautiful day, hot and sunny, you know . . . well, I found myself on the bridge and walking. I wanted to be out in the sun and the wind. Wanted to be a part of this wonderful landscape. If that sounds mad it probably is.'

'Oh no, that's certainly not madness. I know exactly how you feel. So you decided to start living rough?'

'I didn't really make a decision. Didn't plan anything. I meant to spend the day here, then I couldn't be bothered walking back and it was a mild night so I slept out and then just days drifted into weeks and I had fun making a shelter and I got a few things in the shop and after about a week I suppose I thought, well, why not just try to stay here?'

'How ingenious of you! You make it sound so . . .' she paused, searching for words, 'so . . . wonderful!'

'It sort of makes sense, being here. In London I suffered from anxieties, worries, neuroses and here I find that they've gone. Or almost. Of course, I know I can't stay here forever. It's illegal for one thing.'

'Oh, I wouldn't be telling anyone,' she said rather quickly, and put her hand out towards me. I realised she expected me to shake it. I took it and found myself embarrassed in case mine was dirty. If it was, she pretended not to notice.

'Marjorie,' she said, shaking limply. 'That's my name.'

'My name is Gerry,' I said. Her hand was cool, slender. It was my first human contact for months. Names, labels . . . I hadn't thought about my name for weeks. Was it really mine? Hadn't had to use it in conversation. I must, to an extent, have overlooked questions of identity. It hadn't felt like I was anyone other than simply me for the last six weeks because I had internalised everything. Six weeks. Was it so long?

'So you're from round here, Gerry?'

'Originally. I don't want to talk about it.'

'I'm sorry. I didn't mean to be nosey.'

'It's not that. It's just that I haven't spoken to anyone properly for weeks. I'm afraid I'm not ready to talk about myself. It seems odd.' I tried to laugh but it didn't sound right.

'Still in limbo?' she smiled. Then seeing my blank look, 'Last time we met, you said something about limbo. I've made you laugh,' she said, looking pleased.

It was true. I felt light-headed. 'Between the hell of London and my former life in these parts.'

'Was it as bad as that?'

'I had to get out. It's like paradise here.'

'I believe you. I live in the village but I work across the river. I'm a teacher, a creature of schedules and routines and timetables and year after year the same thing, discipline, exams, the sacred syllabus.'

'You don't like it?'

'Let's just say it's not particularly rewarding for me any more. Since my husband died, it's begun to seem rather pointless. I don't want to get morbid. So – changing the subject – is it quite easy to survive in the wild?'

'I suppose it is. Yes, it's amazing how little you really need. And I feel healthy and fit. I get some aches and pains but I think I'm doing okay. I was in the Scouts as a boy and was always interested in survival techniques. I catch rabbits you know and there's loads of herbs and birds' eggs. It's amazing how many different types of eggs you can eat – pigeons' and seagulls'. And there's berries and plenty of fresh water and loads of fresh mussels which you can boil up in a can.'

I was starting to enjoy talking to the woman and she seemed interested. Her face was interesting. Those green-brown eyes were wide and clear, the clean eyes of a young woman, fringed by surprisingly long lashes of a colour darker than her light hair. She was very good looking and not at all old.

'I suppose I thought I might do a bit of writing here,' I heard myself saying.

'Oh, you *write*?' she exclaimed. 'How interesting . . .'

'But somehow it hasn't happened. I think it's because there's no reason to write – in some way this place is just so perfect – there's nothing to write about. Maybe writing is just a substitute for living, I don't know. Anyway I do a lot of reading. I get books from the charity shops.'

'Yes, I think I've seen you in there, too.'

'I go there on Mondays, the day after the church bells, and I also go to the Leisure Centre for a swim. Yes, I know. If I was a real hermit I'd swim in the sea. There's some things I draw the line at.'

Now I had her laughing.

'Actually, in actual fact, I live just around the corner from that charity shop,' she said. 'Why don't you pop in to see me tomorrow after your swim? I'd welcome a longer chat. I have to go now, though. I've to visit my daughter and her family at Errolbank.' She stood up and the log shifted slightly in the sand.

'I've enjoyed your company,' she said. 'It's been very interesting. I'm the white door, number 7A, Butter Wynd, just across from the Ship Tavern. You'll easily find it.'

She offered me her hand again. 'Hope to see you tomorrow?'

I watched her walk back to the path and off towards the village. She had a good figure, jeans tight across her bottom, and I liked the loose careless way she had her hair fastened. She couldn't be all that much older than me. My overall impression was of golden-brown skin and hair tones and wet green eyes. I was left with mixed feelings. Sort of jubilation that I had a friend, someone sympathetic. And anxiety that I was going to be . . . made to leave . . . but this thought was stamped on because I knew in my waters that Marjorie would not tell anyone. She wouldn't have invited me if she was going to tell anyone. I felt that I could trust her.

The day went a little flat. For the first time I was discovering the monotony . . . something I'd never dared to admit to myself. I could have invited her for a cup of coffee at my shelter, but that might have spooked her. Later, when the image of her had faded a little, I found myself wondering if she was only pretending to be friendly . . .

Kylie Morrow hadn't gone missing, or been kidnapped. She had spent hours trying to find someone who was holding. And when she found someone with gear to give her a taste of dragons, she crashed overnight there, at a flat in Baxter Park Terrace, and when she woke up the next day there were other people there and she shot up with the guy's spike and her stay lengthened to a day and then it was Wednesday. Then she'd been too scared of Daniel to ring him up, because she was back on the smack, and she'd promised him. She left the flat and walked about for a bit but there were too many people who knew her. She needed to get her head down. She found out that Daniel had called the police five days ago. Couldn't go home. She got a taxi to Timmy's place near the airport. Timmy was a hairdresser, who'd fancied her since they were at school. The place belonged to his parents, who lived in Spain, a detached villa with a garden, secluded and quiet. She needed to be away from Daniel, needed time to think, to get herself off the smack. She made him promise not to tell anyone where she was. He was desperate to sleep with her but she knew it was better to keep him at arm's length. Days went by, mostly spent in bed, or drowsing in a duvet in front of the TV, taking valium to blurr the edges of the cravings. Everyone said it was difficult to get yourself straight, but she'd always found it easy. What *was* difficult was staying off.

In between the gaps of drowsiness and periods when her dulled senses permitted her to eat and drink in tiny amounts and perform other bodily functions, she was doing some thinking. Marrying

Daniel had turned out to be a mistake. She should have listened to her dad. He had been against it from the start. She had never met *his* parents either because Daniel hadn't wanted to invite them to the wedding in Antigua. Her father had told him to his face that he was 'a fly-by-nighter' and 'a jumped-up joiner flashing his money around to impress the silly people . . . you're not good enough for my daughter,' he had roared at the end, 'despite all your money.' Daddy and his new wife were living at Windsor and they didn't phone or write. It was up to her to keep in touch and she had to do it on the sly, when Daniel wasn't around.

She sat on the carpet watching the *Jerry Springer Show* and eating a sandwich she'd made herself. The TV screen was filled with noisy bloated Americans.

Julius (*was a man, became a woman, wants to be a man again*): 'You're ma woman, Elma!' (biff!!)

Elma (*says she was happily married – SHE LIED*): 'But ah doant love you no mo', Jules' (smack!!)

'Honey, you was a man when ah met you . . . (ouch!!)

'Yeehaa! Go git her!' the studio audience yelled. 'Kick'r butt! Git that LARDASS!'

The 22-stone black woman in the swimsuit laid-into the 18-stone topless blonde trans-sexual as smirking oh-so-horrified Springer leered among the audience. Kylie grabbed for the remote, suddenly sickened. She heard the door opening.

'Hey, Kylie – it's me. I got the afternoon off. What's that you're watching? Oh – gross!'

'Ehm feeling beh'ir thi day, look – ehv jist hud a sannie . . .'

'That's great. Look, I've got something to tell you . . .'

'Eh, wut izzit?' Kylie looked up at Timmy's knees. 'Bliddy hell, lookit thi sez o that wummin!'

'You won't like it . . .'

'Won't like wut?'

'I've phoned your husband. Left a message on his answerphone.' Timmy pulled a face. 'You hate me now, eh?'

'Didya?' Kylie said. 'Tell you the truth, ehm no that bathered.'

'Wow, that's a relief,' Timmy said, diving on to the sofa. 'I thought you'd hit the roof.'

'Eh'd hae ti speak ti um sooner ir lit'ir. Bit ehv decided ehm gonna lave um, fir good, like.'

Timmy opened his mouth but said nothing. The *Jerry Springer Show* was taking an advertising break. Kylie laid aside her plate on the carpet beside the empty drinks cans, and loudly belched.

'See, ehm gettin beh'ir,' she said, and laughed.

15

Gavin sat on the drystone dyke at the back of the cottage looking away over the ripening corn swaying in the gentle breeze, enjoying the coolness between his bare toes. The sun was directly overhead, shining on the green-brown heads which undulated across the wide plain. The river beyond existed as a diffused brilliance through trees. He sucked a lemongrass stalk, the heat pressing on his forehead and shoulders. He could feel the warmth on his eyelids holding out against the lethargy of the early afternoon. The weight of timelessness. This was living! When he half-closed them he saw only a pattern of magnesium explosions against the red of blood corpuscles in his eye sockets. From a distance the landscape looked perfect and between his toes, tractor treads imprinted in the caked earth made a clay border around the edge of the field. A line wandered into his head. Tay waters wash twice a day. Wash what? Life's tumults on the estuary clay, no, mud. And? Thrive unseen da da the bridges between, something something on the ebb and the flood. Ah, wash was too weak. Too insipid, too inactive. Twice a day, Tay's tidal waters wash an estuary's tumults on miles of shining mud. Then? Endless cycles, or cycles endlessly, or something about freshwater and brine?

Gavin took out the battered red Silvine notebook from his jeans' back-pocket and the pencil stub that was inside it. What was the main point? The semblance of calm and tranquillity, the reality of fierce struggle underneath, of nature red in tooth and claw. The dramatic violence of the tides and the need to adapt or die. So, twice a day, Tay's tidal waters turn, tugged by tyranny of the twirling moon and sun. Here, freshwater washes salt on glittering miles of mud.

Gavin wrote this down in his neat small handwriting, then chewed the end of the pencil for a while as he thought about a final line for the stanza and how to rhyme with 'mud'. Flood, obviously. So there had to be an ebb too. Something something something something in ebb and flood. Ah! Conspiring in the murderous tumult of its ebb and flood. And then? Well, then there would need to be something more specific, detail, the lives affected. But nothing immediately suggested itself. Maybe it was more of an epigram. The sun was hot and his shoulders were taking the full blast. He squinted under his hand at the exercise book again. Ach, too tame! Something more like this:

> So, twice a day, Tay's tidal waters turn,
> tugged by tyranny of the twirling moon and sun.
> Freshwater washes salt, in ebb and flood,
> and tooth and claw is nature's law
> on the murder miles of mud.

Grandstanding it? A Comstock effort; Orwell at Errolbank? Better, he thought, if rather melodramatic. He deserved a beer. Gavin eased himself off the wall and crossed the garden by way of the paving slabs and went in the backdoor. It was cool inside and he took his beer into the living room and slumped into the sofa. The murder miles of mud. Nice assonance, hint of Raymond Chandler. Or Elvis Costello: 'Oliver's Army'. Nasty sticky squalid little ends. Things disappearing into oozing holes in the mud. Annelids. Then, drawn out by the torpid heat and the dazzling sunshine, he returned to the dyke and gazed east at the estuary, a shimmering broken line of magnesium explosions that dazzled his eyes. But he was now noticing movement down by the old airfield. He could make out several cars parked in a field. He'd been expecting this, but not so soon. He rushed indoors to get his binoculars.

Adjusting the focus, he saw three men: two in suits and the third in jeans and T-shirt. It was this man who seemed to be doing all the pointing and talking.

He made a rapid phonecall.

'Mrs Summers? Is your husband – is Lewis – there?'

After a few moments, Gavin heard the voice of Lewis Summers, retired history teacher and chairman of the action group.

'Lewis?'

'Indeed it is he, and I am,' said the mellifluent voice. There was a dry chuckle on the line. He sounded a little drunk. At three in the afternoon. Gavin smiled.

'Thought I'd better let you know . . . there's three men down in the airfield. Looks like a planning visit. It's starting!'

'Right-ho, haha hee hee. Is it by gum? Three of them you say? The dastardly shower. Well, Gavin, my lad, thanks for the call. I'll round up the usual suspects as quick as I can and we'll meet you there. Thank goodness some of you young people have got sharp eyes.'

Gavin locked up the house, located his sunglasses, and set off up the farm track. At the main road, he walked quickly east towards the old airfield. He passed the turn-off for the farm of Leys, continued for a further hundred yards to another turning, and walked the winding dusty track, much potholed, between two stunted hedges. He sat on a treestump in a gap in the hedge and observed the three men in the field. They were using the bonnet of one of the cars to spread out a map and were poring over it and pointing. He thought one of the men looked like a councillor but the other two were developers or planners of some sort. After ten minutes or so, he heard Lewis Summers' car. It was unmistakable, a battered grey Peugot that had a characteristic misfire, something of a joke in the village. Summers' vehicle came rattling and jolting down the potholed farm track and Gavin noticed that the three men in the field glanced briefly at it before resuming their perusal of their charts.

The Peugot came to a sudden halt opposite Gavin and he could hear the squawk of the brake pulled on tight. Summers got out, a spry, white-haired man tall and thin, in faded jeans and a belted safari jacket and a tweed hat. Since retiring from a long career as a history teacher, he'd thrown himself into the life of the community. Younger by far than his seventy years, Summers was full of old-

109

world courtesy, being a bit of a hand-kisser to the point where husbands sometimes got irritated with his gallantries.

Scott Rennett, a choleric former accountant, still in his fifties, who walked with the aid of a rubber-stoppered aluminium stick and always wore the same zip-up green padded anorak, was a renowned regular of the Old Anchor Bar. Last out of the car was a man known to Gavin only as Old Tom, a keen golfer, but deaf as a coot. Brandishing what looked like a five-iron, he looked lethal, despite his checked golfing pants and Pringle sweater.

Summers peered through the gap in the hedge. 'Come on then, lads,' he said. 'They won't be expecting an attack from the rear.' He chuckled wheezily and stepped into the field.

'Aye, let's give them a piece of our mind,' Old Tom said, walloping the air with the golf club.

The men in the field must have been surprised to see the deputation striding across the grass towards them.

'Wut ir these clowns upta?' Kevin Morrow asked. The other two looked up from their charts and shook their heads.

'Are you the boys that're going to build a they hooses?' Old Tom demanded, when they were almost up to the cars.

'Wut uv ut?' Kevin shouted. 'Wutzit t' dae wi you?'

'I'll tell you what it is to us,' Scott Rennett said, leaning heavily on his stick. 'We're locals. We live here. And we like this area the way it is.'

'We just came down to tell you you'll no be getting planning permission,' said Old Tom. 'Not a chance.'

'Zatso?' Kevin sneered. 'Wha seys?'

'We do. You'll no find a'body round here in favour o a they hooses. No here.'

Muir laughed. 'I think you'll find we've got very good planning grounds, and what's more this land . . . we already own it.' Bill Muir, newly-appointed chief executive of Loyal Homes, the company that was going to build the project had recognised at least one of the deputation because he was something of a local himself, a self-employed architect.

'Dinna tell thi cunts nuthin,' Kevin instructed. 'Thir naebdies. Ald fogeys. Thi dinna coont. Thi cud deh thi moarnz moarn.

110

Noo . . .' he said moving towards them, hands clenched at his sides. 'Yi ken wut yi kin dae? Z'meh land yiron, so yiz kin jist bugger aff, ir eh'll cah thi polis.'

'You don't own this land,' Gavin said. 'You may think you do. You may have papers and that, but this land was here long before you were, and it'll be here long after you've gone.'

'Wha ziz?' Kevin demanded. 'Ane o thi original Picts? Move yir erse, sonny.'

'We're going,' Lewis Summers said, smiling, 'for now – but you've got a fight on your hands. Nobody in the area supports you. You'll find you have rather a lot of opposition, gentlemen.'

'It's a question of whether the project is good for the area – and we think it is,' Muir said. 'It's a matter of progress. This area is a backwater, stagnant, needs improvement. People need houses. You must move with the times. You folks seem to want to hold back the tide of progress.'

'Sticking hundreds of houses in this beautiful area is vandalism not planning,' Gavin said. 'We want a future but it has to be controlled for the amenity of all. All you're interested in is the massive profits . . .'

Kevin rapidly advanced, flexing his forearms menacingly. 'Uf yi'r no aff meh land in fev secints, eh'll hae t' sling yiz aff mehsel. Sumhin eh'd enjoy . . .'

Gavin backed off. The other three were already at the car doors.

'Bugger aff!' Kevin jeered. 'An eh'll mind yir ugly pus, Pict-features!'

It was a beautiful day and I decided not to make the trip into Tayport. I had convinced myself the woman – Marjorie – didn't really expect me and to avoid any awkwardness, I decided to leave it. At least for a day or two. I walked down the heavily-shaded path through the forest to the lookout point at the top of Kinshaldy Beach. Nearby there's a disused military campsite in a clearing at the edge of the forest. Several delapidated buildings and a corrugated iron shelter inside a high wire perimeter fence. I had originally considered living there but it's near a junction of wide tracks through the woods where too many dog walkers and day-tripper come and go. I didn't want to become a tourist attraction.

The lookout point is set in a secluded clearing fronted by high dunes; a brick room high up on girders reached by dangerous crumbling concrete steps. It's thirty feet above the ground, about ten feet square, with window apertures on three sides. I often go up there to sit in the shade on hot days. You can command almost all of the beach, five miles, and see the spires of St Andrews in the distance.

I had brought my notebook with me, intending to try to achieve some writing, or serious thinking at least. It's not easy. The trouble I've always had . . . getting into the position, which basically means being starboard of the piece of paper at the same place and time as you have a pen or pencil in your mitt pointing to the port side. You come at it to leeward between the buoys, and just to place a line of ink or graphite on a blank page can be cathartic, therapeutic, can give you the illusory sense of progress, of stability. And sometimes even too damn much effort. Start off doodling, lines, squares, hatching . . . even the physical effort of that can be good. Doodling leading to thoughts about the task, about not being able to write . . . self-analysis . . . the difficulty of thinking clearly on paper. And a paragraph, a whole paragraph later, I'd be into something. Digging, scratching, tacking . . . But London had often defeated me. Random thoughts of sex obtruded, forced me off on long crazy meanderings around the streets, looking . . . Those weird expeditions to try to get off. To try to get outside of myself. Moving for hours and hours in a straight line, deviating, cutting back, criss-crossing the centre, miles and bloody miles. From Westbourne Grove to Putney Bridge, from Notting Hill Gate to London Bridge via Knightsbridge, the Houses of Parliament and back via Islington, Camden and Kilburn. Walking out the Edgeware Road to the Brent Reservoir to watch the car head-lights of Staples Corner. It was all there for me, miles and miles . . . adventures of the erotic. My mind was dead then, feeding upon its neuroses and my soul was dormant, cold, but my body on those hot London days screamed for final and

112

absolute release. I was in a state of constant excitation. Permanently engorged, uselessly priapic.

And I stumbled on, into adventures which incapacitated me for days. In Camden Town, a hippy girl picked me up in the street, took me home, a girl in loose flowing dingy clothing. A stud in her nose and straggly long hair. Squat in the Caledonian Road where she lived alone without electricity. Lit by candles. She cooked on a tiny methylated spirit stove. She said she was a lesbian and played bass guitar and wrote poetry and had many friends like Leonard Cohen's 'Suzanne', except it was near the canal not a river and she brought me coffee without milk not tea and oranges that come all the way from China, but she was half-crazy alright. She had a good body I remember now, slender, scrawny, her skin thick and white, snapped back instantly when I plucked it. Her bulbous breasts lolled sideways, nipples stiffening in deep brown pools.

And in the street an hour later, my legs were wobbly and I found a place at the corner that was open and went in and had an orange juice and a cup of milky coffee and after a while realised that I was lusting after a group of girls in the corner booth who were laughing and making a lot of noise. I knew if I lifted up a twenty-pound note one of them would follow me outside. With the smell of her still on me, and almost knackered, I knew then there is no end – no logic, no reason – to desire.

And out again into the street, the dark streets of sheeting rain and I walked endlessly through them, singing to myself, weary and slow, leaden-legged, ten miles through the metropolis to my lonely bedsit, kicking up lines of water from the toes of my busted sandshoes, rain sliding in rivulets down the back of my neck. It felt good then to luxuriate with a neat whisky in a hot bath with plenty of bubbles, steaming and safe, inviolate, empty and weary. To slide off for fourteen hours' sleep in coolness of evening breeze sleep right through to midday behind thick curtains of sleep wafting gently. To wake with a pumping erection remembering the lust of Rebecca – that was her name.

And another time . . . I was walking past a pub; it was a sunny day and some guys outside on seats made a joke and somehow I stopped and got into a conversation. And one of the guys was so

113

witty, a real Oscar Wilde and of course I knew they were gay – it was a gay bar – but it was so, you know, kind of light . . . lighthearted. So I stopped for a few drinks. And they were admiring the new barman, a young guy about twenty and chafing each other about him and it made me laugh out loud. And for the first time I could really see what could make someone attracted . . . He was, there was no doubt . . . gorgeous, lightly tanned, an open white shirt open to the stomach and a slender gold neckchain and tight jeans and buttergold hair, so pleasant, so feminine. His skin was soft and clear . . . But after an hour or two the scene became bitchy, and shortly I let myself be picked up by an older guy with a beard, mainly because I wanted to see how far it would go and because I couldn't be bothered saying no and because I didn't have anything else planned for the afternoon. I was ever a slave to the random principle. We went back in his car to his place in Ealing. A long way. It amused me to think I was turning him on. He slapped on a lot of KY jelly and gave me some poppers to sniff, muttering to himself about splitting me in half, to get himself off. I didn't feel anything. Then the bastard fell asleep. When I could hear him snoring I had a wank on his sheets and thought about ripping off his wallet but couldn't be bothered. It's not good to be having these kinds of thoughts here. A foul intrusion into the serenity I've achieved, and what's worse, they taint me with the sordid memories of London I'm trying to forget. Perhaps I should have gone swimming after all. Gone to see Marjorie. First woman I've spoken to for a long time. I hope I'm not starting to think of her in that kind of way, especially since she was so friendly and sympathetic. But I need to get a carton of milk and I don't want to miss the shop, which closes early. Better walk to the town now. The tide is barely a rumour.

16

Marjorie regretted the invitation to the man on the beach. When he hadn't arrived throughout the whole course of Monday, she had run through the gamut of possible excuses. Her final conclusion before she went to bed was that it had been rash, premature at the least. And looked at in the light of Tuesday morning it was almost embarrassing. So she'd planned to get an early start and go shopping in the city and was outside her front door, wrestling with the Yale lock when she noticed him coming down Whitenhill, counting house numbers. He hadn't seen her. She debated whether to move swiftly to the garage. No, that wasn't the right thing. He'd made the effort. He was carrying a shoulder bag and he looked neater, and clean.

'Going out?' I asked. 'Sorry if this is a bad time.'

'Shopping,' she said, pulling a face. 'Not my favourite thing. Well, come on in.' She led me into the hallway. 'You look as if you've smartened yourself up.'

'These jeans and trainers are new,' I told her. 'And the shirt is. New to me, anyway. I was at the charity shop earlier. And I've been for a swim. Not to mention my shave – the first for a week.'

'Well, I'm honoured indeed,' she said, teasingly.

It was a small flat with lots of plants but gloomy at that time of the day. I felt rather constricted and distinctly odd to be in the flat of someone I barely knew. There was a lack of clutter in the room

115

of the kind that one might associate with a single female, no frilly ornaments, or dinky china dolls or ghastly tack and tat. The bookshelves, though, were filled to overflowing, the floor accommodated piles of newspapers and magazines and the walls were hung with several framed landscapes and seascapes.

'Feels odd,' I said. 'First time I've been in a house for ages.'

'Must be,' she agreed. 'Actually I'm glad of the excuse not to have to go shopping, but I thought you were coming yesterday. Did you mistake the day?'

I hesitated, planning my reply carefully. 'I wasn't sure if I should come. I thought you might have asked me out of . . . politeness.'

'Thought you might think that,' she said and laughed. 'Take a seat.' She had even square teeth and I realised that she was wearing a kind of pink lipstick. I suddenly realised she was about my own age. It was not beyond the bounds of possibility . . . *London thoughts*!

'Thanks.' I sat in an armchair in the bay window. It was soft and deep and smelt faintly of parma violets. 'Also, it was such a gorgeous day yesterday. I went to the beach. I like to walk out on the sands as far out as I can. You can get pretty far out.'

Marjorie frowned, standing over me. 'Isn't that dangerous . . . the currents?'

'That's partly why I do it. You have to guess when the tide is going to change. It comes in pretty fast. I used to do something similar in London. On the bridges, especially Vauxhall Bridge. It has this wide iron rail, about two feet wide. I used to lie across it, at right angles to the rail, perfectly balanced, with my legs off the ground, my arms by my sides and my head and chest off the edge, looking down at the water. Perfectly balanced you see. Like that I could feel every vibration of the traffic on the bridge, perfectly suspended so that the slightest touch, I used to imagine, or puff of wind, you know, would send me over. I used to lie like that staring at the patches of light on the water and the mudbanks and Battersea Power Station half a mile away.'

She hovered in front of me. 'But why?' she asked. 'What was the point?'

116

'I just liked the risk of it. Because it was dangerous it sort of made me feel more alive. Sometimes I'd lie there suspended for ten, fifteen minutes at a time, mesmerised by the light on the water, or the dimpling patterns of raindrops. It was like meditation. I used to train myself to ignore everything else. Shut off all traffic noise, conversations of people passing by, until I could forget myself. Of course, people assumed I was trying to commit suicide – when the opposite was the case – and sometimes they stopped and tried to get hold of me, or even cars stopped and that was why I mainly did it at night. I don't know if I was ever in much danger. Well, I never fell in, although a few times I wobbled . . .'

'I know the bridge you mean,' Marjorie said. 'That must be about a hundred feet . . . And trying to beat the tidal race on the Abertay Sands . . . every year, people drown there. Get swept away.'

'But if you study it, you can minimise the risks.'

'You're mad. Would you like a cup of coffee?'

Marjorie went to make the coffee and I squirmed deeper into the armchair. There was something already familiar about the enclosed space, the comfort of the sofa and armchairs, a table, windows, plants, pictures. It was all so quiet. This also was, in a way, reclusion. I wonder if she saw it that way? A life on the margins, eked out, no risks, no dangers, subsisting alone. A McIntosh Patrick landscape, an Alberto Morocco Mediterranean scene, a J.D. Fergusson – or was it Cadell? There was a functionality about the place, lived-in, unfussy. Few mementoes to the existence here of a man. Perhaps she had moved after her bereavement? This was a widow's nook.

'Nice place you have here. Quiet.'

She emerged from the kitchen, smiling. 'It's not bad,' she said. 'South facing, but until about ten; the light is blocked by the pub on the corner.'

'I saw it, the Ship Tavern.' At her age, whatever that was, wearing jeans would have been unacceptable if she had not been slim. She couldn't be more than five or six years older than me. I liked the way her hair fell forward over her cheek. I heard her from the kitchen:

117

'In coffee – milk and sugar?'

'No sugar.'

Marjorie returned to the living room, placing a tray on the cluttered table.

'How were your daughter and family?'

'Pardon?'

'You said you were visiting . . . at Errolbank . . .'

'I told you that?' She seemed surprised. 'Oh well, they're fine, except for the fact that they live right opposite where some developers have decided to build an enormous housing estate.'

'At Errolbank?' I hadn't been there in years and remembered it as a quaint village. I remembered the church spire, the village perched on its hill. 'I used to visit a friend there, a long time ago.'

'I go there to visit my grandchildren, Susan and Kenneth. Is your coffee alright?'

'Perfect. I wouldn't have said you were old enough to be a grandmother.'

Marjorie laughed. 'Thank you. Of course, I had my daughter when I was only 22 and she had her family even younger. Oops, I've given my age away.'

She threw up her arms in mock horror.

'Not really, because I don't know how old . . .'

'I'm fifty this year. My grand-daughter is eight.'

'*Fifty*. Wow!' I said, opening my eyes wide. I mean, she didn't look it.

'Yes, ancient isn't it? Half a century. I'm almost a national monument.'

'I didn't mean . . . I . . . you look great! I would have said early forties, tops.'

She laughed with her head back and I did spot some white hairs at her temples. 'You're good for my ego,' she said. 'You are.'

'I mean, fifty – and you still look good in jeans.'

'Yes, well . . . hides a multitude of sins. How old are *you* anyway?'

'Forty-four.'

'Are you?' She raised her eyebrows. 'I would have said younger.'

'I would have said younger too, but I'd be lying.'

'Ha!' She offered me the plate of biscuits. 'Anyway, what were we talking about? Oh yes, Errolbank is a lovely place,' she said, and sighed. 'What they are planning will ruin it forever. So I'm trying to stop the development. That's what all these papers are – in case you wondered.'

'You're an activist?'

'Everyone should have something to believe in.'

'I used to. I was a teenage politician. Spent a lot of time leafleting and canvassing in elections, standing on street corners and talking to people through a megaphone. It took over my life – it *was* my life – for years.'

'And what was your cause?'

'Oh, you know . . . independence. Or Home Rule, or self-government as it used to be known. We were very much a dangerous minority at that time.'

'So with the Scottish Parliament now you must feel justified?'

'Hmm. It's all become bogged down with bureacratic compromise. I think it'll come eventually. It's logical. There's really no argument against it, except fear of change and fear itself.'

Marjorie nodded. 'My husband was a supporter. He was related to a man called Douglas Young.'

'No?'

'You've heard of him then? He was a distant relative, quite famous in his day.'

'Yes, of course. That's just amazing. Small world.'

'Isn't it?'

'So do you think you'll stop it?'

'Oh, you mean . . . at Errolbank? We'll try our best. Now there is a Scottish Parliament, of sorts, I think the major political battleground will shift to environment issues, you know – amenity, the pace of development versus conservation, that kind of thing. It'll be the green agenda that will polarise opinion. Trees, quality of the environment, restrictions on planning, recycling, pollution, energy conservation, nature reserves, public access to mountains and the countryside issues – all that. Scotland is small enough that we can set the standard for quality of life right here.'

'Sounds good to me.'

'Carly – that's my daughter – and her husband, Gavin, are countrylovers, hate the city. And now they're to get 2,000 houses built right at their backdoor. In the name of profit. I suppose, Gerry, you got used to lack of amenity and overcrowding in London?'

'You have to. God knows how I stayed there so long.'

'How long did you say you lived there?'

'Ten years, believe it or not.'

'Hmm, long time.'

'When I think about it I really hate the place – cities – and the squalor. It's like a sort of skin, or shell – a carapace you have to put on when you arrive at King's Cross Station or Victoria. And all your perceptions change. It's like the only way you can handle living there is if you develop this carapace. And you can feel it sort of solidifying on your shoulders. But when you're away from London you feel it coming off, you feel lighter and you wonder how the hell you managed to live there.'

'I'm not a great fan of London,' Marjorie conceded. 'My husband and I once spent a week there. We stayed in an odd hotel in the Paddington area. The room had two fridges in it. Neither of them worked. Nor did the shower. The place was almost empty. No wonder. The food was . . . well, it had to be seen to be believed. The chap who owned it was an Arab, Egyptian I think. Nice enough, you know, but he had some funny ideas – tea with hot milk. Breakfast was toast that was entirely white and cold baked beans with a fried egg on top. We were woken at four in the morning by a woman outside the front door ringing and ringing and shouting up at the windows. My husband eventually had to go down and let her in. She was very drunk and abusive. He thought she might be a prostitute.'

'I lived for a time in Paddington. That was where I worked, of course.'

'What did you do?'

'Worked in a psychiatric unit.'

'That sounds interesting.'

'Yeah, I liked it. The pay was poor, but the job was extremely varied, like being in a human zoo.'

'You must have seen a lot of weird things?'

'After a while I found it difficult to . . . well, you had to work hard to stop yourself getting rather depressed. All that mental illness. All those blighted lives and there were more out than in, if you know what I mean. "Care in the Community" it was called. The reality was loads of manic depressives and schizophrenics drifting about, like flotsam and jetsam, sleeping rough. The whole of central London began to seem to me like a vast crawling asylum.'

'You make it sound *delightful*,' Marjorie said, laughing. 'More coffee?'

The venue had been carefully chosen, Luxor's Club in Pont Street, just around the corner from the penthouse suite in Lowndes Street. It was a discreet establishment, entered from Cadogan Place through a doorway guarded by several bay trees in ceramic bowls, a magnificent stuffed tiger and an elderly toothless uniformed Cockney doorman with fallen arches. It was the first time that Daniel, who had flown from Dundee airport, and arrived by limousine, and Kevin, who had travelled by plane to Heathrow from Glasgow and taken the tube, had met since their meeting at the Loch Tay Hotel in Kenmore. Derek Rutherford and Bill Muir had travelled down together on the red-eye sleeper and were due at the club at 7 p.m. At half past, a private investor, an executive of a finance company and a leading venture capital banker would arrive. The purpose of the dinner was to launch Carse Development Investment Associates. It was expected the three investors might bring legal representatives but the formal details would be handled later. The brothers had arrived separately at 6 p.m. for a pint in the bar and to catch up on family business.

The Gentlemen's toilets at the Luxor are palatial in ultramarine tiles and green glass and chrome. Kevin urinated on the steel pedestal and conversed with Daniel, who was ensconced in one of the cubicles. The bistro was empty at that early hour.

'Thi main thing thi niyt,' Kevin said, 'iz ti keep abdee happy things iz on schedule. Mind, ehm no happy wi thi bliddy Cooncul.'

121

'Yeah? Wut's thi score wi thi application?' Daniel asked from behind the door as his bowels loosened under constant effort.

'Dinna ask,' Kevin said, directing the hot stream exuding from him. 'We hud thi planning officers oot t' thi site. We hud meetins aboot thi ootline application an aboot thi different phases an that. Bit thir stull carpin, so ehv no been able ti submit thi fucker yit.' He zipped up and moved over to the sink and began washing his hands.

Daniel rattled the toilet-roll holder. 'Thir gien yi hassle?'

'Eh. Thir bliddy backtracking, ken, on thi hale ehdea,' Kevin said, using the hand-dryer. 'Even though thi new toons scheme cam fae thi Cooncul. Bit ut wiz thi ither lot, ken, afore thi fucken elections. Noo thirz a load a arseholes makin noise aboot tree-felling an such-like. Eh hud a bunch a troublemakers at thi site thi ither day, shouting thi odds.'

'Eh? Load a opposition, like? How d'yi no tell iz, man?' Daniel pulled the handle to flush the toilet. 'Eh cud a gied yi a hand.'

Kevin patted his hair into place and adjusted his silk tie. 'Eh've done thi yaishul preparations, like . . . got thi cunt Molison t' areenj a few meetins . . . thi bastards ir wahtchin ti see wut wey thi wind'll blaw. Phase 1 ootline permissions come up in a couple a weeks. That's the fufteen mil plan.'

Daniel washed his hands. 'Yeah, git that in so thi bastards canna cheenj thir minds.'

'We miyt hae t' loss pert o thi site,' Kevin said. 'Tree-felling. See, maist o thi objections ir aboot a sma wid thit lehs on thi sooth, atween thi site utsel an thi river.'

'Fucking trees? Unbelievable, Kev. See, uf we bided in America, we widna hae a this trouble. Wid beh'ir be gittin back. Derek an thi boy Muir ir due, in . . .' he consulted his Rolex . . . 'in fehv minutes.'

'Aboot Derek,' Kevin said, as they walked through the tastefully-lit bistro, 'eez fuhlly briefed a coors, bit Muir . . . we tell um only wut ee needs ti ken, only when ee needs ti ken ut.'

'Eh, a coors,' Daniel agreed. 'Eez thi boy thi taxman wull be speaking ti.'

They sat down at the tables in the alcove which had been pushed together.

Kevin poured himself another glass of wine.

'Trees?' Daniel muttered, shaking his head in disbelief. 'Bloody trees.'

Part 3

Tumbling Waters

17

Having been out as far as I can go, it was time to come back in. There's a regularity, a given logic in that, an inherent truth of sorts. My aunt, Kathleen Fimister, suspected nothing on my arrival at her semi-detached bungalow in Seaforth Crescent, at the back of West Ferry. We are not a close family. Naturally, she assumed that I had travelled from London that day. Of the intervening seven weeks she knew nothing. Her spare room was always ready for me as and when it was required. A quick whizz with a hoover to stir the dust, the window left open for a few hours and a change of sheets. I have no other home since my mother remarried and went out to Australia, taking my older brother Phil with her. I haven't been to see her. It's a long way. Kathleen, her sister, is a widow, recently retired, and her big thing is bowling.

'There you are now,' were her first words to me on her doorstep. As if I'd only nipped out to the shops, yet it was three years. That miserable embarrassing Christmas and New Year spent here just the two of us. Festive meals for two – an oxymoron if I ever heard one. And of course, the Hogmanay awash with her bowling friends, not a one under sixty.

'Put your things in the spare room. I'll make up the bed later. How about a cup of tea?'

Yes, apart from back pains and some mild rheumatism in her fingers and neck necessitating her wearing a padded neck collar sometimes, the wash of time wasn't treating Kathleen too harshly.

She is self-reliant, not a complainer, one of those leathery thin women who wear laced-up sensible shoes and go on forever. They inundate the links golf courses and bowling clubs of Scotland. Auntie Kathleen spends a lot of time on her kneeling pad in the flowerbeds poking at the earth with her trowel and I suppose that keeps her fit. Her tastes in decoration may run to the floral and she's a terror for the cardigans, but she is resolutely positive, sees the upside of absolutely everything. That time when a quarter ton of granite fell off a building and missed her by inches, landing on her right foot. A broken big toe and ruined shoes. 'Could have been worse,' she said brightly, smiling up at the ambulance medics and the firebrigade officers, 'could have dented my new hat.' I suppose she had a lot of time to practise that level of calm. Married a sailor, my uncle Ron, Chief Petty Officer Fimister of the Blue Anchor Line. Must have been an odd sort of marriage – he came back only twice a year for a fortnight. Suppose the marriage was more a sort of habit. There's a picture of him in his dress whites on the mantle-piece. Like Duncan Law. Or John Law. In the uniform they could have been twins. Brothers under the skin, matelots with lots of mates in every port, jolly rogers and jolly jack tars. The monotony of long voyages, how the routine must have deadened all the initial romance of names of places, labels of the exotic: Valparaiso, Jo'burg, St Vincent and the Grenadines, the Beaufort Sea, the Maldives, Mindanao, Liverpool . . . Just the ëngines churning full ahead. Mechanical, repetitive, and the human element just cogs in the machine. Like being on the assembly line really, one that moves around the globe. Did he write letters? Did she? Or did they just quietly thole the separation? *Thole*. There's a solid Scotch word for you that reeks of Calvinistic acceptance of the grim. Dour and girny, grumbling grief in Gourock, ultradry in Carntyne, lotus eating in . . . Garthamlock, or Riddrie, some kind of a forecast: *It will be nae bad in the west and awfy nae bad in the east and all points north can expect prolonged dour girning for the rest of the week but those of you in the south – youse – will have to thole.* Those shore-leave fortnights must have been difficult. How can you package a marriage into four weeks a year. For thirty years? Makes no sense. Why marry if the pull of the sea is that strong?

The light in the spare bedroom is reduced because the window is north facing, although I could just see the trees of Dawson Park and, in the distance, the hills and fields of Angus. I put down my suitcase and shoulder bag on the bed. It didn't feel like home, didn't feel permanent. I went to the kitchen.

'Three years since I've seen you, is it, son? Your hair is much longer than I remember. I'm surprised they allowed it at the hospital.'

'Yeah. I've been meaning to get a haircut,' I said. 'Maybe tomorrow. Anyway, I packed in the job weeks ago. It was getting to me, making me depressed.'

'I'm not surprised. Some of the things that went on that you told me about last time,' she said. 'Well, I'm jolly pleased you're here. I could do with the company. Now, I'll leave you here for a mo while I nip out to the shops and get something for our tea.' Matter-of-fact, practical realities, no deep questions, no imponderables with Auntie Kathleen. You came, you stayed, you had tea. Every evening.

When she got back we had our tea and watched some television. She wasn't a great television-watcher and not having watched it for some time I was surprised to find how sleepy it made me, the glare and the flickering light acted heavily upon my eyelids. Or maybe it was the confined heat and stagnant air of being indoors.

I was feeling tired when I went up to bed, and lay down and switched off the light, but the room was suffused with the saffron light of the streetlights, a wan half-light, and the bed was too soft, too fluffy. I had to open the window and then the rattling of the blinds began. The minutes became hours and I found that my brain was hurtling round and round and keeping me awake. When you try to get to sleep you're aware that you're trying to get to sleep and the thought that you are keeps you awake and the thought that the thought that is keeping you awake is the thought about how you are trying not to think about trying to get to sleep. Trying not to think. Trying to think of nothing. Impossibilities. I went down to the kitchen and drank several long glasses of water. I was very thirsty and overdid it. What my mother used to describe as 'blebbing', although it's good for you. And the water here is

129

fantastic, liquid ice, not like the putrid recycled trash that comes through the taps in London.

I made up a bed on the floor and I must have fallen asleep at some point because I recall the sensation of waking up. You never know for sure, do you?

So I was back in my home city, among human society, in shelter, under a roof, with the rest of my life ahead of me. In time I might come to think of those seven weeks as a kind of spiritual cleansing, an extended mental fasting of the soul.

I unlocked my suitcase and examined my possessions with great interest. It was as if they did not belong to me. For seven weeks they'd been sitting in the locker at the railway station. The travel alarm clock, an intricate instrument that used to sit on my bedside table throughout my London years, its face turned to greet me on waking. I snapped it shut and listened to its soundless ticking. The MW/FM/LW/SW portable radio, a neat top of the range transistor that can pick up broadcasts from hundreds of stations throughout the world. My brass picture frame with the family group and me, aged about eight, taken outside the pre-fab. *The Spinoza Reader*, well thumbed and annotated, Kerouac's *On the Road*, Miller's Tropics (*Cancer* and *Capricorn*), J. B. Pick's *The Great Shadow House*, Neil Gunn's *Highland River*. My Panasonic stereo radio cassette player, earphones and tapes: Van Morrison's *Astral Weeks, Hard Nose the Highway, Tupelo Honey* and *Moondance, The Best of Nilsson*, Donovan's *Catch the Wind*, the Beatles' *Live at the BBC* four-tape set.

Cistern Tales

Another day another jobbie, as the old lavatory attendant used to say, Moray Neill muttered, replacing the telephone receiver.

He'd phoned Councillor Jock Barclay, a senior opposition spokesman, about a brown rumour floating around in the conversational sludge of the Moorings Bar that a certain pretty young councillor had had her tits fondled quite gratuitously by the Convenor of Properties, during drinks after a conference in Glasgow but wasn't pressing charges.

130

'She doesn't want to rock the boat,' Barclay said. 'I mean, if it did happen, and I'm not saying it did, she's wanting to keep it – or perhaps I should say them – under wraps.' His loud wheezing laugh blocked the phone, then cut itself off abruptly. After a rather moist spluttering silence, Barclay continued darkly. 'That odious toad, Welks . . . she'd need to get them disinfected if he'd touched them, harharrffmmff. But, knowing how you like to keep . . . abreast of what's going on,' he said, almost ending himself at this new witticism, 'I've got a far more . . . succulent story for you to get your teeth into . . .'

And out it all came, in shits and farts, as the cludgieman would say.

'You've seen the bit in the local paper about an inquiry in the Public Services Department?' Barclay asked.

'Three hours – that's some inquiry.'

'Uh, well, we had a complaint from a council employee, well, an allegation really, a sort of did you hear this is going on type of thing. Seems the head of department, Nobby Keirans, is up to his neck in it.'

'Sounds interesting . . .'

'Seemingly, there's a school leaver taken on in the department, in Keirans' office like, a young lassie, just eighteeen. Taken on just as a temp, the usual six-week contract. Except Keirans goes and falls in lust with her.'

'A baldy wee coot like him? He's what . . . late forties?'

'Mebbe not so old as he looks, could be mid-forties. Anyway, the next thing is, and this was the complaint, she was made permanent, and seemingly this just never happens, well, not in just one month, and her salary's going up five grand a year. Five grand. That's a lot of lust, harrffharff. And she's shooting off with Keirans on jaunts all over the bloody place. You name it, they've been there. Conferences about public toilets and sewage management and Christ knows what else, and all on public money.'

'And this was sanctioned by the Public Services Committee?' Moray queried.

'Well, not exactly. Seems rumours have been flying around for a while and the top brass heard about it and had a word with

Keirans. Warned him off like, but seemingly he was determined –
that was the word he used – determined.' Barclay's heavily in-
fectious laugh spluttered over the phone. 'And maybe if your wife
was in hospital and you had . . . you had an eighteen-year-old bird
to go to a conference with maybe you'd . . . harffharff . . . be
determined to go.' Barclay was incoherent with wheezy laughter.

'But . . . harffharff . . . harff . . . this is the funny bit . . . he . . .
harrff . . . Keirans that is . . . had to apologise to the Committee for
asking permission to go after they came back. Retrospective like.
Seemingly this conference in the Bahamas . . .'

'Where?'

'That's right, the Ba–harffharrff–haramas . . . some bloody
urgent conference . . . harff . . . on cludgie maintenance or un-
blocking shitey drains had come up and normal permission
couldn't be obtained . . . if you can believe that?'

'Where else did you say they've been?'

'Ireland, Sweden, Greece – on something called a Euro-sludge
Seminar.'

'Sounds absorbing!'

'But that's all within the last six months. She's only been working
there for six months. Thing is his private life is up to him, but the
allegation is that because he's getting his leg over, he's kind of
promoted her cause, sort of watered her sweetpeas, and that it's
sort of adultery on the rates.'

'Could be hard to prove . . .'

'Well, but he's never hidden that he's having a thing with the girl.
He's been boasting about it all over the place. Maybe you would
too if you were a wee middle-aged baldy like him with a young . . .
harff harff . . . bimbo in your bed. The top brass have told us that
he's claimed it's a long-term relationship. Maybe that just means
till his wife is out of hospital, I don't know. We hoped that the story
about the inquiry would flush out the real story, but it looks like it's
all going to be washed under the carpet. Unless you can do
something about it, of course.'

Another day, another jobbie, as McLean of the soakaway
Scottish Source said to him on the phone. *Another day of dung-
gathering for Dingbat Dynorod of the Sewage and Communica-*

tions Expectorate. Look lively there, matey. All hands around the
mainbrace and man the pumps!

Sharkey dropped by to pick him up, with enough lenses in the
boot to film the NASA space programme. 'I've had the film in the
freezer for a week,' he said, 'had a feeling something was going to
turn up. A good shagging story is just what we need. Where are we
off?'

'North-west. Now, it's near lunch time,' Moray mused. 'I don't
know what this girl looks like, so I thought we'd hang around
outside the Public Services Department.'

'Up by the ring road, Cleppie Road way?'

The Volvo estate sped up the Hilltown and tucked itself into a
newly-vacated space in front of a newsagent's, directly opposite the
front gates of the Council compound, with a view of the carpark
and the office block.

'My idea is to wait and clock Keirans when he comes out. He just
might have the bimbo with him, if not, maybe he'll go to meet her.'

'I hate these stakeouts', Sharkey grumbled. 'Always happen at
mealtimes. Maybe this shop does pies or sausage rolls, eh? I could
murder an ingin bridie.'

'Too risky. If we lose him at the junction we're stuffed. Better
keep the motor running.'

'Oh well. I'll get my kit out in case I've to try a running
shot.' Sharkey got out and began searching in the boot. He
came back with a Pentax camera body and two lenses, one of
which looked suspiciously like the one Moray had dropped at
Trottick. It was fourteen inches across at the business end and
two feet long.

'Murderpolis,' Moray mumbled under his breath.

Sharkey caught the direction of his gaze. 'Na,' he said. 'This is
big willie and it's the business. Use it mainly on football jobs but
the range is terrific. You can read the label on a wonderbra at half-
a-mile with this bastard. Properly used, of course.' He grinned at
Moray's discomfiture 'Heard about your trouble with Ecky Edwards, but it wasn't broken. See, too many cunts think they can
have a go. Course much of the kit nowadays is point and shoot.
Digital. Can be faked up on the screen to make it look better. But

for a real job of work, you can't beat big willie. Fast as fuck. No cunt escapes.'

The pair sat in the car for almost an hour, getting funny looks from passersby who marked them as plain-clothes polis or DSS snoopers or narks from the Child Support Agency. Moray had had to shield Sharkey with a newspaper while he urinated into an Irn Bru bottle, so the car was steamed with the hot fumes of urine. They'd listened to the radio for a while. Elvis Costello's 'Shipbuilding', then 'The Tide is High' by Blondie, then what Sharkey described as 'modern pish – trance or techno shite' with no discernible lyrics at all. So the radio was switched off and they sat in gloomy silence.

They almost missed Keirans when he suddenly appeared at the front gate in a green Range Rover Discovery, barely braked and bounded out turning sharply left. He almost made the green light but pulled in behind the traffic lights. It was a desperate scramble to get across the road and into the left lane.

'Think he clocked us?'

'Dunno.' Sharkey had to work hard to keep the jeep in sight as it careered forward and bowled along Clepington Road, then took an obscure left-hand turn.

'Oh ho, me boy!' Sharkey said. 'And where are you going, chum?'

But the jeep doubled back and out into the Old Glamis Road, down to the Kingsway, and turned left.

'That's a weird detour,' Moray yelped, as Sharkey struggled to keep the green vehicle in sight as it sped fast along the dual carriageway, heading west. 'Where the hell is he going? Not home, because he lives in Douglas.'

'Must be going to see the bint,' Sharkey said. 'We could've just cracked it.'

The Range Rover was seen up ahead to turn off into the crammed busy carpark of Asda off the Kingsway. Moray was panicking. 'How the hell will we keep track of him in here?'

For a few moments they lost the green vehicle in the crowded lanes that threaded the carpark.

'There!' Sharkey grunted. 'For fucksake, he's on to us. *He's on to us!*'

The green vehicle was at the exit lane, making a fast getaway up to the roundabout. Gone. Fucked!

No matter how they scouted around in the next half-hour, they had to face the obvious. Keirans had spotted them and taken evasive action. They'd blown it.

'He's obviously gone to see the bint,' Sharkey said. 'How don't we know where she bides?'

'The only address I have is in Ardler.'

'How didn't you say earlier?'

'Because we knew he was at work.'

'Aw, man, we should've staked out her place. Now we've spooked the cunt.'

They drove to Ardler, in the lee of four towering multi-storey buildings known locally as Bosnia. A security company, hired by the Council to patrol the area when the police declared it a no-go zone, had been terrorised away from the area after four days and had requisitioned tanks and body-armour. The tenants used the windows as litterbins. It was an area with a high number of single mothers. The concrete precincts, at ground level, looked as if they been bombed by massively overfed seagulls, but the white blotches, he knew, would turn out to be used nappies.

The flat they searched for was south of the multi's, across a derelict playpark, in the low-rise housing. It was on the first floor, and Moray moved slowly along an open walkway, dictaphone in hand, allowing Sharkey to get into position, at ground level, kneeling behind a dustcart, abandoned by a council employee outside the public lavatory. It was a very long shot. Worse, Sharkey's view of the door could be disrupted by anyone who came along on ground or first-floor level.

He knocked. Knocked. No-one in. He gave the thumbs-down over the plettie.

He returned to the car. 'Wrong address,' he said. 'Turns out to be someone else of the same name, according to the neighbours.'

Sharkey cursed. 'Let's stop at the chipper and think what we're going to do. You make a few phonecalls. We need her address.'

While Sharkey swigged Irn Bru and stuffed greasy chips into his face, Moray worked hard on the mobile, ringing contacts, ringing the library, getting people to check electoral rolls against tele-phone directories – and he came up with a new address. Not far away.

Sharkey heaved the newspaper raft of chips out the window and started his engine. 'Mingin,' he said. 'The ile was rancid,' he said. 'No time to lose.'

They turned into a narrow street to see the green Range Rover Discovery hightailing it into the distance heading back to the ring road.

Moray groaned.

'But the address we have is right,' Sharkey said. 'An he thinks he's gien us the slip, so all is not lost. Maybe he'll visit her after work. We'll sit tight.'

The flat where the girl was living – the lovenest, in *Scottish Source*-speak – was even more difficult to get to. It had an outer door controlled by an intercom. Moray was finally able to get in when an elderly neighbour came out and politely held open the door for him. He checked the name plate on the first floor. He and Sharkey walked around, trying to clock the best vantage point. It was a narrow cul-de-sac. Worse, at the end of it was a primary school.

'The bad news is we might get arrested for being paedophiles,' Sharkey said. 'The good news is that there's a lot of people coming and going and so we don't stick out like spare pricks at a lesbian wedding.'

Four hours went by. Four hours of sitting bored, trying to sleep, listening to the radio, to tapes, trying to ignore each other's farts, bad jokes, suffering from cramp in the legs, being bored, being bored by boring, bloody boredom. They fantasised about the perfect sequence of shots. Keirans parking getting out, she coming to meet him in the middle of the street, kiss, kiss, snap, snap . . . A fantasy that would allow them to knock it on the head and go home and stretch out horizontal instead of being folded in half in the car seats, staring ahead at the quiet bloody dead-end street. Sharkey sat with a Nikon and a 220 lens across his lap, but he'd lost interest even in fiddling with it. In the back seat under a newspaper was the Pentax clipped on to big willie.

After four hours of torture, it began to happen. The green Range Rover was coming up the street, looking for a place to park.

'Down,' hissed Sharkey. 'The cunt mustn't see us!'

They peered over the dashboard and saw Keirans enter the building.

They allowed themselves to sit up.

'Did you see?' Sharkey exulted. 'The cunt has a *key*. We'd better get into position. I'm going to move the car across the street behind that red Lada. That'll give me a clear view of the front door. Your job will be to impede them. Block them from getting into the Range Rover until I've got the shots I want of them together, preferably holding hands. Maybe they'll come out like that, in which case, you try to ask them questions. But your main task is to force them together so I can compose a tight shot of them. Get me?'

'Yeah? So what do you think I should ask them?'

'Fuck knows,' Sharkey snorted incredulously. 'You're the words man. "How does it feel when your boss is on top?" or "Do you always go for baldy wee gits . . . ?" Think of something.'

And their great moment came less than ten minutes later when with the urgent ecstasy of euphoria, and the clarity of an action-replay, Moray seizes exactly the moment after the lovers emerge holding hands and step into the street. With the perfection of a moment in history, they look expectantly towards him – and Sharkey's big willie resting on the bonnet of the Volvo – the pair smile vaguely (turning to scorn) when they spot the dictaphone and hear the words he's uttering and leap in the doors of the big vehicle which clatters to life and speeds away leaving him with the dictaphone clicking noisily (later revealed to be at the end of the tape so it didn't catch any of the swear words anyway), but Sharkey is finally and totally and absolutely fucking orgasmic. Moray is beyond it, into dizzy mode, fainting with hunger and the tension of the past few hours.

'I'll mac loads of these to McLean,' Sharkey says, 'and we'll be on a big score! You've got the story all knocked out, yeah?'

'No, but it'll only take me ten minutes. I'll fax it.'

'Mind if I leave you here to make your own way home? I'm

137

fucking desperate for a crap, man. I'll just about make it before I shit myself. Phone me later, eh?'

Sharkey roared off urgently as Moray walked out to the main road to find a cab home, composing tabloid paragraphs in his head.

18

The Old Anchor is a low-ceilinged drinking howff on the north side of the main street at Errolbank. Low-set windows admit sparse light of a suffused, underwater, or below-decks quality. Mostly, light is provided by large brass lanterns suspended from the brown ceiling. The second of these had never worked and having never been repaired, swings eccentrically from its electrical cable. New customers often bang their heads on it, to the glee of the locals, who watch for such eventualities. The floor is polished timber of the kind that moves minutely beneath the weight of feet and this queasy sense of gravity is transmitted by the turned wooden legs of the ricketty chairs and stools and is more pronounced nearer the bar area, so that customers standing at the bar often felt a slight tilting that might slop the top half-inch of froth from their glass. The maritime theme is continued on the faded wallpaper, which features jovial dolphins and octopuses at play in the deep. Numerous brass implements of a nautical appearance are bolted to the woodwork, and a large lifebelt suspended from hooks greets customers above the door to the toilets, which the owner, Bob, a retired Merchant Navy officer, refers to, obscurely, as 'the foc'sle', and which has a porthole in its timbers. If the whole effect of the bar is of a confined space, it's a familiar and comfortable one. The Old Anchor stands against the tide of progress. Yellow 1950s formica of the circular wooden tabletops had flaked to create a patchwork of blackened wood and rotting fabric improved by the burnt ash of cigarettes and the sharp points of ballpens or penknives. Patrons did not have to endure the irritations of fruit machines, videogames, one-arm bandits, cigarette machines, mobile phones, jukeboxes or piped muzak. None of these intruded into the murmurs of conversation, the rhythmic creaking of the brass lamps in a slight draught from the door, the delicious slurp of a cask draught ale pulled by hand-pump. The sure antidote to any sense of nausea the dingy enclosed atmosphere might induce in the first-time customer is the quality of its locally-brewed draught ales. The Earl of Errol's Frolick and Megginch Dew were of the highest-known specific gravities and Carthagena Cordiale, imbibed by the unwary, would ring the bells all night. After several pints of these, the most confirmed land-lubber acquired such a pair of sea-legs as could withstand any unpredictable weather.

The owners of the bar were a florid middle-aged couple, known merely as Bob and Elsie, whose families had lived in the area for as long as anyone could remember. Bob, an old salt, had the tattoos to prove his long acquaintance with the sea and the quaint turn of phrase that could encompass customers as 'shipmates'. Previous generations of both families had owned the bar and its predecessors in previous centuries, when it had been a coaching inn, a hotel, a tavern and a lodging house. Two rooms above the bar were still known as 'the lodgings', although no-one could recall them ever being let even for a single night. But the hand-drawn yellowing card offering 'Lodgings – See the Proprietors' remained on display among the upturned bottles on the gantry. The sons of the owners, Coughlan, the eldest boy, a dark taciturn youth with long side-burns and thick hair and a gold earring, and his younger brother Jamie, a lively, even cheeky boy in his late teens, known universally as 'Jim lad' served at the bar with local girls who assisted from time to time.

'Well, confusion to our enemies and fair wind to our friends,' Lewis Summers said, hoisting his pint glass in the direction of the almost full pub, with his back to the bar.

'Land ahoy, me hearties,' Gavin pronounced beneath him on a rickety stool.

Summers swivelled to place his tumbler on the table and perched

140

himself on the tall stool in the corner, a gangly figure, his thin legs astride the stool until he pulled them up on to the rung. He unbelted his safari jacket and leaned back against the bar. His bony knees in his jeans were at the same level as Gavin's face and several inches of his thin red ankles could be seen in the gap between canvas and suede shoes. The levels in the optics above his head plunged. The lifebelt swung on its hooks as the door to the toilets slammed shut. The brass lamps were swinging in the draught from the open door, the floortimbers trembled to the movement of feet.

'So the groundswell of opinion,' Summers announced, reclaiming his whisky glass from the bar, which he sniffed appreciatively. 'Is that a deputation should be sent?' He sipped the whisky and closed his eyes in mock reverence. 'Ah Gavin, that's nectar – Cameron Brig. The *cratur*! Now, what were we about?'

'Ach, well,' said Scott Rennett, leaning back against the dolphins and octopuses, 'we'd to persuade the doctor boy to send a deputation to the next Council Planning meeting.' He glowered under his eyebrows. 'It's what we agreed.'

'I won't deny it, Scott,' Summers said, nodding. 'Though quite why we should have to persuade Dr Grant-Gilford when he's chairman of the community council is beyond me. It would have been agreed right off if he wasn't so steadfast about sticking to the proper channels.'

'Stick-in-the-mud, more like, he's such an old Tory,' Gavin said. 'Doing anything is not his thing. Nor is making decisions.'

'Aye, talking is what he prefers, the auld gowk,' said Old Tom, lighting his pipe. 'Ye know he came in here? Just the once, mind. Asked Bob what sherries he had. Sherry? He never came back as I know.'

Summers chuckled, 'Aye, that would have put his nose out of joint, alright. Anyway, tonight we fairly caught him on the hop. He was ready to wrap up the subject with no action decided.'

'You'd better stand for the chair next time,' Gavin said, to nods of agreement. 'I think he's got water – or sherry – on the brain.'

141

Ordure in the House

And Sharkey had got, by pure good luck – although he would swear it was professional skill – the perfect shot of Mr Swick emerging from a doorway with one hand reaching down to check his flies. He looked a dodgy geezer and the caption said it all. YOU'LL HAVE HAD THE RENT, THEN? Randy Landlord's Midnight Visits: A *Scottish Source* Exclusive:

BIG NOB IN FINANCIAL SECTOR

Jeremy Swick is a big nob in the financial sector, where he acts like a toff, owning hundreds of flats in Angus, Perthshire and Fife. He's a millionaire with a wife and two kids, and the kind of power to open any door. He makes it his business to select female students or single mothers as tenants.

When your landlord is a randy renter with the keys of your flat, what can you do to stop him? You can lock the door, put the baby in its cot, the water's running for a shower, you're slipping out of your bra and knickers and you turn around and there's your landlord . . . "Sorry to call at an inconvenient moment," he says, "now about your rent arrears . . ."

This scenario is all too familiar to scores, perhaps even hundreds, of former tenants of Mr Swick over the years he has been operating his property-letting service. One former tenant, Jilly, a hairdressing assistant, described his methods.

JILLY'S STORY

'You see the adverts in the paper, flat to let or room . . . or whatever, but you have to stand outside it at a certain time and there's usually a queue. Then Swick arrives and everyone gets shown the room and he speaks to you one at a time, asking details, you know, name, address, job . . . and takes your phone number then says he'll let you know. He makes you feel as if you'd be lucky to get the bloody poxy flat. So when he rings up and asks if you want it, you

feel, like pleased, ken, and so you go down there again and meet him, and he gives you the keys but it starts right off sort of asking like ASKING IF YOU'VE GOT A BOYFRIEND. Well, it doesn't seem like there's any problem, it's only later . . .' Jilly, who

asked that her surname not be revealed, for fear of reprisals, claims that all four of the flats in her block were tenanted by young single women. 'It was a bit o a surprise, when I got to speak to them,' she says, 'but I soon found out what was going on.'

VISITING HER TWICE A WEEK AND SHE WASN'T PAYING RENT

He was visiting the girl in the end flat about twice a week and she wasn't paying any rent. She didn't come out and admit it right off, it was like she was kind of ashamed about it. She was a very good looking girl, gorgeous really, and he'd started pestering her and eventually she'd given in. She hated him, she was kind of feared of him really. There was another girl, an Asian, had a very good job and she'd threatened to get the police to him when he started saying

things to her and HE STARTED GRABBING THE ASIAN GIRL. But she'd done it with him too and SHE CLAIMED HE'D DRUGGED HER, you know, put something in her drink . . . I left after a month, but I heard of loads of other girls and they all had a story to tell. The man's a monster and you see him in the street, poncing around like he's a respectable . . . ken . . . he's just an animal.'

ANGELA'S STORY

'At first he seemed like a nice bloke and I was glad to get the flat and the rent was very reasonable. He didn't start bothering me for two weeks and then he said there was a problem with the water pipes.

He said he'd have to get men in to sort it out. Wanted to know when I would be in. But it was him that came and he said he would do the job himself. I was in bed because it was my day off so I had to

143

get up to let him in. But I went back to bed and he came in and HE WAS STARK NAKED AND HE STARTED GRABBING ME . . . HE PULLED MY NIGHTDRESS OFF. I was terrified of him and he said nobody would ever know and it was my word against his. I never went to the police. I didn't want my boyfriend to know . . .

SIOBHAN THE STUDENT

'When I told my friends at College I was having trouble with my landlord, they all went like, him! And they all knew about him, it was all around College. He's been harassing girls for like years and nobody's ever done anything about it.'

BRENDA THE SINGLE MOTHER

'I had trouble paying the rent. It's not easy bringing up a kid on your own when you're not working. He knew that and he was always hinting and making remarks. You see I had to pay him in cash every fortnight when I cashed my giro, he said it was easier if he came round to collect it and he always hung around, talking and that, trying to be nice to me. I just ignored him really. Then he didn't come around for I think four weeks and I spent the cash and ended up in arrears. That was what he'd been wanting of course, so I started letting him . . . you know, to PAY OFF RENT ARREARS WITH SEX . . . we had sex when he came round. But I met this boy and he got angry about it and I ended up moving out. It made me feel cheap, MADE ME FEEL LIKE A SLUT, he's a total bastard and I hope someone can stop him.'

The *Sore-arse* gleefully ran the story across its centre pages with the faces of real tenants inset against a montage of images of seedy closes and scantily-clad models sitting on beds and, of course, the large picture of Swick himself. One of the former tenants agreed to pose for a topless shot. McLean was orgasmic over the telephone. This was exactly what he wanted. The paper was flying off

144

newsagents' shelves all over the country. Moray Neill and Sharkey stuffed themselves with curry at the Serang of Hoogly and got through four bottles of the house red on the day the piece appeared. It was their biggest success to date. A real triumph for Scottish journalism.

'That Grant-Gilford seems to have friends in higher places,' Scott Rennett grumbled. 'Mostly it seems to be him that has the ear of the councillors . . . and maybe even . . . the planners'. His brows darkened. 'Aye, maybe even the planners and the developers too. Why the hell would they no?'

'Possibly,' Gavin said. 'Wouldn't put it past him.' He sipped from his pot of Megginch Dew and wiped his lips.

'Ach no,' Lewis Summers intervened, 'our good doctor is no a traitor.'

'How can ye tell?' Old Tom inquired, puffing rapidly on his pipe. 'It's deeds not words that matter. He's done nothing so far, except talk talk talk about opposing the development. And time is rolling on.'

'And he doesn't even live in the village,' Rennett said. 'He'll not be affected.'

'Ah, he will, he will,' Summers said. 'Be fair, lads. He knows the opinion of the village. It was he who first suggested the survey after all.'

'Ach, survey ma arse!' Rennett exclaimed. 'That wisna muckle help. The man's a feardygowk. Needs a stick o dynamite up his bum afore he will dae onything at a.'

There was noisy agreement at this from around the huddles of tables. 'He's right,' said Jim McAvoy, the postman, sitting on the left of Scott Rennett, 'the survey was the very least you'd expect a community council to do. It was just a testing of the waters, not actually anything to do with opposing the thing.'

'Hear, hear, Jim, well said!' Rennett agreed.

'I mean it wasn't even a petition . . .' McAvoy said.

'There was the petition . . .'

'Aye, but no by the community council . . . it didna come frae them at a,' Old Tom said.

'That's why it was the best thing to form the action group and keep it separate from the community council,' Gavin said.

'Aye out of reach of Grant-Gilford and the silly auld Tory wifies,' Rennett said. 'Nothing would get done in a million years if it was up tae that lot. They'd be at loggerheads over the tiniest detail. Choppin and changin – ye know how contrary they can be? An half o them disnae even live in the village, disna even come into the village.'

'Disnae shop here, disnae use the facilities. Or amenities,' Old Tom agreed. 'You're no wrang.'

'Well, if we can turn to other matters,' Summers said dryly, contemplating with pleasure the golden meniscus in his tumbler, 'now that we've torpedoed poor Dr Grant-Gilford and the loyal ladies of the community council. Has anybody had a word with Councillor Douglas since last Tuesday?'

'She's still on holiday,' piped up a man in dungarees at the next table. 'Cooncillor Douglas is still awa, but I bumped into that ither ane, Cooncillor Hogue, Jill Hogue, in Perth on Saturday past. In the street like.'

'What was she saying, Jeemie? Anything new?'

Jeemie Thom, a stonemason, and an elder of the parish church, was widely respected for the reticence and rectitude of his opinions. 'Well, ye ken, it wis jist a wee chat I had wi her but the gist o it wis she's ca'ed oot a tree expert laddie, for tae mak a report . . . ach . . . well, ye ken . . . she wants the boy tae survey a the trees that follow the shoreline frae Seasyde tae Daleally. It's an ancient woodland, ye ken, according tae her, and they canna jist cut them doon wi'ooten special permission, ye ken.'

'Aye, Jeemie, that's grand,' Summers said, 'but did she say if this expert . . . this tree specialist . . .'

'Arborealist . . .' Jeemie added. 'That's whit the boy wis cried. An arborealist, ken, a specialist o trees.'

'But Jeemie, is this specialist employed by the Council?'

'Aye, is he a council man?' Rennett asked. 'That's whit we need tae ken.'

'Naw, I'm thinking she said he was an independent, a boy that paddles his ain canoe.'

'Aye, well,' Summers said, 'the Council employs its own tree conservation officer – I've seen his name in the library on posters. We'll have to have a word with him. He's based in Stanley I think.'

'If he's employed by the Council, it's likely he'll be thick with the Planning Department,' Rennett said. 'Ye ken whit that means . . .'

'Not necessarily, Scott, not necessarily,' Summers said in a mildly chiding tone. 'Don't make enemies of people who might be our allies when the time comes. Now, I feel this action group needs to let the wind out of its sails just a little. Another of these Cameron Brigs for me I think, Gavin, if you can shout on Cap'n Bob or Jim-lad.'

19

After a week or so at Auntie Kathleen's, a full night's sleep still eluded me. I found the silence, the absence of the tide on the shingle, oppressive. I would get up in mid-morning feeling as scuzzy as when I went to bed. I felt cooped up, constrained, dissatisfied like a caged animal. During the daytime I barely knew what to do with myself. Auntie Kathleen had not once asked me what my plans were, or whether I intended to find a job or sign on. Visiting the flats of former friends proved unproductive. The old haunts were knocked down or changed out of recognition. Even the city centre was unrecognisable: new shopping centres, new thoroughfares, no focus. The 3-Js coffee bar had gone, a bistro standing on the site had itself closed down a month before, according to an official notice on the window. A new coffee place further up the street, with red tartan carpeting and fake-antique claymores on the walls, seemed to be the meeting-place of old ladies in bonnets. Up the west end, a few of the old pubs were still there, the Taybridge Bar, the Campbeltown and Mennies, but others had suffered drastic makeovers – Laings had a beer garden now and was doing scampi-in-the basket meals. The Tav in the Hawkhill had been knocked flat and where it had stood was now a sports centre. The Scout and Frews were gone, the former renamed Slattery's while Frew's site had a new ring road running through it, or probably, it was hard to tell precisely. I felt like an alien. Was it only ten years?

Even the faces of those whom I thought I had known seemed

changed when I looked closely at them. Was that really the person I thought it was? I spoke to one or two of these casual acquaintances I had known from pubs and parties long ago, but none knew me. I wasn't offered any pints and no-one seemed interested in comparing memories. The fleshy shapes of their faces seemed to dissolve somehow in front of my eyes and change into the faces of total strangers. He might be . . . whatshisname . . . ? And isn't that . . . ? But I could not be at all sure. My memory was not up to this game of trying to pin down shifting resemblances from ten years ago. I spent a lot of time in the new bookshops, but did not have money to buy. The town seemed out of joint, out of sympathy with me. I had no connection, no focus, no-one to see. Auntie Kathleen went out and I found myself staying in, to avoid the depressing pointlessness of wandering around the city centre. Which was every bit as pointless as hiding out in the woods at Tentsmuir. I needed a change of scene. Some hint of a motive to recharge my batteries. London had been traumatic and even the seven weeks in the woods hadn't anaesthetised the whole metropolis experience. I was living too much inside myself and that is never healthy.

I told Auntie Kathleen I was going north to visit a friend in the Highlands. I had no friend in the Highlands but almost managed to convince myself how much fun we would have at a reunion.

'And where does this young man live?' Aunt asked, as she poured water into the teapot and placed the green woollen cosy on it.

'Ullapool. Well, nearby, on a kind of croft,' I said. 'Yes, he's become a crofter, you know, lives on a small holding. Has a few sheep and . . . and hens . . . that sort of thing.' I had the distinct feeling that she knew I was lying, but was giving me the benefit of the doubt.

'Well, I hope he'll feed you alright,' she said. 'And you'd better take warm clothes. Which train are you getting?'

With a loose arrangement to come back in about a week, I got the bus into town and got off opposite the post office. Another bus took me to the Charleston estate. I got off at the terminus and walked through the dull monotonous council housing to the Kingsway and down to the roundabout just north of Invergowrie.

149

I walked out to the petrol station and began hitching. Even just being clear of the city made me feel looser, freer, almost light-headed. I remembered my hitching in France and Spain and later in Italy. Hard to believe it was twenty years ago. It isn't so easy now; people are more wary. Most of the hitchers you see on Scottish roads are foreign students.

Almost half an hour, no time at all really, before a car juddered to a halt in the layby. A dinky little Ford Ka, green, like an aphid. Half an hour. I could imagine twenty years ago how impatient that would have made me! *Then* it was all go, go, go. Anyway, it's a guy just like myself, this driver, early middle age, and he tells me how he used to hitch all over.

'But these days I don't have the time,' he says and smiles rather sadly. The car is full of kiddies' things, toys and that.

'I know what you mean,' I say. 'This is the first time I've hitched for . . . well . . . about six years.'

'I used to like it, right,' he says. 'Me and the wife went all over. Scandinavia, France, Holland. Where are you making for?'

'Visiting a friend up at Ullapool. Hitching just seemed more . . . sort of convenient.'

He dropped me in the centre of Perth, and I had to walk out to the A9 roundabout at Almondbank. Luckily, I only had a leather shoulder bag. I can't stand being encumbered by luggage. That first long hitch to the south of France I had tent and sleeping bag and cooking stuff and most of it I junked along the way. Who needs it? All you need is a sturdy polythene bag you can crawl into on top of the heather, one that folds small, spare pair of underpants and socks you can easily wash, a spare T-shirt if you really want to push the boat out, small towel, toothpaste and toothbrush, Bic razors and soap, notebook, paperbacks and the jeans, trainers and leather jacket you're wearing. If it weighs more than five pounds you've over-packed. Stick it all in a comfortable shoulder bag and no matter what country you're in, you can forget about accommodation if you have to. Sit up all night, or walk the streets, or lie on a park bench and count the stars. It's fabulous the freedom you can get in this tiny and shrinking and absolutely beautiful world just by roaming freely and forgetting all the inessential shit that clutters

150

your life otherwise. I'm thinking all this in the comfortable seat of a fast car speeding up the A9. The driver, Neil, a thrusting, business-executive type has already apologised for his speed. He's late for a meeting in Pitlochry, so he's taking chances on bends and cutting up oncoming lorries. It's a dangerous stretch and several times we get flashing headlights from oncoming traffic. I guess he picked me up just to show off. He likes an audience. Probably isn't his car, more like his dad's, and he's probably just a business studies student anyway.

Pitlochry is a bonnie place, a perfect size for living in, except it's usually overrun by tourists, which probably pisses off the younger folk. They probably can't wait to get shot of the place and get out to university. But I get Neil to drop me off at the bridge over the river just before the town and walk back to the slip road. All around are gorgeous mountains, or hills really, and forests. Traffic seems to have hit a mid-afternoon slump and only the occasional vehicle appears and most take the Pitlochry turn-off. A half-hour becomes an hour. The sun slips into a thickening bank of cloud. It's so silent I can hear the occasional splash of fish in the river under the bridge.

The councillors arrived at the small Indian restaurant in the quiet streets of St Andrews in the hired minibus. There were eight of them, full of cheery bonhomie. Six were of the administration and two were from the major opposition group, but with the prospects of an evening's free drink and food all party differences had been set aside. In any case, only one of their number had any pretence to being a politician, and even he had progressed no further than membership of a few Regional Executive Committees of his party. The others were of the kind of decent, ordinary local worthies who get elected almost despite their political labels on the basis of being known to be halfway sensible – safe hands on the tiller – and, best of all, being unlikely to cause any great upheavals. They were local men, men you could have a good drink with. They had no superior airs, weren't likely to baffle you with science or make you look like a fool, and were elected every four years and promptly forgotten – till the next time. So Harry and Sid and Alasdair, Henry, John,

Jimmy, Erchie and Don tottered out of the minibus at the door of the Shiva Tandoori ready and willing to make the best of the night away from their wives. Away from the gaze of all who knew them. Away from all council responsibilities and political loyalties. Just eight middle-aged – verging on elderly – men from a rural area who had no difficulty enjoying each other's company, as long as someone else was paying.

The Shiva is a discreet and welcoming establishment, and the silverware and wine glasses gleamed in the dim red lights which coloured the napery pink. The waiters were most attentive and fussed over the guests as they were seated at the large table at the rear of the establishment behind a red velvet screen. The table had been set for twelve.

'Ach, we're on the early side,' said Sid, loosening his braces. 'They'll be here, ah've nae doots aboot that.'

'In twa shakes o a lamb's tail,' said Erchie, the retired farmer.

'Boys, ah'll hae tae exercise the dog,' Harry announced.

There was general glee. 'A'ready, min? Ye've had naethin yet tae drink?'

'It's ma age, ye ken. The wee fella comes and goes. Comes and goes. Aye, jist when he's a mind tae.'

This tickled the crowd who fell to discussing – in his absence – whether Harry had a colostomy bag or not. They were still discussing this when a waiter appeared ushering in their four hosts, smartly dressed younger men.

'Ah cooncillors, yir here a'ready! That's brah!' one of the new arrivals said cheerily.

'Aye, we're a wee early.'

'Yon minibus didna half flee owre the hills,' said another appreciatively. 'Up and doon a the wey!'

'Good, good,' said the shorter, dark-haired man. 'Now, I think we should get the introductions out of the way so we can all relax and enjoy ourselves.'

'That's a grand idea, man,' said Harry, emerging from the direction of the toilets. Some of the councillors had stood up, others remained seated. Harry introduced himself first and his colleagues, and there were handshakes all around.

The four arrivals introduced themselves. 'Ehm Daniel Morrow, a director o thi Carse Development Investment Associates. Z' meh brither Kevin, wha's Managing Director. Derek Rutherford iz thi company secretary – fir eez sins – an Bill Muir owir on the riyt iz thi Chief Executive o Loyal Homes. Thir gonna buhld thi hooses on thi site.' Daniel paused and smiled broadly at them. 'Mibbe. Mibbe buhld thi hooses. Assumin that wir application iz approved beh thi Cooncul an yir guid sels.'

This was exactly the right tone, and Daniel could see the councillors relax, some even laughing. They weren't here to discuss planning matters, he knew. Not really.

'Eh'll no be makin a lang spiel . . .' he could see the smiles at this. 'Bit eh wid like ti thank yiz a fir comin an eh hope thit we kin answer any questions yi miyt hae aboot thi development, ir any ither problems yi wush t' raise. Bit o coors . . . thi main pert o thi niyt iz jist ti see thit we . . . thit we a hae a bliddy brah time . . .' There were loud expressions of agreement now, so he wound up quickly. 'Waur's thi drink?' he said. 'Eh? Wuv bin here mair than fehv minutes an nae drink!' They wouldn't have laughed louder at Billy Connolly. He sat down at the head of the table. The waiters came in bringing a tray of bottles of champagne and started to take drinks orders. Daniel looked around carefully at each of the councillors in turn as everyone began chattering excitedly. Yes, they looked right, they'd be loyal to each other when the time came. It was going well. In an hour, or maybe an hour and half, they'd bring in the girls. And, at the end of the evening, Derek had a brown envelope for each of them to take back on the bus. Yes, a good evening in prospect. A successful evening. He sipped a flute of champagne. *Brah!*

Finally, after an hour and a half, a car comes on fast and as it passes me, the driver sees me and kind of reacts. Swerves off on to the Pitlochry turn-off as if it wasn't what she was planning. This only occurs to me a few minutes later when I see the same car emerge from the south slip road and come towards me again. This time, she stops and holds the door open.

'I guess I kind of got a bit lost,' she says, once I'm inside. She's a

153

brunette, about mid-forties. Smart short hairstyle, an elegant woman, respectable, discreetly perfumed. Nice legs and a skirt that's dark blue and rather short. Middle class, perhaps even upper middle. Director or company executive, or the wife of one. She reminds me a little of Marjorie Braid, but somehow more brash and there's something nervous about her, guilty almost. A different story soon starts to emerge a few miles further north. She tells me her name is Christine and that her husband is away on a course in England. 'Lost' – my eye! I can see the signs, and it's not the first time this has happened to me. Whereas my younger self would have had no problem with it, now I'm far too wary. I watch and wait. We talk about this and that, fashion, holidays, tourism, London. But there's something else going on.

A few miles further and it's 'Oh, it's so hot in here, isn't it?' and she's undoing a button. It's not that I don't fancy her and god knows it's been ages since I had sex with a woman, but these things can turn very nasty.

'Must have a drink of water,' she says soon, slowing down and driving off the road into a wide forestry track. Somewhere near Calvine, I think. She switches off the engine, unbuckles her seat belt and – perhaps deliberately – her skirt rides up her legs as she's drinking mineral water. All around are trees and small birds swooping over the car. Then she's all over me kissing my face. I sit there and let my mouth go slack as she wet kisses my lips. I keep my hands by my sides. She's very excited and hot and forces her leg over mine and gets on top of me in the tight space of the passenger seat.

'Christine,' I say. 'Ehm, Christine, you're very sweet, but . . .'

'What?' she asks looking at me, her lips pouting wetly. 'What?' Her lipstick is smeared over her upper lip and her hair is mussed. She's breathing heavily and is flushed in the face.

'It's just . . . my girlfriend wouldn't like it,' I say tamely. 'You know.'

'Oh,' she goes, closing her eyes. 'My husband wouldn't like it either . . . but . . .' she pauses, then gasps, 'Gerry, I need you in me, *now*!'

It makes me laugh, it just sounds so false. 'No, honestly, look . . .'

But she's smothering me with her kisses and dry riding me, pushing her bra into my face through her flapping blouse. I feel the car shifting under the weight.

'Come on, oh, come on . . . ohhhhh!' she gasps, totally beyond control.

There's nothing I can do because she clings on to me, gasping and nuzzling under my chin. We sit like that for a few minutes.

She sits up. 'Gerry, I don't know what came over me,' she says finally. 'What must you think of me?'

She gets off me and with difficulty gets back into the driving seat and starts doing up the buttons of her blouse. There's a hot wet patch at my groin where she rubbed herself against me.

'Honestly, it's okay . . .'

'But you've got a girlfriend?'

'Well, I do . . .'

'So what's her name?'

'Eh – Marjorie,' I hear myself saying.

'That's nice,' she says insincerely.

She drives on; we're like a pair of strangers with a guilty secret. It was companionably quiet for a few miles to the turn-off at Dalwhinnie. We kiss again as I get out and make vague promises. She gives me her phone number. Somehow I find myself wondering if it is genuine.

As soon as she is out of sight, I tear it up and throw it into the ditch. I inspect the wet sticky patch on my jeans and wonder why I mentioned Marjorie. That was odd. I almost believed it myself. The hitchhiker's fantasy. I remember that time in Italy, between Florence and Bologna, when I'd been picked up by a girl and a hitch had turned into a day and a night stay at her parents' mansion. With her feeding me from the kitchen and her parents in the other wing of the house not even aware I was there. Forty-eight hours of almost non-stop sex! And another time, somewhere near Oxford, when three girls took me home to stay at their flat and we all ended up in bed together just for a laugh. Stoned out of our nuts! One of them called Gillian, I think. Those were the days when you didn't need to worry about condoms. And that time when I was wearing my kilt coming back from Stirling, the Bannockburn Rally, a beautiful black-haired Canadian girl ten years older than me who'd been at the Rally too. Making it on the hillside like Rob Roy! What *was* her name? God knows. I must have been about eighteen. Not my first time though. God no.

Anyway, concentrate, it's early evening and I'm starting to get hungry. So I walk to the village and into the transport café that looks like it belongs in a Wild West frontier town. I order a fry-up and a big mug of milky coffee. Hardly anyone in the café; just a big empty space with two teenage waitresses giggling behind the counter. Maybe they could smell my wet underpants?

I walked back to the A9 and began hitching again. The cars had their headlights on. It began to get colder. Just after 8 p.m. an old guy in a Ford Escort van. I could smell drink on his breath and he was quite talkative. He took me all the way to Aviemore and let me out at the station. It was dark and there were a lot of lights. The place seemed a lot busier than I remembered. I gave up my ideas of going further and had a pint in a warm red-lit bar with piped muzak and a fake coal-fire, thinking, strangely, of Marjorie Braid, and how nice it would be if she were here with me. Then I walked out on the Carrbridge road a little and stepped off into a wood, just a little way in. I found a soft piece of grass under a tree and unfolded my polythene bag and stepped into it and lay down. I used my shoulder bag as a pillow and, looking upwards through the dark leaves of the trees to the deeper dark, studied the con-stellations of stars, the streetlights of the Milky Way and, grasping that thought steady like a binnacle, felt myself canted, lifted, and dropped on the white horses of deep sleep.

20

But hitching had lost its appeal. It was bloody cold and mostly raining. There was a more substantial reason. It was pointless. I didn't like to admit it was boring. There were no real problems to overcome. You stuck out your thumb and after a while, long or short, you got a lift. And everywhere you went seemed to be the same. In this mood, I made it to Inverness in a couple of lifts and walked through the cold streets. I bought sandwiches and took them to a bench near a footbridge over the Ness. It was almost, but not quite raining, grizzling and foggy, the grass by the castle lush and green. Traffic was swishing in and out of the Caledonian Hotel carpark. It was more than twelve years since I'd been in Inverness and it seemed to be bigger, a lot busier.

When I'd eaten my sandwiches, which neither filled me nor assuaged the coldness that racked my bones, I walked along Church Street, contemplating going into a pub. I walked into a pedestrianised part of the High Street and saw a cluster of telephone boxes. I was thinking of Marjorie Braid and her cosy little flat at Tayport. It'd be nice to phone her. Why not?

'Of course I remember you.' Her voice sounded calm but far away. 'I was wondering what you were up to . . .'

'I'm in Inverness . . .'

Her laid-back, sympathetic manner soon made me feel comfortable. There was no sexual element. Well, that's not entirely true. I fancy her I suppose, but somehow I don't have to admit that and we can just have a normal casual friendship without any

157

hang-ups. We had become friends quickly, strange when I consider how isolated I had been, how paranoid. Talking to her I
could forget some of these anxieties, these preoccupations, my
motivelessness, incipient depression – whatever it was. I was glad
to have her as a friend. Having her as a friend made me feel
pleased with myself.

Inverness was a bore, grizzling and nondescript in the rain. I
couldn't be bothered looking for somewhere to stay. Much easier
to hitch. North? South? It didn't seem to matter.

Dispatches from the Latrines

This time the tip-off had come from McLean. Some responsible
citizen had dialled the *Scottish Source* news line. Well, they had this
teaser in the inside front saying if anyone knew of any stories, give
us a bell and you're quids in. A lie of course, just another way of
cheating Joe Public because there was a get-out clause. Which
punter could ever truly claim ownership 100 per cent, because if it
was a story, well, odds on someone else would have it too? Sorry,
chum, no dosh for you. Boo hoo hoo. Ah, but that clipe line, as the
boys and girls at the sore-arse knew it, was a great well of untapped
material fuelled by hatred and its minions, envy, spite, greed, and
the absolute need to shop any uxorious bastard getting away with
something they didn't ought to be getting away with. You'd be
amazed what Moray Neill had learned of human nature in every
shift at the Sore-arse. Most of the best exclusives were obtained
under base motives, particularly spite and envy. The readers could
identify with the spite and envy of the story and enjoy the 'bring-
doon' of the mighty, the pompous, the overbearing, the uppity,
sharing in the triumph of the anonymous and humble 'bringer-
doon'.

The caller – from a payphone – had simply said 'See thi Public
Works Depertment? Thirz a boy sellin a thir stuff t' thi Typhon, bit
naebdies pressin chairges cause eez got a wee black book . . .' And
that was it. The story in a nutshell.

'No helluva lot to go on, fucksake,' McLean as good as conceded. 'You could start with the Police Press Officer boy.'

'Aye, well,' Sharkey said, later. 'We'll have a job getting this one to stand up. Some guy stealin wood? Hold the front page!'

'Sarcasm's the lowest form of wit,' Moray countered. 'We've to look into it. McLean'll be on our backs until we do.'

'Aye,' said Sharkey, 'but let's not lose sight of the fact that we're talking here about a bloody department that built Glenrothes – as a homer.'

''I've heard that rumour. There's not a word of truth in it.' Moray winked. 'Even though the Director got a golden handshake in his thirties when the councillors looked into it. Anyway, I phoned the Police Press Office.'

'And what did the polis say?'

'Investigations are continuing.'

'Great,' Sharkey snorted, smoothing his sideburns. 'That'll be the headline.'

'Aw, fuck off! But they did say they had a report. A complaint was passed to them. A man is helping them with their inquiries.'

'Na? I've crapped myself out of sheer excitement!' Sharkey said sourly. 'Look – I know a guy knows a guy who works there. I'll give him a bell and see if I can get a name. Your job, of course,' he concluded. 'I'm just the snapper; you're meant to be the words man.'

'I'll give you a word,' Moray said. 'In fact four. Get your finger out.'

'Wow! A verb *and* a noun. In the same sentence! You've been practising.'

'Yeah, yeah!'

Sharkey laboured mightily and on the third day produced a name.

They sat watching busy Reform Street from the window of the Pancake Place, a busy coffee joint despite the fake antique claymores on the walls and the violent red-tartan carpeting. Moray sipped a steaming glass of hot blackcurrant to clear his tubes.

'I think I'm coming down with something,' he complained, wiping his nose with a tissue.

159

'So long as you're going regular, you got no worries,' Sharkey announced. 'Missed appointments in that department and you're fucked. In my humble opinion, of course.'

'Thank you for that medical insight.'

'Don't mention it.'

'These matters come easily to you, don't they? No qualms of any kind?'

'I'm just the snapper. Are you going to eat that muffin?'

'Have it.'

'Great. The name we've got is . . .'

'*Must* you pick your nose like that? I might have been just about to use that teaspoon.'

'Wouldn't advise it, mate. It's got snot all over.'

'You were saying,' Moray prompted, 'about this name you've got?'

'A Mr Arthur Flood, used to work at the Stobswell Depot. Sacked for gross misconduct. No notice. The polis are still looking into it – as you said – but he's not been charged. Word is it's something to do with the Masons.'

'Perry or James?'

'Ho. Bloody ho,' Sharkey grimaced.

'Odd to be sacked without notice . . . just for stealing some wood. It was wood, was it?'

'Oh, yeah, a lorry load of wood. Just the one. But what's more interesting is this black book. He's been bummin his load in the Gairfish Bar in Midmill that he's got loads of evidence on council officials and councillors. All their wee scams. Seemingly he threatened to blow the gaff if he was sacked. But he's leery just yet of the tabloids. What I'm told is that he's trying to blackmail the Council into giving him his job back. He doesn't want to use the wee black book – if it exists.'

'What was his job with the Council?'

Sharkey grinned. 'That's just it. He was a foreman of the public works. The very boy to know what's coming in and what's going out and where and to who. Best of all though, he's been employed since the days of the old Corporation.'

Moray was thinking hard. 'So – he was sacked without

160

notice . . . but surely he could use the disciplinary procedure . . . even the tribunal . . .'

Sharkey took off a cowboy boot to massage his stockinged feet. At this, even old ladies sitting nearby who'd survived the war were seen to blench. 'Oh, aye, of course, but the one guaranteed thing about that is that it takes months, even years. He could be dead before he gets a hearing.'

Moray covered his nostrils with a paper napkin. 'So what do you suggest . . . ? Must you do that, *here*?'

Sharkey had the boot on the table to inspect. A waitress in the non-smoking area dropped a metal tray with a loud crash. A crowd of foreign tourists gathering outside to stare at the menu in the window were plainly much diverted by the sight of the boots on the tabletop.

'Are you really going to eat them?' asked an elderly wag passing by.

'I'm going!' Moray announced, getting to his feet. 'If you can't be civilised. Farting, nose-picking and now this . . .'

'Yeah, I'm a talented guy.'

Moray slapped coins on the tabletop. 'This'll cover my drink. Bye.'

The Carse Development Investment Associates were having a difficult time as they went through the processes of incorporation. One of the major investors had to drop out due to liquidity problems; another was querying terms and conditions. After the deadline expired, Derek Rutherford wrote a sorrowful memo to Kevin Morrow detailing the extent to which the company was undercapitalised.

Kevin faxed his stockbroker, his financial manager and, finally, Daniel. All three came back with the same advice: if planning permission was granted, the project was certain to be hugely financially profitable. Kevin decided to increase his personal investment in the company, and advised his financial holdings manager to facilitate transfer of funds into the capital account. Kevin's finances would be stretched over the three projects he was simultaneously involved in, but he'd been in the position before,

161

and each was likely to exceed forecasted profit. There was risk, in the short term. His main concern was to get the development started before winter set in. Once it was, he felt sure there'd be no shortage of investors looking to buy their way in. His main problem was obtaining outline planning permission for phases 1–3 and marking obstacles in the water so that he could circumnavigate them.

21

I t wasn't often mother and daughter went shopping together. Neither was keen on trekking around the city centre and it was rare for Carly to get a Saturday off. Gavin had taken the kids to Perth Leisure Pool so Carly drove herself into town to meet her mum at Boots' corner.

The city centre was in uproar. Clowns stalked the streets on high stilts, jugglers juggled, acrobatic tumblers tumbled. A band, fronted by three girls in black cocktail dresses, played a hot-tempo Latino dance number from a raised stage with a striped awning. A crowd had gathered underneath. Elderly ladies shrieking and giggling, twirled each other in time.

'You look really nice, Mum,' Carly said. 'You should wear make-up more often.'

'Says you!' Marjorie retorted. 'Who never wears any.'

'I like the way you have your hair done. I mean up like that, shows off your neck. I've always said you've got a lovely neck.'

'I was amazed how expensive these hair places are nowadays,' Marjorie complained. 'And I had to wait for three days before I could get an appointment in the first place.'

'Where?'

'The place you suggested, on Sunday, dear, you know, Oscar's, in St Andrews – where you said your friend Sarah went.'

'Oh yes,' Carly said. 'They did a good job though. And I like the butterfly clasp.'

'It was fifty pounds. Imagine! I still feel a bit guilty about the

163

cost. I never bother for school and – I suppose also because of my voluntary work . . .'

'You were going to phone them – to give up one of your evenings.'

'I never got around to it. I'm still doing two evenings but I do the soup run later now on a Monday, it's been moved back to 11 p.m.'

'I don't know how you've kept it up all this time,' Carly said. 'Mind you, I'm proud of you for doing it.'

'It gives me something to do,' Marjorie said. 'When your father died, I promised myself I'd do something. Something real to help the homeless. It's taken me this long to get involved. I used to be very active before you came along. I still feel I'm not doing enough.'

'I think it's brilliant what you do.'

The singers stepped up to the microphones and the band began to swing.

. . . I'll try . . . for a kiss . . . in the garden . . .

Some couples at the front began to waltz across the paving and people were clapping along.

'Great singers,' Marjorie commented. 'I think I've seen this lot on TV.'

'Glamorous too,' Carly said enviously. 'Look at those legs.'

'Thir local lassies,' a woman said proudly. 'Awfy brah singers, ir thi no?'

'Here, come on, we'd better make a move,' Marjorie said, tugging Carly's sleeve.

'Okay, where first?'

The Overgate Centre is a temple of glass with moving stairways and glass chandelier lights and mirrors. They spent time in Debenhams, where Carly tried on jeans and tops. Marjorie searched for a winter jacket. Shoes – they both tried shoes, in various places. Sales assistants smiled at the resemblance of the two, clearly mother and daughter, the mother taller and slimmer and the daughter with a nose stud and her hair in braids with coloured beads. They soon tired of the constant bustle and the trying-on, and queues for the changing rooms. When Marjorie looked at her watch, it was nearly 2 p.m. They had achieved so little.

'We'll head up to the Wellgate,' she said. 'For one more push. But first, we'd better have some lunch. On me. Where d'you fancy?'

'Pub? Or restaurant?

'I just want a sandwich and a coffee,' Marjorie said. 'Got to watch my figure.'

'Oh, mum! You know there's nothing wrong with your figure! I wish I had your shape! You're the size 12, remember, not me.'

They emerged carrying their bags and on the stage in City Square a different band was about to play.

'Let's watch this for a minute,' Carly said.

'Okay, just a minute.'

An ungainly middle-aged man with wrap-around black sun-glasses stood poised at the microphone, looking over his shoulder. A leather-clad man behind him hoisted a saxophone to his lips. The rest of the band stood behind keyboards, drums, or strapped themselves into guitars. An announcer declared, *and now, ladies and gents . . . in a rare public performance . . . St Andrew . . . and . . . and . . . the woolly mitt!*

The speakers chugged under the sizzling weight of a mega-bass beat. The singer rapped in Dundee dialect.

'What a funny name for a group,' Marjorie said, turning away. 'Come on, dear, your mother's hungry.'

They escaped the turmoil of the High Street and sat in the café at the Art Gallery, in an alcove table. The place was almost empty. Outside, the bronze politician silently legislated above the flower-beds and the square rear of the bronzed Empress of India cast a dingy shadow.

'So what have you been up to then, Mum?'

'Just the usual . . .' she hesitated. 'Oh, well, that is . . . I did meet someone . . . a new friend . . .'

Carly looked up from her plate of soup. 'Oh? New friend? That sounds mysterious. Is it a man? Well, come on, out with it, Mum . . .'

Marjorie smiled archly. 'It's just someone I met when I was out on a walk.'

Carly pretended to be scandalised. 'Mum! You've not let your-self be picked up in the street?'

165

'No, no, nothing like that. He's a friend. Phoned me the other day. He's up in the Highlands just now. I probably shouldn't have said anything to you; I knew you'd get the wrong idea. We're just friends, that's all.'

'How long has this been going on?'

'Now, nothing's going on, dear. I met him and we had a chat and I invited him for a coffee . . . if he was passing and he came by a few days later. And we had a chat and that's all there is to it.'

'He's been to your house?'

'Yes, just for a cup of coffee. He's far too young for me anyway.'

'Ah-hah, so he's a toyboy?'

Marjorie laughed. 'I honestly don't think you could really call him that. He's way too serious and . . . earnest. Takes himself very seriously. Something of a writer.'

'So what is his name?'

'Gerald, calls himself Gerry.'

'And he's not married?'

'No.'

'Well . . . what did you talk about?'

Marjorie smiled. 'Oh, lots and lots of things. He's been working in London for ten years and is a bit fed up. He was living rough . . .'

'Mum! I don't believe you!' Carly exploded. She leaned forward and spoke confidentially. 'He's one of your tramps, isn't he? For heaven's sake! One of the down-and-outs?'

Marjorie was taken aback. 'No, no, dear. He was living rough at Tentsmuir . . .'

'Oh, that makes a difference does it . . . a better class of tramp . . . ?'

'He's not . . . He's a bit lost just now, confused, that's all.'

'He was living rough?'

'Well, yes, but he has an aunt in Dundee and so he's staying with her. Now he's gone off to visit a friend in Ullapool.'

'I see what you mean about "confused," ' Carly said. 'He doesn't seem to know whether he's coming or going. Your toastie's ready. Will I get it?'

'Thanks.'

When Carly returned, she resumed her criticism. 'Sounds like he doesn't know what he wants. Is he coming back? I mean will you . . .'

'I don't know, dear. Maybe, maybe not. He said he has a friend who lived at Errolbank. You might know . . . somebody called Stephen Brack.'

Carly sat up in surprise. 'Oh yeah! Stephen and Fay Brack. They're friends of Gavin's. They live at Bridgend of Cardean now, near Meigle. They're coming down for the protest meeting.'

'There you are then,' Marjorie said. Then she mused: 'Hmn, maybe Gerry would like to go to that too? He's very concerned about the environment. In fact, we have a fair bit in common.'

'Mother! You scandalise me! You really do. What would Dad say to all this?'

'Now, that's not fair, and you know it. And where do you get this "tramp" nonsense from anyway? "Homeless people" that's what they're called. As in "people" without a home. Just ordinary people trapped by circumstances. Honestly, you can sound so middle class sometimes, Carly. So self-righteous.'

'I didn't mean to be narky, Mum, just . . . well, I worry about you. You're a bit naive . . .'

Marjorie snorted. 'Me – naive? Huh? You want to have to teach 4G every day of the week – they'd give you naive! In some respects I can be as hard as nails – as well you know. Who was it who . . . ?'

'I *was* just kidding,' Carly interrupted, 'Just kidding, but don't go overboard. Hard as nails – no way! But you can be . . . well, I worry about you being a bit vulnerable, taken advantage of, you know. Coming into contact with all that sort . . .'

'Now what sort would that be?'

'You know, dossers, the homeless, what Gavin calls the underclass . . .'

'Oh does he? The underclass . . . I suppose that's what university has taught him?'

'Yeah, of course, Gav likes to think he's part of it . . . the underclass. Financially he's about right.'

'Nothing came of that application then. For the university library part-time job?'

'Well, he said he applied, but you never know with Gav.'

'Something will turn up for him. And when he gets his degree, there will be no stopping him,' Marjorie said.

On the way out of the Art Gallery, they stopped at a noticeboard and read various leaflets and posters of forthcoming events.

'Gavin would be interested in this,' Carly mused, 'a talk about the Picts in Angus.'

'Yes, he would, wouldn't he? Sounds interesting. Might go myself. Who's doing it?'

Carly examined the small print. 'Somebody called . . . Dr Stella Auld, of St Andrews University.'

'When is it? Aw, that's the date of the Planning Meeting in Perth.'

'Date is right, mother,' Carly teased. 'Outrageous at your age. You should be sat at home in your old rocking chair crocheting or knitting . . .'

Marjorie pulled a face. 'Now you're being sarcastic.'

'Bloody right I am, Mum!'

22

The sandstone buildings of the Council Chambers overlook the river and the little wooded islands that swim in the stream beneath the bridges. The estuary here is a surging shallow river a hundred yards wide. During daylight hours, cars in metered spaces, facing iron benches, line its banks beneath giant trees and traffic wardens prowl relentlessly. The main entrance used by councillors is on the High Street, close to the river, beneath ornamental streetlights.

Almost a hundred noisy residents of Errolbank stood around the steps on the evening of the Planning Committee Meeting. The mood was jocular, optimistic. For most it was a night out in the town, with a pint in a local hostelry to follow.

'A grand turnout, Scott,' Lewis Summers was saying to all who would hear. 'Just grand, my my. Indeed.'

'No many o the auld Tory wifies,' Rennett said, leaning heavily on his stick, 'an yon Grant-Gilford is suspicious by his absence. It's maistly locals here.'

'Aye, it was good of Bob and Elsie to lay on a bus,' Gavin said above a chorus of hissing.

'Who's that?' Rennett demanded. 'Ach, that Muir fella. Boo, hisss . . . Ye traitor!' he shouted, waving his stick in the air.

'This number of objectors,' Gavin said, 'will surely have an impact on the committee?'

'We'll mebbe no a get in,' Jim McAvoy said. 'The Chamber's quite sma.'

169

'Damn shair an ahm getting in!' Rennett declared. 'An getting a seat. If these bliddy cooncillors can hae a seat . . .'

'Hush, Scott, hush man. I'm sure we'll be alright.'

'The polis is here,' Old Tom announced. He'd found himself a perch on the metal rails, and was puffing scented tobacco smoke above the heads of the crowd.

'It's what ye'd expect. Ah, here's the lassie Jill . . .'

'Cooncillor Hogue . . .' a photographer appeared, tugging at her arm, 'how's about a picture wi some of the delegation . . . for the *Advertiliser*?'

'Aye, delegation . . .' Old Tom said. 'The Grant-Gilford creature is no here. I doot it'll hae t'be yoursel, Lewis.'

'Ah'll come wi you!' Rennett said, waving his stick like a claymore. 'I'll soon give them a piece o my mind . . .'

'Steady, man, steady! Ye'll hae somebody's eye out with that,' Old Tom said, grasping the stick.

'Ah well, Scott,' Lewis said, 'that's good of you to offer, but I think young Gavin should . . . after all he lives right next to the site . . . and he's got the words, being a university man . . . What d'you say, Gavin, are you game?'

'*Gavin Cathro!*' a loud voice boomed from the crowd. 'How are you doing, man?'

'Stephen! And Fay! Over here.'

A heavily black-bearded man wearing a black fedora and a long black coat was pushing towards Gavin's group. In his wake, a petite woman with long shiny black hair, a pale delicate beauty, almost saint-like.

'Good to see you!'

'And you, man!'

'Fay – you look great! Lewis these are my friends, Stephen and Fay Brack. They use to live in the village.'

'Pleased to meet you. And *you* – gorgeous lady!'

Lewis Summers fetched up one of Fay's hands and began kissing her fingertips. 'Beyond doubt one of the most beautiful ladies . . .' he began. Gavin turned to block further gallantries, though Fay was smiling indulgently. Lewis could overdo it a bit. He was always spouting his philosophy that the world needed more hugging. 'We should be proud of our emotions, Gavin,' he was always saying. 'We're different from the English, more like Europeans, the French . . . they haven't got any of this embarrassment about touching and kissing and weeping. That's what the world needs, believe me – more hugging!' There was no sexual element. He simply wanted more intimate contact, on a more comprehensive level. He hadn't an enemy in the world. His wife was disabled and Lewis was her carer. She was always berating him for his attentions to other women and his drinking, but he took it in good part. Late in the evening, he would get up to use the payphone behind the bar. 'Better check in at the guardhouse,' he would say, winking. 'See if the rottweiler is awake. Tell her I'll be home before dawn and not to wait up.' His most renowned gambit when he phoned someone, anyone, male or female, was his opening line: *I just called . . . to say . . . I love you . . .* followed by a prolonged dry chuckling before he would proceed to the matter in hand . . . *Lewis here . . .* His phonecalls could be lengthy and not altogether serious.

'Thanks for coming, guys,' Gavin said. 'Carly's coming separately, with her mum.'

'So are we winning?' Stephen asked. 'There's certainly a lot of people here.'

'We'll know in a minute. There's an usher.'

'Some auld wife has taen a tumble on the steps,' Old Tom informed them. 'Lost her footin. Whoa, she's up again. She's alright.'

A diminutive bald man in a blue blazer with the council badge on the breast, stood on the top step. His words were drowned by a great cheer from the crowd and everybody was pushing up the steps into the council chamber.

Gavin stood on the top step looking down the street to see if he could see Carly and her mum.

'We'd better go in,' Stephen said. 'Maybe they're having trouble parking the car. We did.'

'Gavin!' Lewis waved to him urgently from inside, over the heads of the crowd.

'You're right. We don't want to miss it. I might have to speak as part of the delegation.'

'Gavin – that's great! You'd be good,' Fay said, leading him inside.

The crowd shuffled into the foyer and up more stairs into the main council chamber. It was like the drawing room of the Palace of Versailles, opulent in crimsons and purples with gilt-edged cornices and polished oak benches. Council officials in blue blazers kept the crowd moving and sat them in the rows of benches around the walls of the chamber, behind the desks of the councillors. Most of the councillors were seated and looking around in wonder at the large number of the objectors. Others stood in knots at the other entrance to the main chamber.

'They must have some back way of getting in,' Scott Rennett groused. 'None of them passed us, I'm damned sure.'

Gavin sat beside Stephen and Fay, in the row behind Lewis. As soon as he sat down, he saw Dr Grant-Gilford standing with the local Errolbank councillor, Janet Douglas and two others whom Gavin did not know. He also noted Bill Muir, the Chief Executive of Loyal Homes – the enemy! Leaning over the desk of a councillor whose ruddy complexion and startling white hair was set off by a bulbous mottled nose. His eyes roved the public gallery as if searching for enemies.

Jamie the barman, sitting in the first row, grinned over his shoulder and gave Gavin the thumbs-up. Gavin noticed Carly and her mum with a tall man he didn't know, filing in at the back and being made to stand against the wood-panelling, beside a display of flags. The place was packed. He couldn't attract Carly's attention. The man with Marjorie, in an open-necked black shirt, must be, he realised, the man she'd met at Tentsmuir.

Disturbing Reports from our End

Moray Neill had been unable to contact Flood or budge the immovable obstacle in the Press Office at Tayside Police. Complete impasse. Nor had he had any contact with the scatological Sharkey. He'd phoned McLean and received curt sympathy.

'Fucksake, he is a shitey cunt at the best of times. But I need you workin as a team. Sir Philip de Cundy's here all week. I need to show him there's some good stuff in the pipeline from your end. Get on it, pal.'

Moray had, by this time, established a vague network of contacts in most of the leading organisations in the area. Mostly this operated out of self-interest. People would phone him to grass up their rivals. The Council was a hot-bed of intrigue and back-stabbing. The administration's majority had been wiped out over several elections and stood on a knife-edge. But as usual, the enemy was within the party.

The Moorings Bar at the bottom of Crichton Street at the back of the City Chambers was a good place to pick up malicious gossip. Though not many elected members went there, it was a prime location for the hangers-on, the detritus that sticks to the heels of every political group. Leading combatants could infiltrate juicy tidbits into the public domain by airing it in the presence of one of the fringe members of this *demi-monde*. Within hours it would be all around the town as firmly established rumour. Moray had uncovered gradations of rumour-mongers in the Moorings. There were those whose gossip tended to be more inspired than fanciful. There were mere repeaters, second-rate retailers. And a third level, who repeated only part of, and partially, and sometimes, hilar-iously skewed tales they'd heard at third or even fourth hand. W was a reliable leaker of tittle-tattle from one political group because he attended the same bowling club as Councillor X. Y was a particularly good source close to the leadership since his cousin's brother-in-law was Councillor Z, the group whip. But anything W said about Councillor Z was liable to be spiteful tosh and anything Y claimed to know about Councillor X was no more than bilious hearsay.

The problems with over-frequent attendance at the Moorings were that you might be told tales which would transpire to be the diminishing echoes of the same tales you heard the last time you were in the pub, and that you yourself might become implicated in the tales. Moray generally attended less than once a week, timed to coincide with major committee meetings or sessions of the full council and always washed his hands thoroughly afterwards.

He pushed through the old-fashioned saloon swing-doors into the dimly-lit bar area and looked around. There were several sad faces he knew, mostly of the type he wished to avoid, so he went straight to the bar and ordered a pint. The council meeting was still in session, he concluded.

A greasy red-faced little man in an ancient anorak, whose eager gaze Moray tried to ignore, sidled up. Pustulent sores erupted on and around his nose, and some of his hair was lying on his shoulders.

'Heard thi latest?' he wheedled.

Moray almost imperceptibly shook his head. The other man coughed and wiped his nose upwards over his forehead.

'Yi dinna hae a fag on yi?'

Moray didn't smoke but knew to carry a packet of cigarettes on his trips to the Moorings.

'Thanks, pal, yir a good scout. Eh wiz gaspin . . . gaggin . . . meh throat wiz . . .'

Moray recognised the familiar gambit. 'Want a pint . . . Jim?' he asked.

'Z'no Jim.' A grubby hand was proffered from the pocket of the anorak. 'Turdie, that's wut thi creh iz.' Moray shook it without looking too closely at it. *A slippery customer.*

'Aw, yir a wee gem,' Turdie said. 'Eh, go on, eh'll hae a pint a Maclays ta . . . meh giro's late this week. Ehm a buttie impeculiar, ken, bit eh'll pey yiz back ahriyt.'

'That's okay.'

'They bastards at thi broo shid be hung beh thi bollocks fae thi Tay Brig.'

'Yeah. The latest you said . . . ?'

'Aw, eh . . .'

'Well . . .'

'Hear, eh ken yir a journalist boy, bit eh dinna wahnt meh name in thi pippers, ken. Ehv meh ain reasons . . .'

'No names, no pack drill,' Moray grinned.

Turdie smiled ingratiatingly and fumbled at his sleeve. 'That's thi gemme. An uf it's worth sumhin t' yi . . . ehm only lookin fir a wee tap . . .'

174

'Well, I have to hear the story first.'

'Aw eh, a coors . . . a coors. First, eh.' He peered over each shoulder suspiciously. 'Look, ehm no wahntin abidee . . . yi ken . . . wa's hae lugs, like . . .'

'Okay, there's a table over in the corner. I'll join you in a minute. Have to go to the bog first.'

Gavin watched as a bandylegged little man in a council blazer ambled into the Chamber bearing a silver mace across both his forearms and declared, *Ladies and Gentlemen, the Lord Provost!* and everybody was getting to their feet.

The Provost, a red-faced, wide little man in a tight, blue, double-breasted suit strutted in, looking harassed, followed by two tall implacable flunkeys, holding up the ends of his red robe.

In front of the audience, the little man, who seemed short of breath, shrugged himself out of the robe and with effort climbed puffily up into the mahogany chair with the high ornate scrolls on the back, squirmed a bit in the seat then donned a hat that reminded Gavin of something out of HMS *Pinafore*. He banged a gavel on the top of his desk and everyone sat down. Such a little man, such a large hat, was Gavin's irreverent thought. He felt like laughing. The two tall men stood with great dignity on either side of the Provost's chair.

'Cooncul is noo in session,' said a squeaky voice that seemed to emanate from the Lord Provost. 'Clerk?'

A tired-looking man in a crumpled grey suit was on his feet at the head of the table beneath the Provost's high chair. He spoke so quickly it was difficult to follow: 'Lord Provost, councillors,' he announced. 'View of large number delegations concerning item 4 on agenda of Planning Committee, recommended this item be taken first.'

There was a muttered chorus around the room: 'Agreed!'

The Clerk continued: 'That being agreed, now proposed hear item in public for delegations, then in camera.'

'Agreed!' went the mutter around the room.

'Not agreed!' said a few dissenting voices. The clerk queried the source of the dissent. Councillor Jill Hogue was on her feet.

'Member Almondvale,' intoned the Clerk.

'Yes?' queried the Provost testily.

Jill Hogue, an ample woman of middle age, stood behind her desk on which was prominently placed her large leather handbag. She wore a green tweed suit and black spectacles. She had an intimidating air of authority.

'Not agreed, Lord Provost, fellow members,' she boomed. 'In my view this item is best dealt with in public . . .' she glared around the room, '. . . in its entirety. A large number of electors have travelled some distance to be here this evening and are entitled to hear the deliberations of the committee in full.'

'Aye, well,' muttered the Provost. 'Seconder?'

'I second,' shouted Councillor Janet Douglas, half-rising.

'Good old Janet!' Lewis Summers whispered loudly.

'Very well. Vote,' mumbled the Provost.

The Clerk rose to his feet again, quickfire: 'On motion proposed the Committee Chairman delegations be heard public session, there being amendment proposed Councillor Hogue, seconded Councillor Douglas, business pertinent item 4, Planning Committee agenda be taken in public session. As procedure, please show for amendment first.'

Councillors' hands shot upwards. Six. Only six.

'Motion?'

Twenty, more than twenty.

'Amendment falls, 24–6. Chairman.'

'Thank you,' the Provost muttered. 'We will proceed . . .'

A voice was heard clearly shouting: 'A bliddy stitch-up!'

Gavin recognised the angry tones of Scott Rennett.

'We want to hear the whole debate! That's what we came for . . .' Angry murmurs around him seemed to offer support. But council officers were already extricating Rennett from his seat and barging him inexorably towards the entrance.

'I'm an old man!' he roared. 'Watch what you're doin!'

There were a lot of smiles as Scott Rennett could be heard loudly remonstrating with implacable officialdom. Inside, business was proceeding rapidly.

'. . . agreed hear several deputations each side . . .'

'Agreed!'

There was a delay as a microphone was tested at the front and Dr James Grant-Gilford was ushered over to it by the little man in the blazer. An expectant hush fell over the room.

Cludgie Confidential

Moray sat in the cubicle of the Moorings Bar providing descant on several roundels of the call of nature. Two men came into the toilet to use the urinals. He heard the whisper of their waters. Some overheard words tumbled into his shell-likes.

'That cunt Fairbairn's on thi take,' said a low voice.

'Eh,' grunted another. 'Broon-envelope joab. Wha's thi buhlders this time?'

Moray suspended his breathing but, strain as he might, could not decipher the two-syllabic grunt of the reply. He heard the sound of zippers being pulled up, feet departing. The loud flushing of waters almost masked the sound of the door closing. *Fisticuffs Fairbairn, Deputy Leader of the Council?*

In the bar, he could see Turdie's eyeballs rolling around the room. Moray's rule was that no tale was worth more than one pint and several fags. He sat on the greasy edge of the cushioned bench in the corner. *Fairbairn?*

'Yi took yir time,' Turdie groused. Moray saw Turdie's glass was empty except for the dregs. What was baffling was that his own glass was half-empty. He waved to the barman behind the bar and held up one finger. The barman nodded.

'Have my pint if you want,' he said to the tout. 'I think there's a fly in it.'

'Zir?' Turdie went through the motions of inspecting it briefly before taking a huge gulp. 'Eh well, mair protein . . .' he wiped his lips with the sleeve of his anorak.

'You know Freddie Fairbairn, yeah?' Moray began.

Turdie made a moist noise with his lips and teeth. 'Coors. Word iz eez bin takn dosh fae thi buhlders, ken.'

'That's old news.'

Turdie's face sagged. 'Yuv heard ut?'

'Everybody's heard it. But what I'm not sure about is who the developers are.'

Turdie leaned closer. 'Z' thi Morrow brithers, eh heard.'

'The Caldrum Street development?'

'The tout's face screwed itself into a grimace. 'Nut. That yin wiz gied thi thumbs-up beh thi Cooncul lang afore. Na, thi Morrow brithers ir ahent a hoosing plan fir Errolbank. Eh heard thoosants wiz dishd oot!' Turdie grinned sadly. 'Clortay bastard, eh widna mind gettin mi mitts on that kind o dosh mehsel!'

'But what has Fairbairn to do with Errolbank? He's not a Perth councillor.'

'Yi ken yirsel, laddie, thir a in ut thigithir. Must be sumhin t'dae wi . . . gettin thi Labour lads owir yon ti back thi ehdear . . . ken, a *financial* matter, like . . .' Turdie's raw hand slid over the tabletop to Moray's wrist. 'Bit thirz mair,' he said, smiling crookedly. 'A lot mair. Gonna git iz anither pint? Z' gone awfy dreh in here, zit no?'

23

I was glad to get out of the place. The heat of a hundred and fifty bodies, the hard-to-hear mumbling, the incomprehensible rituals. The dazzling chandelier lights winking off the silver mace and the gold braid of the Provost's ridiculous hat. The stuffy, hot room, all the people and raised voices and the never-ending drone of that guy on the microphone. So I was glad to get into the streams of people abandoning the meeting for the wet night air.

'What did you think of it?' an elderly lady in a headscarf quizzed me as I stood on the pavement, looking for Marjorie. 'Surely they cannot support the application.'

'I really don't know,' I said.

'Na, ye can't trust bloody councillors,' a little man in a tweed bunnet and green waxed jacket grumbled beside my shoulder. 'Bunch a chiselers! A in it fir thirsels.'

'Gerry – this way!' Marjorie called. 'We're going to a pub. Will you join us . . . ?' She smiled, 'We don't have to go if you . . . if you . . .'

'No,' I said. 'Good idea. Anyone seen Stephen Brack?'

'I'm right here,' said a familiar voice behind me. Now bearded, long black hair fastened in a ponytail under his black hat, Stephen Brack! Shorter than I remembered, more squat.

'I'm not believing *this*!' he roared. 'How you doing, man?' He almost pulled my arm off, shaking my hand. 'Hey – this is my wife, Fay. Darling – this is my old mate Gerry, whom I haven't seen since the days of Benvie Road.'

179

Fay offered me her hand.

'Calls for a drink!' Stephen said. 'Which pub we going to?'

'I'll find out,' Marjorie said. 'Wait here.'

'This is really great, man, seeing you again,' Stephen enthused. 'Hey – we had some great times, didn't we? Yeah! Remember the time . . . Bob Erskine – Big Bob's chair broke in the old Tav? And Pete had him thrown out for fighting?'

'Yeah, I remember people talking about that, Stephen, but I wasn't there that night.'

'Could've sworn you were. Mind you it's a long time ago.'

'So what have you being doing with yourself? Apart from getting married of course. Sorry I missed your wedding.'

'Would have been great to have had you there, man.'

'Still writing?'

'I'm thinking of giving it up.'

'You were saying that in Benvie Road!'

Brack pulled a lugubrious face and his hands came up at his sides, palms uppermost in that oft-recalled gesture of being non-committal.

'How long have you been married?'

Fay said, 'Six years. Would you believe.'

'Any children?'

There was a sort of an embarrassed silence which Brack broke with a loud fart. 'Oops, sorry!'

'Stephen!' Fay said, frowning. 'Can't take him anywhere. No, Gerry, we have no children.'

'Must have been those chilli beans,' Stephen said. 'Hey, Gerry old boy – are you and Marjorie . . . ?'

Marjorie came back then. 'Everyone has gone to the Watermill, just round the corner,' she said. 'C'mon everybody.'

'Right.' We set off across the street. *The black river, undine, coalescing, under dim fronds of streetlighting*. I fell into step beside Stephen.

'Dig the hat, man,' I said. 'Hebraic!'

'It's from Homburg,' he said and laughed. 'The Susquehanna Hat Company.'

'These books of yours?' I said. 'So you made it? Into authorship, I mean.'

180

'Not quite in the way I would have liked. *C'est la vie*. Anyway, what about your pentin?'

'Pentin? I haven't been interested in painting for . . . more than ten years. Since I went to London.'

'You used to be so keen,' he said, walking on to the street to avoid a lamp-post. 'Or maybe you were just green on the scene. Ah man, I missed having you around, those great times we had . . .'

The Watermill was (it said on a plaque at the entrance) a converted granary, its vast interior sprinkled with neon lights and red chandeliers. It had chrome banisters, dim-lit alcoves and ye olde fruit machines. Piped music of a noxiously insipid kind leaked from hidden loudspeakers.

Marjorie approached, smiling, and tugged my sleeve. 'Gerry? Drink? Perhaps you could help me at the bar?'

'Of course.'

We stood together at the crowded bar.

'Long time since you've seen your friend?' she asked. 'His wife is very pretty.'

'Stephen and I go back a long way,' I said. 'A lot of dreams and hopes. I don't know what happened to it all. All those ideas, those . . . I don't know . . . ambitions. We were going to set the world on fire. I don't suppose now we ever will.' I don't think she heard much of what I had said because she kept nodding even when I had finished, then in a lull of the noise, said:

'There's always time,' she smiled, 'for a new start. Heavens, I'm not about to give up now. I'm only fifty, for God's sake. And you're only in your *forties*!'

The conversations all around us were about the planning application and the meeting.

'That Grant-Gilford, man . . . someone should have tellt him tae speak up! I'm sure half the cooncillors couldna hear him.'

'Ach, he wis boring. A dreich little man. Time he was kicked oot as community cooncil chairman. He jist droned on and on . . .'

'Aye, but he did put the case . . .'

'Ach, that blatherskite couldna . . .'

Marjorie put her cool hand on my wrist. 'I'll take these over, Gerry. Gerry? If you could wait and get the rest on this tray . . .'

181

'Okay.'

Somebody said: 'And as for old Lewis . . . man . . . he didna want to stop. They had to take the damn microphone aff him. He's a bonny fechter. I thought he said his piece awfy braw. I saw some of the cooncillors nodding.'

'Aye, nodding like donkeys! Half o them wis asleep, man!'

I loaded the drinks on to the metal tray and carried it over to where our group were seated in the corner. Stephen patted the seat beside him. 'Sit here, Gerry, boy,' he said. 'I want to hear all about your adventures. Take it you're not married yourself?'

'No. Never married. Lived with someone in London for a while . . .'

'So you're back here to stay, are you?' Fay said.

'We'll see.'

'I hope that old lady is alright,' Marjorie said. 'The one that fainted at the back. They really should have more seats in these council chambers.'

'It was a grand turnout, indeed,' said a sprightly white-haired man in a camel-coloured safari-jacket hovering over our table. 'I think we've every reason for confidence, wouldn't you say? You, young ladies . . .' he said, bending over the back of the seat, to smile at Marjorie and Fay, 'am I right in thinking you're young Gavin's mother-in-law?'

'Yes, that's right, I'm Marjorie . . .' she blushed, or it seemed to me she blushed. 'Lewis? Isn't it? Good speech . . .'

'Ho? My name it is known far and wide . . .' the man sonorously began to declaim, 'for miles around where I bide . . .' holding aloft his whisky glass. He stopped abruptly, perhaps realising the ending was rude. 'And this lovely lady I know already,' he said, smiling at Fay.

Gavin and Carly arrived, bringing with them a blast of cold air.

'Couldn't find out where you'd gone,' Gavin said. 'We've been into four pubs looking for you.'

'That's an acceptable excuse,' Lewis said. 'Indeed, it is loqacious, the laxative for logic . . . something or other . . . lovely lady,' he beamed. 'I will return. Must go to see a man about a canine.'

'Gerry – this is Gavin,' Stephen said, 'another old chum . . .

Gerry is a mate I've not seen for years. We used to have great times, in the old days. Ho, man!'

'Pleased to meet you, I said.'

'Likewise.'

'I used to have long hair like yours. Had to get it cut, like, for work, in London.'

'Makes you weak, cutting your hair,' he said. 'Gotta get myself a pint. Back in a mo.'

'Gav's the original Pict,' Stephen said. 'Direct in line from Calgacus. Who defeated the Roamings at Mouse Gropings. Mons Graupius. D'you still do that with the words, Gerry, you know, puns and rhyming slang? Like we used to?'

'Not so much. Well, cheers!'

'Aye – lang may yer lum reek,' Stephen said, lifting his pint aloft so that the light sparkled through it. 'And may ye be in heaven an hour afore the deil kens ye'r deid. Aye, and to our king o'er the watter . . . may all yer troubles be little ones. May all yer winds be behind you . . .'

'For heaven's sake!' Marjorie exclaimed, laughing.

'To all of us Cratchit's each and every one!' Stephen concluded.

'To all of us,' Marjorie echoed, sipping her Pernod.

Everyone drank, but suddenly Stephen raised his glass over his head again and roared. 'Bless this house and all in it,' he said.

'Bless this house,' we intoned, preparing to drink.

'May the sun always be at your yardarm,' he declaimed. 'When you sit at prayer in the cludgie . . .'

Gavin arrived from the bar. 'Kids are okay,' he announced. 'Mum says Kenny's out like a lintie and Susan's watching TV.'

'. . . and may you be forever young . . . You're not supposed to break a toast!' Stephen complained. 'Means bad luck. Aw, well . . .'

'Good,' Carly smiled. 'It's not often we both get out – together.'

I had a very odd feeling, sitting in the corner with Stephen Brack and unable to talk to Marjorie, who was deep in conversation with Carly and Fay. Gavin sat quietly by himself, listening, introverted, contented. I felt absolutely alien, an observer on the younger me who seemed to figure highly in Brack's colourful reminiscences. I

183

didn't feel I belonged in any of the tales. And I could barely remember any of the events he described.

'You have a photographic memory, of course,' I reminded him at one point.

'Did have. But you *must* remember the time I gave Ian Wayward-Small a hammering over that girlfriend of yours?'

'Of course, though I'm sure you've embellished the tale.'

Brack laughed. 'Me? Embellish? Ho-ho, how well you know me! Hey, remember Ben . . . got the job on the bins and used to put on his old school blazer and hang about sweeping the streets outside the Heh Skail – just to show the place up – until the Rector complained to the Council about it? Ben's dead now, overdose, acccidental. Yup, like quite a few of the old crowd, Gerry. We're the survivors.' I sometimes bump into Don Phinn – old Phinny – in the street and old Petros too. Petros Liliburain. Padraig Littleburn, Pedro Lubber. Hey! However you configurate it, he's the same old Peter. Boy is he a fighter! He's had cancer, a heart by-pass, TB, about a dozen other serious diseases and still comes up smiling in that Zen way he has. And he's younger than you! And wee Bob is still around. Remember that awful band he started, Louettic Louie and the Dripping Dicks, or something, just when punk came in, and none of them could play a bum note? Wee Bob was the first punk in Dundee. True. The first. Then there was Bread Poultice and the Running Sores . . . remember that night at the Art College Union, when Bread came on stage in a coffin carried by two janitors . . . and climbed out dressed in a bin liner?'

'No, not me, I'd left by then. But I heard of Bread. He was one of the Steves? There were three Steves. Not counting you, yeah?'

'Four, not counting me. Falconer, Reid, McDonald and Knight; this was Falconer. He's still around. But Jog, their drummer, died recently.'

'I met Steve Knight in London once,' I said. 'At the Moonlight Tavern in West Hampstead, during a gig by the Skids. I think Reid was there and all. That was in the days of the Associates. Billy MacKenzie.'

I could sense Stephen had lost interest. He's a sixties music man. He gazed into his pint. 'Ronnie Kegan's still unmarried,' he told me. 'I see him a lot these days. Hasn't had a girlfriend for yonks. His hair's gone white now. Remember his continual vows of chastity?'

'Funnily enough, I do, Stephen. Didn't girls used to think he looked like David Essex?'

'Well you know he did. One time in his flat – you might remember – there were two girls upstairs, Jill and . . . Sally . . . I can't remember . . . both about seventeen, fancied him like crazy but he just ignored them. They invited him upstairs to their place and disappeared. He's sitting in the living room for ages on his own and then he needs to go to the bog, which is off the bedroom, so he troops through and there they both are – starkers – on the bed and they grab hold of him but he just goes to the bog and when he comes out just sits and chats and then goes away. Mind you, they were rather sluttish . . .' Stephen caught sight of Fay looking at him and lowered his voice, 'but they had fantastic bodies. He had incredible self-restraint. Of course after that the girls put it about that he was a poofter. Mind you, he didn't always use to be so saintly.'

'What I remember was his aristocratic attitude that everyone and everything was quite beneath him, dear boy. Always wore those linen gloves everywhere . . .'

Stephen roared. 'Yeah – until Freddie Beckett asked him if he was a burglar!'

'Freddie Beckett? Carol's brother?'

A grey-faced ugly man of middle years in a zip-up leather jerkin leaned over us. 'Seez that ashtray, Jim, eh.'

'This?' Stephen said. 'This seashell thingy?' It was a plain flat oystershell or scallop. I was reminded of my exotic shell at Tentsmuir sands. *Echoes.*

'Eh.'

'She sells seashells on the seashore . . .' Brack said. 'Hey! that reminds me. Meaning to ask you. There was a lot of hoo-hah last year about a book you'd supposedly written . . . well actually written . . . I mean there was a book . . . a, um, manuscript I read which was supposed to have been written by you, about the old times in Dundee.'

185

'*I'd* written? I've never written a book. Not one that's been published anyway.'

'That's what I thought. I had a visit by an archivist. She let me read it. Quite short but a lot of the old days were described in it. Mind you, she didn't have your name . . . there was no name on the thing; it was anonymous, except that the narrator was a guy called Gerry.'

'Weird.'

'The manuscript sort of petered out in Spain somewhere. You went to Spain, didn't you?'

'Yeah, hitched. Lived there for a few months. But things didn't work out, so I headed back to London.'

'Well, that's in the book. So if you didn't write it, who did? I mean, it had loads of detail about me, and loads of others from the old days. Details that only a few people could know.'

I felt an eerie feeling in my spinal column. 'When I was in Spain . . .'

'Yeah . . . ?'

'I had this diary . . . I was living in Minorca . . . in a sort of commune . . . used to make notes and sketches . . . just anything that came into my head. There was this other Scottish guy there. Frankie. We used to talk, and get drunk together and swim at night you know in the Med and get out of our heads . . . Well, when I got to London, on a long coach ride from Alicante . . . long, long coach ride . . . Well, I didn't have it, the notebook, I mean.'

'So maybe this other guy? Is that what you're saying? But was he from Dundee, because that's where the book was found?'

'I don't think so.'

'I might start to believe I wrote it myself, when I was asleep!' Stephen said. 'Who knows?'

'What are you two going on about?' Fay said, laughing. 'Sat here like a pair of old men reminiscing . . . I'm going to help Marjorie with the drinks. What'll you have?'

Before they could get to the bar, there was a commotion and we saw the councillor, Jill Hogue, coming in the door, in the midst of a knot of mainly elderly people. Everyone gathered round. We stood up on our seats.

186

'Oh, this is it,' said Carly.

'*Shush*, please . . .'

'*Be quiet*, everybody!'

Councillor Hogue put her handbag down on the seat behind her. I could tell by her face, it wasn't going to be good news. Like us, some people were standing on seats around the room to get a better view. There was an excited air as everybody crowded round to hear the result of the council debate.

'I'm afraid it's not good news . . .' she began grimly. There was a slump of disapproval, tremors of defeat. 'The application has been approved – by quite a large majority.'

'Oh . . . *no*!

Growing uproar manifested itself in a torrent of anger and hubbub. The Councillor held up her hand.

'The vote was 19–10. I have to say never in my years on the council have I felt so disgusted! I strongly suspect that some members may have received inducements . . .'

At this, fury broke out; loud accusations were shouted. Fists waved in the air, others loudly swore . . . then there was a hush.

'Of course, I cannot prove anything – as yet. Some of those who voted for the application never even opened their mouths tonight. And as for Janet Douglas . . . it gives me no pleasure to say this . . . I've known her all my political life . . . but can you imagine, the ward councillor . . . and she *abstained*!'

There were hisses and turbulence among the crowd. Councillor Hogue was obscured for some time, when the crowd were quietened down, she said:

'Afterwards I couldn't get any sense out of her. I have to say I think some members may have voted for the application because it would stop any large developments in their own areas.' She pursed her lips and light glanced off the panes of her spectacles. 'Now, it's very disappointing I know, but we will just have to fight on. This is only an outline permission – and most certainly it will be called in by the government. We must not lose hope . . .'

'Bloody nimbies!' someone shouted.

'Aye, bastards!' shouted others.

'Councillors will stab you in the back as soon as look at you' said

187

someone close by our table. I could see Gavin was white, and Marjorie looked on the verge of tears. I wanted to be over beside her, and stepped down.

There was the sound of breaking glass and a commotion over at the bar.

'He's fainted!' someone shouted.

'Marjorie . . .' I said, moving into Carly's vacant seat. I put my hand on her shoulder. 'You can fight on.'

'I suppose so. Though the law's on their side. It's the thought of the irreversibility of it. And those beautiful trees.'

'They won't get permission to chop all the trees down,' I said. 'Not in this day and age. You'll see.'

Gavin, who had gone to the toilet, came pushing through urgently. 'It's Lewis. He's collapsed . . . they think it's a heart-attack . . .'

Part 4

Undertow

24

Kevin Morrow sat high in the midst of penetrating noise. Even the earphones he had been given could not stop the vibrating whine of the helicopter engines, the hollow sweep of the rotor blades in the thin air above the estuary. High above the water, strapped into the narrow seat, Kevin saw for the first time the extent of the land he owned. Behind him sat the technical bods who would convert his dream to reality, the minions who would do his bidding. He caught a reflection of his head in the perspex; his tiny eyes sunken in, peering from the casket of shiny skin that domed his skull and thrust out above his jaw.

'We'll go lower,' the pilot said, his words crackling through the earphones inside Kevin's helmet.

The helicopter descended unevenly to hover above the vast mudflats. Sunlight bounced around the cockpit, glancing across and into his eyes, as the helicopter swung in air. Looking down, Kevin saw the giant rings of displaced water around the crater the helicopter was making. The tide was in, but he was in control of it all. From his chariot, he commanded. The technical men in the seat behind were marking their charts and words of their conversation trickled through his headset. It wasn't up to him how they surmounted the problems of cutting a permanent channel through the sandbank, as long as they did. He caught various phrases like 'stabilisation' and 'retraction walls'. It didn't interest him. He felt inordinately pleased, like a Roman conqueror must have felt, surveying the disorder of the barbarians. The jumbled fields, the useless trees, the lazy miles of reeds. He was the progenitor of a new colony at the frontier. He would build a new Rome.

'We'll move inland a bit,' the pilot said. Kevin gave the thumbs-up. Not Rome exactly, he thought, but something on that epic scale. Something unquestionably grand, something *historic*. But Morrowville or Kevingrad would not be accepted, would bring ridicule, and it couldn't be Carsetown, too easily amended by vandals to 'arsetown'. On the other hand, it lay behind that vast sandbank, the Carthagena Bank, below. Carthagena. *That* sounded historic. That was the kind of thing he was after. Kevin had gone to the trouble of looking up the word in dictionaries and knew that its meaning was 'New Carthage' and he had even looked up that in the *Ladybird Book of the Romans and Greeks*. New Carthage – built by Kevin Morrow. A mighty city of the future that would surpass all the little towns and soon fill the entire Carse and swallow up Dundee and Perth. It would be a bright place, a happy place, above all a young place, with no bad memories, no gory histories or mouldering ruins. Yes. Kevin knew that there was a slight problem. He remembered from the *Ladybird Book* that the great city of Carthage had been destroyed by the Romans, not built by them, that in fact, they had ploughed it into the ground. So what? It just went to show how history was bunk. He was the Roman in the gloamin who was going to rebuilt it, right here in the Tay estuary.

Kevin stared down at the shore: water, mud, trees. There were the barbarians, hiding behind their foliage, their stinking mud-banks and reeds, like black rats. They used the landscape as a weapon; its disorder was their method. Well, he would bring a civilisation there, and he would make millions out of it and give people jobs. First, he had some calls to make to get wheels in motion, to programme the juggernaut of which he was in sole and absolute command.

'Ehv seen enough,' he spoke into his helmet microphone. 'Tak iz awa.'

Beneath the leafy screen was almost entirely noiseless when the helicopter swayed sideways and swung back out over the river.

192

Silent as the graves of history, thought Gavin, his back against the bole of an oak, as he looked south on to the swaying ocean of reeds. For several miles, the narrow strip of trees, barely forty feet wide, extended along the top of the ridge that separated the solid ground from these wet reed beds. It was a mixed wood: oak, beech, hazel, rowan, sycamore, chestnut . . . melodic with birdsong and nest-making. For decades, centuries, the narrow woods had been developing towards a harmony of competing boughs and branches, long since reaching a peaceable equilibrium. These trees had slept through the years listening to the song of the tides, wind rustling in the reeds, steady flicker of rain on leaves, rain dancing wistfully on the waxy-cuticles in moonlight, in sunlight, in snow and ice, on haar-saturated days when no-one came to walk . . . they had been here. Gavin stopped to examine an infantry line of ants running vertically with precision, up a chasm of the bark. To the ant, a tree was a city, the copse a vast continent, and Scotland was inconceivably vast, an abstraction; if ants ever thought about it at all, and who was to say they did not? Gavin had not till now looked, looked closely at this thing he loved. He studied the deeply crenellated skin of this living thing, this phallic outburst from the soil, this emanation of ancient spirits leaking from the graves of the old ones. His fingers explored its ridges and undulations. He inhaled its peaceful mossiness.

'Come *on*, Daddy!' Susan called from further down the track. The wind tested the outer leaves and provoked a groan and creaks and a deep restful sigh, above and all around him. 'Their mossy homes in field and briar' were the words that came into Gavin's head. Poem by Shelley. Probably 'Adonais', the elegy for Keats. But the Romantic poets' love of trees was an abstract thing, too pure. His was tempered by an urge to hold back the flood tide of human ignorance and willfulness in wrecking its playpen. His urge was atavistic, anarchic, a little selfish. He couldn't stop people burning and uprooting rainforests in far-away places, but he could throw a bloody spanner in the works, here, on his own doorstep against Loyal Homes. Think global, act local, that was it. If he chained himself to this tree . . . or climbed to the top and refused to come down . . . would others join him? Would it work? It seemed futile.

He hurried to catch up with the others. They were in a sort of covered clearing in deep-green shadow, a flat soft-littered space between four enormous sycamores, carpeted with a flourishing moss that looked like grass. A kind of makeshift shelter had been constructed by someone below the bank; several sheets of corrugated iron supported by beams had been driven into the soil beneath the exposed roots of the trees, with a view over the reeds. The sides of the shelter had been constructed from polypropylene sacks. Kenneth was sitting inside it like a Red Indian chief and Susan was trying to pull him out.

'Mum! Mum – Kenneth's getting all filthy . . .'

'It's okay,' Gavin said. 'I'm going in there too . . . Is there room for a big one?'

'Yes, Daddy,' little Kenny said, making space.

But the wind made a funny noise in the corrugated iron and the little boy soon rushed out shrieking and laughing.

'Daddy fart!' he shouted. 'Bad Daddy!' He began capering around, gathering handfuls of crisp leaves. Susan sat on a log higher up the bank with Carly, who was unwrapping the sandwiches.

'Hey, come here!' Carly said. 'Kenneth! You'll get your hands dirty.'

'Aw, he's alright, Leave him be.'

'I'll get him, Mummy.'

They ate their sandwiches and Carly fed Kenneth and they looked out rather glumly at the reeds. Later they began retracing their steps to New Farm. They didn't say much, but it was on their minds that this might be the last time they would visit these trees. Gavin's thoughts were racing ahead. He arrived back at the old sycamore and waited for the others. A ladybird was slowly working its way up the smooth north side of the tree. Gavin remembered that was how if you were lost in the forest, you could tell direction; the north side of the trees were always rougher, darker and less foliated, because they got less light. The ladybird walked head on into a green aphid. At first it seemed to want to climb over, but the aphid seemed to shrink and then was gone. Ladybirds 1 Greenfly 0. The ladybird didn't look any bigger. He couldn't see any more ladybirds.

The others caught up. He showed the ladybird to Kenneth who feigned interest then, when he thought Gavin wasn't looking, tried to hit it with a stick. He was told off and burst into tears. Gavin said nothing. He wondered why little boys had this urge to harm living things, a sort of innate sadism. Like when he deliberately dropped the binoculars as if he wanted to see it break, or to provoke outrage . . .

'I wish I had the money to protect the trees,' Gavin sighed. 'Buy those bastards off and make them build their houses elsewhere,' he said.

'Maybe they'll leave some of them.'

'Once they fell them, it's forever.' They would descend like Jurassic monsters belching diesel fumes, scoop out the earth around these great living things, loosen the anchors on these guarantors of human certainty. Their magnificent patience had reassured humanity over centuries of change. Gavin remembered from one of his tutorials that in his old age, Yeats found his most lofty philosophical inquiries into the timeless spirit of humanity aided by his walks among great trees. A sixty-year-old smiling public man among a golden choir of leaves. *Yeats, the great-rooted blossomer*. But it wasn't enough. Men who had never heard of the poet – who didn't want to hear of him – sweating thoughtless, insensitive robots, stinking of tobacco and morning breath, mounted on great rutted wheels and iron treads would press levers and throw switches to haul swivel chains to remove the dead lumber hour after hour, and, by remote control, haul it away across the grey mud by its smashed elbows and armpits and knees and shoulders, and pile it in great mounds of bare broken limbs. They were even going to dredge the mudflats and the reeds.

Gavin touched the bark, a gentle caress, then leaned in and kissed the gnarled old patient skin. 'Let's hold hands around this tree,' he murmured, eyes moist. 'And send it a message of farewell. Come on, all of you, Kenneth . . .'

'What is it, Daddy?' Susan asked, taking the earphones of her Sony from her ears.

'Daddy's sad about the trees,' Carly told her.

195

'I know,' Susan said. 'Mrs Tomlinson says they're going to make paper out of the trees so we can all have new schoolbooks.'

'Is that what she said?' Carly asked. 'What an odd thing to say.'

'But I think I'd rather have the trees.'

'*I know* – ' Carly said. 'Why don't we do the tree dance?'

'We can be like trees . . .' Susan mimed the actions of a stately oak. ' Look at me!'

'Trees! Trees!' Kenneth capered.

'Come on, silly,' his sister said. 'We dance around the trees.'

Carly was last of all to join, returning to take the hand which Gavin offered and reaching for the hand of Susan. And there, around the sycamore they held hands and began to sway and slowly dance around and round the tree, stepping carefully on the twisted bosses of its powerful roots.

25

At Auntie Kathleen's, I watched too much television and knew I should be making better use of my free time. Slumped on the sofa, my eyeballs followed, despite a complete lack of interest, some football match, some horse-racing. I'd been semi-comatose since getting out of bed in mid-morning. Made some toast. When I was in London, even when I was out at Tentsmuir, my aunt's house and this city seemed to be entities, places I could think of, visualise as spots on the surface of the planet, geographical locations, but now I'm here, it's sort of nowhere, a limbo, not a place . . . well not a terminus, like, you know, on bus journeys, when you do some travelling and you arrive at the terminus. And you know that must be somewhere because the bus doesn't go any further. Is it like this everywhere? That when you get somewhere after travelling, somewhere you think you want to be, you find that you want to go somewhere else? The planet seems to be a void marked by the sort of stains you could miss, labels that rub off, spoken words that dissolve in the wind. Bees navigate by a complex sense of geography, sort of innate radar, orientate themselves in space by a coded series of manoeuvres: fifty wingbeats then veer ninety degrees SE, then fifty wingbeats . . . thirty . . . to the pollen in the stamen of the flower. But imagine being a bee that had its memory wiped. The world would be a void, meaningless . . . That's how I feel. I want to go wherever I'm not, somewhere else . . . Being with friends negates this feeling of emptiness. Yesterday, seeing old Stephen again, first

197

time for eight years, and being with Marjorie, somehow reminded me of when I had a sense of belonging.

In 1947 my father travelled from Jamaica to New York to steam 2,000 miles north-east on the *Queen Mary*. My mother steamed 6,000 miles north-west from India, via the Suez Canal, on the *Empire Windrush*. Two years later they meet for the first time in a corridor in Aberdeen, and six years after that, I was born. What does it mean, this randomness? This oscillation on the surface of the oceans, continued within human tissue? Constantly emptying, diverging, convoluting. Now thwarted, now detouring around the obstacle, liquid, solid, gas, then throbbing in air. Are we merely sensate fingers of blob thrust out and isolated? The biological truth, or is there more? Is our life-history a story of yearning to reconnect with the mass of blob that we've emerged from? Does humanity owe everything, our cities, encyclopaedias, cultures, languages – love – to the valence and eccentric spinning of a few hydrogen atoms? Do the narrative threads of our lives reconnect to their beginnings? Will the continents rejoin, magically interlocking shorelines, to restore the perfect land of Pangir? Will we identify ourselves when we come around again, having gone around once? And if we do, does this prove our destination is the same as our source, and if so, how can we tell whether we are presently travelling forward or in reverse? Like my shell on the beach, is it on its way north, or south, and will it come again, or has it already been?

I switched TV channels, a murky old film, the black and white 1950s, wait . . . Marilyn Monroe, always worth watching, something morbid, I don't know, as if only she is dead, in a more final way, more affecting, than anyone else I know. Knew. Why? Because it is a death constantly alluded to, reiterated, so public, and because Marilyn keeps cropping up, lively – and lovely – as ever. We each feel we knew her personally, but at a distance; we knew none of her faults. We knew her as a perfect, one of Plato's Ideals, a goddess, the symbolicisation of a woman. Dead for thirty-seven years, she has the stored-up orgone energy acquired from decades of admiration, in the electronic age to be able to transcend time, space and death, to be able to sing (she's singing now).

198

It's like you can hear the throbbing of her heartbeat in that husky, breathy voice. Close to your ear. My spine is crawling. The song of the dead. I need to cheer up, get a life. Go out, walk, think of nice happy things, get into a singing mood. I put on the second-hand black leather jacket, extra-large size, that I bought down Dens Road Market for a tenner. The leather is thick and soft. It's the best leather I've had since my Nico Spitfire that took me all over Europe, which is in my wardrobe but is far too small. I'm taking up more space in the air than I used to; my shadow is larger; there's less white enamel visible in the bath when I'm in it and more water displaced.

It's a blustery dry day, trees are leaning sadly, a sharp wind stripping leaves like confetti. The light is altering with each heavy passing low cloud. I feel my spirits lift or 'rising in the lift', as wee Shuggie MacDiarmid would have it. The Scots word for the sky or the heavens, as if the spirit is tugged upwards out of you by the low pressure. Metaphysical. Three craws sitting on a dyke, chewing eyeballs. First craw: 'Caw!' Second craw: 'Caw-caw, caw!' Third craw: 'Yes, yes, chaps, dirty realism is great, but magical realism gets more laughs.' The sound of one hand clapping. Walk down the wide roads, high-walled, lined with trees, unmade, soft grit, to the main road with the view of the river beyond and Tayport. Lived there once. I feel good to be going somewhere, even if it is just getting a bus into town. Which is more than poor Lewis Summers can do. At least he's alive. And still wisecracking. Warned off the booze by the doctor, he grins and says he will henceforth be known as 'long dry Summers'. Stephen was pretty cracked up about it. Unduly sensitive to death. And Marjorie's son-in-law, Gavin Cathro, was close to the edge too. A likeable old rogue, Summers. He'll see many summers yet. I should have said that.

The town is busy, it being a Saturday, lots of milling and sauntering and idling. Everyone looking at everyone else but pretending not to see. The city of the stare.

'Lookin at me, pal?'

'Ji wahnt t' mak sumhin o'it, like?'

'Fansy a square go? Yir jist gaggin fir a scone in thi pus.'

199

'Zat a joke, like, yi wee cunt? Eh cud fuckin batter yi wi one ehrum.'

'Wha'r yiz trehn ti kid, yi shitey wee midget?

'Eh cud skelp yir pus . . .'

'An eh cud rattle yir ja . . .'

'Ach, awa'n keech, ye bumhole!'

'Up yours! Yi mental cunt.'

As I got into the Murraygate, I heard the wind-blown notes of electronic music. A small crowd hovered indecisively in front of a plastic bucket of coins. With one eye between them, the middle-aged couple were huddled in the doorway of the closed-down Nautilus Sportswear shop. Perched on a fold-up stool, the large, bald, sightless head of the man in the navy-blue anorak, stubby fingers in torn woollen gloves flailing his keyboard, the turbulent sound of guitars and drums reverberating through an amplifier. His wife, possessor of the eye, sings hoarsely into a microphone clasped close to her blue lips as if unwilling to risk spilling her words . . . *Sand . . . in meh sho-oo-es.*

I spent some time examining new paperbacks in Waterstone's. A slow stroll as far as the Overgate, looking for familiar faces. In the Murraygate the singers are still there . . . *when meh dreamboat . . . comes hame . . .*

Sanctum Oratorio

Moray Neill had spent most of the day sitting in a borrowed car outside the home of Daniel Morrow. It was no fun on his own. Hungry, dispirited and bored, also needing to go to the lavatory, he returned to the city centre. He had just left the car in the Seagate carpark when he ran into Bobbing John. The tout was heading in the direction of the Moorings Bar in his characteristically tentative manner in unlaced training shoes, which were not a pair (Adidas and Reebok). He was keeping a weather eye out for anyone he might know. For him, knowing is owing. His speed proved him to be in possession of the price of a pint (at least) which was burning a hole in his flapping tweed trousers. His hair was innocent of the efforts of barbers – or the effect of water – in the present millennium. It was fastened into a ponytail with a short length of white pipe-cleaner.

'Hallo, Bobbing John!' Moray greeted, laying an authoritative hand upon the grubby white fairisle.

He jumped upwards and turned round in the same odd movement, terrified, but plausibly prepared. He had probably expected a uniform. Bobbing John liked to expose himself in public and had a bad police sheet as a peeping Tom. Despite his appearance, it was he who sometimes inexplicably possessed the one crucial fragment of the story that everyone missed. His was the word that was picked up off the pavey and stuck in a pocket for later resale.

'Yirsel?' he said, unsurprised. His overshot jaw relentlessly ground his front teeth. A facial tic convulsed itself beneath his one good eye, which he fiercely focused with contempt upon Moray Neill. 'Lit iz awa. Ehm needin a swally. Eh owe yiz nuthin.'

'It's worth a fiver maybe,' Moray said firmly.

Bobbing John stood his ground, jaw champing, his hen's eye fixed on the reporter's face to determine the truth of the offer. His head slowly turned and launched a gob of spit to the pavement. 'Fehvir?' he repeated. 'Ji wahnt?'

'The Morrows.'

The tout's expression didn't change. It was impossible to say whether he did have something in his mouth. 'Eh,' he said at last, mournfully. There were spots of saliva at the corners of his mouth among the grey stubble.

Moray abstracted his wallet and under the stony gaze of the little man, delicately removed a blue note. 'Bribery?' he prompted.

'Fuck-eh,' BJ confirmed. 'Young lass, blondie . . .' he spat again . . . 'shiz a junkie or that . . .' He started jerking his arms. Moray was alarmed, believing Bobbing John was going to give a public demonstration like when the schoolgirl had asked him for the time and foolishly waited for him to get his watch out of his pocket – except it wasn't his watch, and like him, it only had the one eye.

'Eez wife's doon it thi Rivervister . . . shiz sellin irsel.'

Moray realised that in his unco-ordinated way, the tout was trying to mime the actions of a junkie shooting up. In that instant,

Bobbing John had it on his toes with the fiver in the direction of the Moorings Bar. He was not sorry to see him go. Inside a minute his fiver would be in the till. Could it be true, he wondered? Could Daniel Morrow's wife be a junkie and would she be selling herself for drug money? Far-fetched . . . He'd look into it. He could imagine the ghastly visage of Bobbing John smeared against some window-pane watching these kind of carnal transactions with relish. He'd heard rumours Morrow's third marriage was on the rocks. Time to bite the bullet and ring the Sharks.

'Fuck you, man,' Sharkey said. 'I heard you were badmouthing me. I'm on a good screw now with the *Recorder*. I need you like I need twa holes in meh erse.'

'The *Recorder*? Thought they had their own snapper in this area?'

'Eh, but he's got cancer of the colon, so I'm it.'

'I've got a story . . .'

'Look, man, let's go our own ways, eh? I can't help you forever.'

Moray realised he'd have to work alone. Which meant buying some kind of equipment, because nobody was going to lend him cameras after his disaster with Ecky Edwards' gear up at Trottick. McLean was unhelpful:

'You've driven Sharkey away. He was reliable until you wound him up. I told you to make it up with the cunt.'

'He's with the *Recorder* now.'

McLean went ballistic. He's with the . . . the . . . fucking . . . Fucksake, right, I've had it with the cunt. The fucking *Recorder*, fucksake! Of all times to jump ship!'

'What's so special about now?'

'Because the fucking *Recorder* has just been nominated for a Golden Urinal Award for Mendacity – again! I mean, they got one last year, fucksake! Sir Philip's gone apeshite. Had all the staffers in for a bollocking. Told us to plumb the depths more effectively and improve our channels . . . get more mainstream sources . . . fucksake . . . or our bonuses are in our pants!'

'That's a pisser, eh?'

'Fucksake, that's putting it mildly.'

Moray reluctantly invested in a miniature digital camera – more money down the drain – and set out for the Rivervista Hotel, which stands directly opposite the filthy railway station and the old boat which the city is always boasting about in the brochures. Formerly a fashionable residence listed in the accommodation guides and having an alcohol licence, the Rivervista has been on a long slide into notoriety. Presently it is divided into bedsits populated by tenants whose rent is paid direct by the DSS. Who improve the city's image by making a display of drying underwear in the windows for tourists to photograph. Moray was aware that the company which owned the Rivervista was Swick Properties Ltd, sole proprietor: Mr Jeremy Swick.

He approached with some trepidation and a black wig under a Man United tammy, mauve nylon shellsuit, and ultra-drongo plastic trainers. He was disguised as the mankiest of minks.

As he approached the deserted main entrance to the building, he saw a woman darkly under the streetlight, leaning against the wall, one leg tucked up behind her. Mumsy Morrow. Cursing Bobbing John for a total blow-out, he crossed the road, and took a seat in the bus shelter to observe proceedings. Mumsy was blatantly accosting the occasional male passersby, directing them inside the hotel. She wasn't going in with them. Odd. He moved nearer and took several pictures of her importuning men at the hotel entrance. So far, so good, but would she recognise him?

'Teenage blonde,' Mumsy wheedled close up. 'Real sexy . . .'

Moray averted his eyes from her face, stuck out his long jaw and muttered assent.

'Room 520, press thi bell, ask fir Lucy. Here – dae eh no ken yi fae sumplis?'

'Nut.'

The stench of urine hovered in the lift, which was scrawled with obscene graffiti. It jolted and jarred when it reached the fifth floor. The door was open. It was a small room, disordered, and with a fetid smell of laundry and fag-ash. The girl was curled up on the bed under a grey blanket. Her movements were deliberate and mechanical as she rose naked from the bed. She looked about thirteen. On the other side of the bed, he could see the sheen of used condoms on the carpet. She was out of it, almost. Could this really

203

be the wife of a property millionaire? When he saw that she wasn't aware of him, he took out his Sony and put it on the bedside table. Its red light glowed.

'Ji wahnt iz t'dae?' she mumbled, sitting on the bed.

'Kylie,' Moray asked, kindly. 'Kylie Morrow?'

'Eh?' She was frail, her body looked unwashed, her hair was mankit and straggly. She looked up suspiciously, bloodshot eyes being the only sign of colour in the pale face. The eyes had no pupils and were the deadest thing he had ever seen. 'How d'yi ken mi name?'

'Look, I want to help you.'

'Twin'ay fir a shag, ten fir a blowjob.'

'Sit down,' Moray said, pushing her backwards.

'Here – wha ji hink yir pushing?'

'Daniel sent me,' he said.

The name dimly registered. 'Wut'z ee wahnt?'

'To help you.'

'Tell um ee kin buggir aff!'

'How long have you been on the game?' he asked.

After ten minutes, the girl drifted off into something like sleep. Moray took pictures of the room, the bed, the girl, the used spike, the smack in its tinfoil and other junkie paraphenalia. Once he'd filled up the disk, he picked up the mobile phone and rang the police. He ran down the stairs. Mumsy Morrow hovered in the doorway.

'Yir lassie's no conscious, like,' he mumbled. 'Eh think shiz deid.'

Mumsy flew up the stairs and disappeared into the hotel just as a police car arrived at the end of the street. Moray moved off until the police went in. Two brawny cops. Then he waited at the bottom of the steps with his camera.

A City's Chambers Flushed with Prominent Members, High Peers, and Other Commodious Gentlemen of Rank Certain to Achieve Success in the Cabinet in Times of Siege

He barely glanced at the lurid headlines on the front page of the *Scottish Source*: PROPERTY TYCOON'S WIFE IS JUNKIE

TART, alongside the picture of Kylie and Mumsy struggling with policemen, a montage of Kylie on the bed, and her works and used condoms. A front-pager – with his byline on it. He was flying! And he was still on the case. He'd been parked on the main road outside Daniel's house for an hour. It was the obvious follow-up for the next edition. A picture of Morrow taking Kylie home for a good seeing to/taking her to a private drug clinic/promising to forgive her . . . Picture and caption says it all, page nine, 200 quid!

Moray was mildly puzzled no other tabloid guys had shown. Not even brown-nosing Sharkey, Lord of the Single Reflex Lens. He wondered if they were lying around attracting flies at Police HQ. Daniel Morrow was in. He knew that because he'd phoned him half an hour ago to tip him off, anonymously, about his wife being held at the police station. He'd expected to see Daniel drive out the gates immediately at full speed and head over to Police HQ. What was keeping him? He'd give it another half-hour. He didn't want those tabloid piranhas to get a sniff of his story.

Where he sat he had a view of a section of the river visible between the high walls and trees. It looked blue, cold and . . . wet. Almost instantly he needed to urinate. He tried to suppress the urge but its insistence grew. Nor could he cross his legs in the confined space of the driving seat. Opening the door and glancing at the kerb, he saw a gutter grille further down. Releasing the handbrake, he rolled the car over it. He scanned the road and his mirrors. Apart from intermittent traffic, there were no pedestrians or peering eyes to see. He undid his seat belt and cautiously unzipped his trousers. He flipped onto his side, like a seal on a beach and opened the door so that he could urinate directly into the grille. He was just about to . . . when he became aware of movement in his left eye . . . a car at Daniel Morrow's gate . . . DAMN!

The gates to the grounds of the luxury mansion were still opening when the grey Aston Martin loped out and, almost without pausing at the main road, turned towards the city. Moray slammed the door with his trousers and seat belt undone. He had to hit the accelerator hard to keep Morrow's car in sight. The Aston Martin finally parked miles away on the outskirts of the city, in a carpark deep in the woods of Camperdown Park, near the golf course. Then Morrow got out and began to walk. He was carrying a large plastic bag. What was going on? Moray wondered.

He zipped up his trousers and kept Morrow in sight as he walked along the narrow tarmac road that winds through the trees. Walking with a burstingly full bladder is difficult, and even more so when it is incumbent on you to remain concealed. The park was deserted. Not a single person in sight. The hapless hack longed for the opportunity to relieve himself. A minute later, he noticed a black limousine crawling along the road towards Daniel Morrow. It was like something out of a mafia film, he thought, but he had no trouble in recognising the city's official car! With the council crest above the number plate, and the little pennant, and driven by a liveried, white-gloved chauffeur, it was very recognisable. It stopped opposite Morrow and the first thing Moray noticed, staring through his zoom lens, was the chauffeur's face. It was Brady, the former school jannie! He watched in amazement as Morrow handed in the plastic bag at the limousine window. He was near enough to see the tattoos on the knuckles of the hand that accepted the bag and placed it on the backseat. The limousine accelerated, tearing its tyres on the gravel. As it swept past the tree where Moray was concealed, he recognised the leonine, gratified, unsmiling head of Freddie Fairbairn reclining in the backseat.

He managed to catch up with the limousine again a few minutes later as it sped west along the Kingsway. The official car drove to Perth. It parked in the designated space at the council offices. Fairbairn disappeared into the building with the plastic bag and when he came out ten minutes later, he was empty-handed. Only then could Moray Neill abandon his mission in pursuit of toilet facilities. He had a full disk of images to download.

McLean phoned him back once he had the images onscreen.

'Yeah?' He was noncomittal. 'So this guy is some councillor?'

'Deputy Leader of the Council. You can clearly see the bundles of dosh on the backseat.'

'Sure, yeah, but . . . where's the doll?

'Doll?

'The doll, yeah, the bimbo, the skirt . . .' McLean insisted. 'You can't have a shagging story without a babe.'

'But this is a major story about council corruption,' Moray told him.

'Naw – it's just a picture of a man in a car seat. None of these guys are shagging teenagers – girls or boys – I don't suppose? Can we no link him to that wee hoor you got yesterday? Now, she was a piece! Fucksake . . . that's what sells newspapers . . . not eh, politics . . . Who cares who's gied who a bung . . . Local government is corrupt, fucksake, that's what it is . . . no-one expects . . .'

There was no point in arguing.

Later that day, Sharkey phoned. 'Congratulations, man, I hear you're taking pictures of car seats. Howsabout, look – I have a great picture of an old setee . . . any good to you, man?'

'Drop dead!'

'No man, seriously. It's a three-seater, maroon plush velvet . . .' He laughed. '*Freddie Fairbairn*, for fucksake, man, you kill me! D'ye no ken who Freddie Fairbairn is?'

'Course I know who he is!' Moray snorted.

'I don't mean his name, mugwump, I mean *who* he is.'

'An ignoramus with tattooed fingers and lots of previous convictions . . .'

'You amateur! He's only the bagman for the party in the whole north-east *and* the right-hand man of the biggest loanshark north of Edinburgh. The bungs he gives Sir Philip de bloody Cundy you wouldn't believe. You'd never get a picture of him in the *Source*, or any other paper. You eegit! My advice: you'd better lock your doors and buy some stainless-steel underpants. And don't mention my name when they come to talk to you. Good luck.'

207

26

'Miss Braid, Robbie's sleeping . . .' One of the girls complained. 'Like, I can't read because of his snoring.'

'Robertson! Wake up!' Marjorie said, rapping her desk. 'You're
supposed to be reading the poem.' She added in a softer voice, 'I
know it's very hot but we all have to do our best.'

By mid-afternoon, the heat in the second-floor classroom of
Bellrock Academy in Marine Gardens in the Dryburgh estate in the
north-west of the city had sent most of the second-year pupils into a
doze. Marjorie could see the heads droop over the desks. She had
opened the windows as far as possible, although several were stuck
and turned down the radiators – although hot air still belched out
of these. An Education Department edict had ordered these to
remain on all year, with the exception of the long summer holiday.
They had been switched back on two weeks ago and were building
up heat for the winter. If the cleaners had left the windows closed,
and one entire wall – south-facing – of the classroom was glass, the
heat was unbearably oppressive. Even without the heatwave the
east of Scotland was presently experiencing. This city of baking
souls. It was difficult to teach in such conditions. She had taken her
mid-morning class outside on to 'the grass' – the baked strip of
scrub that used to be, and was still, called grass – but the
labyrinthine, bureaucratic difficulties of obtaining mats from the
gym meant that she couldn't repeat the exercise. And the class had
been distracted by a group of youths who appeared outside the
fence and began wolf-whistling at some of the girls and making

crude remarks. Later, when a single mother in a very short skirt went past, and stopped to bend over her pram, the boys took a great interest, falling over each other in that exaggerated way they had and getting them back to the work in hand was all nigh impossible.

'Has everybody read to the end of the poem?' she asked, well aware of the storm of protest that would result.

'No, Miss, not yet . . .'

'It's a long poem, Miss . . .'

'Right, I'll allow five more minutes, but I expect you to be able to answer questions on it then.'

The heads went down. Marjorie went over to the open windows and looked out. There was a clear view of the concrete gym block and she could almost smell the powdered stone baking, desiccating in the sunlight. Beyond that, the council estate of Menzieshill shimmered whitely in a heat-haze. There was almost no wind. The temperature was making everyone flaky. In the staffroom it had intensified the usual bickering and territorial infighting between the fossils, who had been in service since the building was built, and the ossifiers who were gradually turning into fossils themselves and resented the fossils more because of it. And it had been like this for three weeks, something of a record. Not a drop of rain for three weeks. The bushes and grass in the playground were wilting from lack of water and shade. The arid smell of dust was everywhere. Blackboard chalk came away in your hands and crumbled on the board and became difficult to read. The books on the shelf by the door, usually inaccessible to the sun, had had to be moved into the cupboard. The plant-watering rota had to be doubled up, although the tray of cactus plants was unaffected.

'Please Miss Braid,' came a girl's plaintive voice from the side of the room nearest the windows.

'Yes, Julie?'

'Miss Braid, can I go for a drink of water? This heat is killing us.'

'It'll be break time in fifteen minutes, Julie,' the teacher said, aware that every eye in the room was observing hopefully her request.

'Aw – fufteen minutes!' Julie said, rolling her eyes. 'I might be dried up like a mummy by then!'

This provoked laughter. Marjorie fancied she heard Stephen Steator make a nasty crack about 'single-mummies' or something, but she paid no heed.

'Okay, time's up,' she said. 'Yes! You've have plenty of time to read the poem. Now let's see what you thought of it.' She turned to the blackboard and wrote: 'Snake' at the top with 'D. H. Lawrence' underneath. 'Now, who's going to be first to tell me what they thought of the poem?' Of course, because she had her back to the class when the question was asked, there were plenty of volunteers and half-whispered remarks, of which 'shite' was the most common. When she turned round of course, no-one had said anything. The heads drooped again.

'So, what is this poem about?'

Norman Dobells saw his chance and thrust his hand up. This was a question he could actually answer.

'Yes, Norman?'

'It's about a . . . a snake, Miss,' he said proudly.

'That's right. And what can we tell about the snake?' she asked. Norman's face fell and he looked glum. She moved on. 'What kind of snake is it? What description does the poet give . . . ?'

Later, she questioned them about the encounter of snake and poet. 'On a hot, hot day, and I in pyjamas for the heat,' she declaimed. Marjorie became aware of sniggers from some of the boys at the back. 'Come on, wake up!' she exclaimed, 'it's not bedtime yet. Yes? What is it, Georgie?'

'Please, Miss,' the girl said, 'please, Miss, Martin's after saying he bets you dinna wear pyjamas . . .'

'Eh did nut!' the boy exclaimed. 'Yi wee liar!'

'Did sut!'

'Did nut!'

'Did!'

'Right stop that! That's enough. Now, Martin, what do we learn of the poet's first attitude to the snake?'

The minutes to the bell dragged slowly in the thickening heat.

The sun was glaring full on, glancing over the tinderblock roof of the gym, making the room a white sun-bleached desert.

'The bell must be late!' somebody said.

'I heard it! Please, Miss, eh heard thi bell.'

'Didnae!'

'No, Thomas, you didn't. Sit down!'

A small knot of boys were squatting by the side door on the tarmac playground beneath, focusing the sun's rays with a magnifying glass, trying to burn the edges of a book. But they straightened up and walked away when Mr Mangel appeared, sniffing the air for smoke.

Then the bell finally went: 3.10 p.m. The room erupted like a volcano. Within a minute, everyone was out and jostling down the corridor. The school echoed with the jeers and shouts of boys heading for their sports' class.

Julie Meadows came up to the desk, with Deborah Parry in tow. 'Please, Miss, my brother Danny's got a snake in the house. Will I ask him to bring it in?'

Marjorie smiled. 'No, Julie, but it was a nice thought. See you on Monday.' She gathered up her books, hearing the recognisable shouts of some of the boys already in the playground heading for the football pitches. Marjorie felt the delight of being able to get out into the fresh air no less keenly than they did.

When she reached the car in the carpark at the back of the school, she removed the windscreen protector but the interior of the car was roasting. She opened both front doors and waited for the accumulated heat to dissipate. One of the few good things about being a teacher was that occasionally you could drive home in mid-afternoon, before the rush hour. The bridge tolls would be quieter, smaller queues. With luck she could get home in twenty minutes. Maybe Lewis Summers had put some kind of curse on the weather: 'long dry summer' was right. How appropriate, she thought, as the DJ on the car radio announced the Dinah Washington song, 'Cry Me A River'. She was preoccupied with worries that Carly and Gavin might move away from Errol. Gavin's friend Stephen had said there might be a cottage available near them. Meigle. A little bit further to drive to see her grandchildren. And those trees they were going to cut down. Phew! It was hot, though, she murmured to herself for the hundredth time that day, glancing at the evaporating river and the enlarged black shape of Fowler's Rock as she waited for change at the Bridge Tolls.

'Twenty p, love,'

'Thanks.'

. . . well you can. Cry me a river . . .

Effluvium Purgatory

The cludgiemen were on strike throughout the city, and things were getting worse. The entire Public Services Department was out. According to Moray Neill, it was more than a matter of bins unemptied on every street in the city; the entire system trembled in the heat, on the verge of total collapse. The cludgiesookers which normally traverse the roads in the early hours siphoning off the liquid from cesspits and drainheads in extruded steel tubes stood idly in unwashed lines at the depot. The scarabs which whizz jauntily around the pavements in the central area with their rotating brushes snatching up dung and droppings are abandoned in the departmental carpark. The men who operate the bin lorries are in the pub. Nothing's moving. There's a blockage, a dire and intractable obstruction, a hardening and solidification of the entire sewage system.

And, to make matters worse, groans the hapless hack, he hasn't had a decent motion for a week. Since McLean phoned. Not a turd. He can't work, the pain is too bad, solid, gut-wrenching pain. He's taking aspirins on the hour and senokot and sennapods and figs and prunes. Boy, is he taking prunes! But *nada, rien*, nil. To the wee room, every hour, on the hour. Sit. Press. Squeeze. Occasionally a little fart. Everything's at stalemate.

The men of the Public Services Department know time is on their side. They're spending relaxing days with the strike committee in the Commodore Lounge. *Whose round is it? Have one on me. Go on then! Another?*

'I'm still getting the feeling you're trying too hard,' McLean had said. 'Fucksake, you're not Woody Bernstein. I've had nothing from you since your front-pager. Just get me some picture stories. Circulation's down in your area . . . Maybe something to do with this sewage strike? Anyway, anything from your end will do . . . anything. Get your finger oot.'

And as the men drank and swapped stories in the Commodore, the bins filled up, the drains began to overflow and a queer kind of consternation began to affect the city. At the sewage treatment plants the solid matter filled up the communitator drums. The liquid waste material was backed-up as far as the catchment channels. The outflow pipes which stretch out into the river from Invergowrie Bay to Monifieth dried up and produced only a little green trickle. The gulls that clustered around the pipes at regular intervals during the day flew off elsewhere in search of richer pickings. Commercial premises had resorted to emergency measures. Public toilets were shut down. The health officer issued a bulletin advising that no paper should be used in domestic toilets. The Council requested that as much waste should be burnt in the garden as was practicable. The system was backed up into every single domestic cistern. When people pulled the chain, there was no water to flush and what was in the u-bend became thicker and more smelly as the hours passed. Nothing was moving. Except Nobby Keirans, the boss of the department, who was on an ill-timed fortnight's holiday in America. The staff received a jolly postcard from him on day three of the strike, sent from Flushing Meadows, VA. But in Dundee, everything had ceased. In outlying rural areas, septic tank collection was cancelled. Assorted containers of faeces were being discovered in unlikely places. Human turds were popping up in school playgrounds, behind bus shelters and in community centres. Councillors were discovering unpleasant surprises outside their own doors because of their laxity in ending the strike. Councillor Welks, Convenor of the Public Services Committee, received considerable odium, in the form of unwelcome packages in large brown envelopes, and a distinctly unpleasant Special Delivery.

And the bastards in the pub rub their hands in glee. *Mine's lager, and a wee nip. Magic! Hullo, hullo . . . we are the Union boys . . . hullo, hullo . . .* They find that in a long hot summer a cold beer goes down nicely in a beergarden to the sound of the PA playing Louis Armstrong, old Satchmo himself . . . *lazy river* . . . The Union representatives of the Professional International Sewage Services Organised Friendly Federation, the Cludgiemen's Registered and Associated Public Service and the British United Movement of Sewageworkers strive in vain to produce accord. The Council were implacable. They would not be moved. Neither side would budge before the other. Neither wished to give way first, to let something slip out to the other's advantage. Motions were passed in the strike committee of course, but these were generally of the 'no surrender without improved offer' variety.

But people had to go – somewhere – that couldn't be altered. The middle class were fortunate, having gardens. The premises of Neptune Bathroom Furniture in Dens Road were raided in the night and the office staff entered the gates to find large specimens in every completed toilet bowl on the assembly line. The cludgiemen knew they held a city to ransom. And the strike continued. A second postcard arrived from Nobby Keirans, posted from Thunder Bay in Canada. One of the deputy managers quipped that Keirans was moving for the entire city, but no-one in the office laughed. It was too serious for that. Their jobs were literally going down the pan.

Moray Neill was preoccupied with his own problems. He was trying the hot-water bottle treatment, upending himself on top of two hot-water bottles while drinking very hot coffee without milk. The pain of constipation is the worst there is, he was thinking. Right at the back and sides, hard, solid, just behind the spine and ribcage. He was able to think of nothing else. That and fantasies about drawing a sharp razor across the bulging tautness of his belly to let all the hard caked crap fall out like lumps of coal. It looked like he was pregnant. There was no sign of it easing. He couldn't bear to be seen. For two days he'd lived on sips of water. It was no longer obvious to him whether his personal situation was connected in some way to the strike, whether as cause, or reaction, real or ironic.

The strike began to get reported on the national media. It's tenth day. The army were on standby at Barry Buddon. Performing training manoeuvres which were more than a paper exercise. The local newspaper advocated urgent emergency action without restraint. Mention was made of the costs of reducing the accumulated backlog. Everyone knew what that would involve. You didn't need to be a blackleg to understand. The stink of the city grew. Flies proliferated. The army sent in sharpshooters to tackle rat plagues. The authorities delayed, in hope of reprieve, while the talking continued. Rumours swept the city of a working toilet in the City Chambers for the exclusive use of the councillors.

The tension grew. The pumping stations were overrun. Experts fulminated about whether they might be beyond repair. Moray attempted to give himself a hot-water enema with a rubber gardening hose fixed to the hot tap. He succeeded only in flooding the bathroom.

And then, and then, when hope was almost lost, on the eleventh day, it was over. Cheers resounded throughout the city. Public toilets were reopened (although not yet for use by the public). The sunshine re-emerged, toilet cisterns began to clank as if water would soon flow. A third postcard from Nobby Keirans arrived in Dundee. A picture of the massed mounds of the Rockies, sent from Great Falls, Montana.

Moray experienced the intense joy of an explosion in the bowel which fired skitters and liquid into a dozen squirts in the bowl (possibly the cleanest bowl in the city). His system was so backed up that he began to vomit a thin yellow scum, whose smell was so awful that it made him repeat, vomit, move. His large bowel creaked and wrenched. His groans were heard in the street. But an hour later, it was running freely, gusts of yellow liquid splattering into the bowl. The flush wasn't working, but Moray was too overjoyed to care. He sat on the toilet all day and was up often in the night. His copious fundament. By the next morning he was able at last to eat. He walked slowly and stiffly to the local newsagent and bought a selection of redtops. All of them had made a meal of the strike. The headline in the *Stunna* was 'Flushed Out: Sewage Strikers Pull the Chain'. The *Horror* had 'Ordure Restored After Strikers Crap Out'. The *Recorder*: 'Helloo, It's Over: Normal Sewage Will Pee Resumed'. McLean and his acolytes had come up with: 'Council Po-Faced in Strike Shitty: Lid Closes on Bog Strike.'

Returning to the house in the strong sunshine, Moray enjoyed the pleasure of a fart, secure in the knowledge that his stainless-steel underpants remained dry. Slowly the city returned to something like its normal existence, input equalled output without accretion. All surplus was removed, processed and eliminated without question and the cludgiemen, 6 per cent better off, were flushed with success achieved without major effort or strain.

Part 5

Flood Tide

27

The tinkling wisping interferences in the roof beams and slates, which had sent Gavin into a restful sleep, woke him when it stopped. A freshening breeze rattled the slates and brought distant thunder, pleasantly distant, its dim echo around the hills on either side of the Carse. Then the sound of downpour, drilling down in slanting lines, bouncing off the slates into the guttering, the downpipes, the rain barrels, making a musical tinkling as it descended to the drains. There was a slight breeze, and with it a scent of ozone, of heat released, stirring the curtains. Gavin felt the abandonment of sleep fetch him.

In the morning, rain was falling as if it would continue the whole day. It was very welcome, after weeks of unabated heat. Looking out of the dormer window in the bedroom, everything was green. Gavin could see puddles formed on the caked earth of the fields. If he squinted through one eye, the puddles could be made to link up with the river. The sky was heaving, bulging with rain, occluding the sun; the daylight was grudging; it was a very dull and grim Saturday.

Saturday, 14 August, 8.00 a.m.

On the building site, the construction workers of Typhon Contracts Ltd, brought in as usual on the convoy of lorries, huddled in the encampment of portacabins, unable to work. Each of the dozen cabins was full of men smoking and swearing, playing cards on makeshift tables. Cigarette smoke trailed upwards from the metal

219

doors. The window panels were white with condensation, the wooden floors slippery with mud. Battered blackened kettles boiled merrily on calor gas stoves. At eight-thirty, greeted by some jeering and jocularity, the site engineer arrived and, accompanied by the foremen, walked a little way into the site. Mostly, this was just for show, they could see from the site office that it was an impassible morass where bulldozers, far less workmen, might get stuck. Nothing could be done until it dried out. The men were loaded back into the lorries and sent home.

11.00 a.m.

The officers in the operations room at the Forth Coastguard Station at Fife Ness, which covers the coastline from Berwick to Montrose, were aware that the tides entering the estuary in a matter of hours were the spring-tides, the equinoctial springs – highest of the year – a flood tide which surged in and remained at a high level for almost eight hours. The rainfall over the last fourteen hours was already within sight of the monthly total and, unusually, the entire Tay Catchment Area had had the same weather patterns for several days. There was an alarming quantity of water building up in the system. It all came down to timing. The coastguard officers knew there would be flooding, but not where, how much or when. They spent a lot of time examining computer displays of the rain-gauge statistics on all the tributaries. They initiated contact with the Hydro-Board about spare storage capacity in the reservoirs. If necessary, water from the western end of the flood plain could be drawn off into the mighty reservoirs. There was considerable capacity, even though the reservoirs were quite full, but the problem was that only overflow from upstream areas could be diverted in this way. Most of the reservoirs were too high up to be of much use because the problem was going to be in the estuary.

1.00 p.m.

By lunch time, a belt of heavier rain was sweeping across most of central Scotland with occasional thunder and lightning. The weather bureau at BBC Radio Scotland put out a general prediction of further prolonged rainfall, especially heavy in the east. This was broadcast by Radio Tay, Wave FM and Grampian TV. The weather pattern over the whole of the Tay remained steadfastly similar.

3.00 p.m.

Standing in the wheelhouse of a small crab fishing boat from Arbroath that was labouring across the mouth of the Tay estuary some hours after the rest of the fleet, two fishermen were aware of exceptionally heavy swell at the tidal bar. Hunched in yellow sou-westers, they had listened to the coastguard's warnings of the spring-tide and were peering through the mist watching for on-shore lights and yellow buoys that marked the dangerous Gaa sands off Monifieth. Visibility was poor.

'Can't see the Spit buoy, Jeem,' said one. 'She's usually to starboard.'

'Aye, min. There's a recht swell running. Surge tide. Look's like it'll be a heh ane. Just like the coastgaird boy said.'

'Whit – no hear ye . . . ?'

'Ah said, it's a heh ane. The tide . . .'

'Ach, we'll be a'recht . . . get roon . . . the Buddon Ness.'

'Aye, likely . . .'

'The ither lads will a be tied up the noo.'

'Haein a pint in the Harbour Bar.'

'Ach – there's the foghorn. We must be ower near. We'd better get a bittie further oot. To come in fae due west . . . ye ken.'

'Whit? Aye, aye, let her oot as far she goes . . . an hud on!'

6.00 p.m.

Gavin spent the day around the house, mostly reading in the living room. Carly was working till early evening and had taken the car, dropping Susan off at her friend's house on the way. Little Kenny played quite happily at Gavin's feet. The rain slid down the panes in translucent wavy lines. Once, he went to the back door and stood watching the watery scene through the high iron-mesh fence which had been erected six feet from his garden wall and which ran around the site on three sides right down to the river, a total length of about four miles. Daylight had barely appeared and there was a smudged fogginess low over the devastated fields. The ditch which ran around the gable end of the garden was flooded with a tumultuous current of green muddy water. The fields were patterned with large puddles gradually seeping together to form vast lakes. The building site was an abandoned swamp as far as the river. No working there this weekend. The barges anchored off the shore were deserted. Gavin could see right across now to Balmerino, some pinpoints of faint yellow lights. In among the maze of trenches and concrete foundations, which resembled the ruins of an ancient city abandoned to history, the pile of massive lumber and tree roots marked the levelled ridge where the ancient wood had stood. Gavin wondered if this rain was nature's revenge. He grinned at the thought, and went back indoors. One up for Mother Nature, and it was still raining! He hoped it would rain for weeks.

Carly came back, rushing indoors, and divested herself in the hall of the blue poncho cape. 'Soaked – and that was only from getting out of the car. When is it going to stop?'

'Ach, it's just rain.'

'What's bothering you?'

'Nothin's bothering me. I've had a nice peaceful day.'

'Kenny been good?'

'Ach, he had a wee tantrum earlier when I had to feed him, but he's had a little snooze and now he's okay again. I've got the tea on.'

It was still raining when they went to bed. Gavin glanced out at it as he pulled the curtains. 'If it keeps up like this,' he said, gleefully, 'there'll be no work on that building site well into next week. Isn't it great?'

'As long as we don't get flooded out. We're quite low here.'

'We're alright, we're still twenty feet above sea-level you know. Anyway those floods in Perth and the Earn valley were in February because of lots of melting snow. We're high enough here and that

222

wee burn takes all the flooding in the fields away from the house anyway.'

11.00 p.m.

The new shift at the Coastguard offices at Fife Ness entered the ops room out of the blustering rain. The three men removed their dripping sou'westers and studied the roster chalked on the slate while the kettle boiled. Computer screens continually updated columns and rows of rain-gauge and harbour statistics.

'Spring-tide is full on now across the Forth, Eden and Tay,' the shift supervisor said, wiping his spectacles. 'Aye, it'll be high at the harbour at Dundee,' he predicted. He glanced at the clock. 'Twenty-three hundred hours.'

'You're right,' the chief agreed, coming into the ops room on a late visit. 'This heavy rain will fair boost the tide levels. The estuary's big enough to hold it. If there was going to be a problem we'd have heard from Bracknell by now.'

'The problem is the water-rate,' said the younger man, putting his specs back on. 'And that's one thing we can't measure. If the rain water runs off fast in the stormwater ducts, and if the current is strong, it could clear the harbour bar before the incoming tide has a chance to push it back. On the other hand, it could be stopped by the incoming salt water.'

'Na!' snorted the chief, and gave a short laugh. 'That's no how it works. See, the water flow in the lower estuary is much, much slower than it is in the upper river and the tributaries. The velocity of the current in spring-tides is approximately six knots per hour at Broughty Castle, ye ken, but only four knots from there to the tidal bar.' He cupped his broad, flat hands to demonstrate the theory. 'Stands to reason, narrower channels create faster flows. But the estuary is so wide and flat it acts just like a brake, slows down the flow.' He moved his hands in a line expressing width. 'I mean, it's two and a quarter miles wide at the road bridge, and, okay, only a mile at Broughty Ferry but nearly four miles at Invergowrie. The sheer scale of the thing is what prevents serious flooding. It can absorb millions of gallons nae bother. Millions. Different, of course, in the flood plains of the Earn and north of Perth. As ye'll mind from 1990 and 1993.' He glanced into the mug of coffee that one of the junior officers had handed him and added milk from a carton on the tin tray on the filing cabinet. 'And anyway, there's lots of different tidal movements, ye ken, tidal races and channels, and the flow is different in every part of the estuary. I've sailed a bittie there myself. Tricky waters,' he concluded.

'I still say there should be a system of flow meters for the lower estuary,' the junior officer persisted. 'That's where it matters for the shipping and the like.'

'You'll both have noticed, by the way,' the third man observed, on his way out of the room, 'that the Tay tributaries warning levels have moved from yellow to amber. It says on the screen that the NFU and the Department of Agriculture have been informed.'

'Uh-huh,' said the junior officer meaningfully, tapping a pencil on the screen, 'that means flooding on farmland areas is inevitable.'

'Aye, the claims will be going in,' said the supervisor quietly, looking out to the smudged lights across the Forth estuary, 'again.'

Thursday, 19 August, 10.00 a.m.

It was several days before Kevin Morrow was able to see for himself the devastation. Like everyone else, he had seen the astonishing helicopter footage shown by BBC Scotland. It had given him little more than a general impression of overturned Portakabins and floating logs. Bloated dead cattle like used tea-bags. The estuary extending a mile inland into the Carse. The mud had wiped out the distinguishing features of the building site, made it seem like an extension of the sandbanks offshore.

The police finally authorised an inspection visit to the site. The A85 was back to full operation, but the small roads in the Carse were impassable. Westbound traffic on the A85 was sluggish as it headed out of the city. Some parts of the road were slick with mud and sand. Kevin drove cautiously, thinking about the complicated consequences of his predicament. The majority of the investment lost was his own. And it *was* lost, gone, dissolved into the river, flushed into the sea. He had no need to phone insurance companies to discover that the disaster came under the heading of 'act of God'. There could be no payout – even if things had been done by the book, which they hadn't been. And there was the sodding Killick Report, which suggested vast and ruinously expensive flood barriers, reinstatement of the river bank, floating booms and God knows what else.

The minor road that led to Errolbank Station was discoloured with mud. The hedges had acted to filter all the disgusting detritus that had floated this way, which was starting to smell bad. A hundred yards further on, the road became indistinguishable from the fields on either side. A council dumper truck and several workmen were standing in high rubber boots near a police Landrover. He saw the heavy-duty tractor vehicle he'd hired from Typhon Construction, standing in what looked to be deep mud.

Kevin parked the Jag behind the police car and began to put on the thigh waders. He got out of the car and slid into ankle-deep mud. The policeman came squelching over.

'Can't go any further, sir,' he said. 'Too dangerous. There's parts there that are three or four feet deep.'

Kevin told the policeman who he was, adding 'and ehv hired that big tractir.' He fetched his binoculars out of the car.

'Well, you'll no get much further than the junction,' the policeman said, shaking his head. 'It's a bad idea, but I cannae stop you.' He pulled off his radio to make a report. 'Or where the junction used to be,' he added. 'Trouble is the ground slopes steeply there, so it'll be deep. I'll radio in and get them to have an emergency vehicle on standby. Good luck to you.' He indicated to the tractor driver to back up.

Looking south to the water from the high cab of the vehicle, all Kevin could see was an enormous mud slick, shining in the wan sunshine, with what looked like upturned boxes and treetrunks jumbled about in it. The white specks were, he knew already, the bloated corpses of cattle. Amid the desolation were the roofs of several isolated houses and farms, surrounded and invaded by the sea of grey mud up to at least their window level. Of the security fencing there was no sign.

225

'Sure you still want to go down there?' the driver asked Kevin, as they adjusted their helmets and earphones. Kevin would sit behind him. 'It looks unstable and right dangerous.'

Kevin looked at the man's side-turned face, the red, patient middle-aged face of a local. 'Your name is?' he asked.

'John Cameron,' the man answered. 'Aye, they cry me Cammie, Mr Morrow.' There was no trace of irony or gloating in the man's voice or his eyes. Bill Muir had chosen the man well.

'Well, Cammie, eh need ti see wuthir thi mud wull run aff soon, ir iz ut gonna stick. Ehd like t' see wut thi story iz at thi site buhldins tae.'

Cameron's eyebrows raised just a fraction but he rubbed at his nose vigorously with his heavy-duty gloves. 'Right you are, sir. We'll tak it slow. Anything deeper than four feet and I doot we'll hae to turn back.'

'Ahriyht. Jist dae yir best.'

Cameron released the hand brake, engaged low gear and the monolith began to roll heavily forward, engine roaring, mud sputtering from its eight twelve-foot diameter wheels. Smoke poured out of the two upright exhaust pipes. Kevin noticed a crowd of sightseers standing on the rise at the outskirts of the village and wondered if they had come to gloat. The juggernaut rolled forward, churning and beginning to lurch and tip into deep mud. The driver accelerated. The smoke thickened.

'Easy does it,' Cameron shouted above the engine noise. 'We'll get there, boss.'

Kevin noticed that the mudslide looked shallower to their right and saw that that was the tarmac road that led up the hill to Errolbank. He tapped the driver on the shoulder. 'Treh ti git iz up ti thi road,' he ordered, 'so's eh kin hae a shuftie wi thi binocs.'

'Right you are.' Cameron was quite happy to extricate the tractor from the mud and soon the wheels were coming almost clean out of the mud. 'How far up?'

'Here wull dae. Stop.' He opened the side window and began to scan the landscape.

11.00 a.m.

Further up the hill, among a group of locals, Gavin Cathro and Jed Arthur watched the progress of the tractor up the hill.

'Boy's stopped,' Jed said. 'Engine's aff. He's looking oot wi his binoculars. He'll be the developer boy alright.'

Old Tom leaned on his stick. 'Aye, no a braw sight for the boy.'

'He'll be insured,' Gavin said. 'There's no skin off his nose. It's me who's had to suffer. I'm the one who's lost my home.'

'Ah, yi can stay as long as yi like, man, yi ken that,' Jed said.

'That's appreciated, but Carly and the kids are at her mum's over in Tayport, and I'd rather we were all together, no offence.'

'Aye, right, man, that's obvious like. But as ah telt yi, ah'm sure they could a fit in, ye ken . . .'

'Ah, it's Carly, Jed . . . she . . . you ken what I'm saying?'

'That damn man and his bloody big ideas!' Scott Rennett said. 'Damn and blast him. I'm going to give him a piece of my mind.'

'Good idea, man, let's all go,' Jed said. 'Coming?'

The knot of locals, some dozen or so, descended the hill towards the tractor, led by Scott Rennett and Old Tom waving his walking stick. The policeman who was sitting in his car saw what was happening and got out and tried to catch up. The Grampian TV crew sitting in the Outside Broadcast Unit heard the commotion.

'You're that developer fella?' Old Tom shouted up at the tractor. 'The ane that's caused a this disaster . . .'

At first it looked like the men up in the cab would ignore them. The sun sparkled on their domed helmets. Then a side window was slid open, and the man in the rear took off his helmet and shouted down.

'Wut a loada crap! Eh didna cause nothing. Ut wiz an act a God, man, an act a God. Naebdee's ti blame.'

'If you'd no torn oot a they trees man, ' Jed shouted. 'An took awa the bank . . .'

'Aye, you've no lost anything,' Gavin said. 'It's me that lost my home. See that cottage there – that's where we lived, yeah. Me, my wife and the kids. We could have drowned in there . . .'

'Aw, 'z yirsel, Pict-features?' the man said. 'Fir thi last time, this wiz naethin t' dae wi thi buhldin ir meh company at a. Noo bog aff, ir eh'll ca thi polis. Aw, here thi come!'

11.10 a.m.

Kevin sat beside the driver as the tractor sloughed through thick mud and slowly returned to the police checkpoint where he had left his car. He had seen enough. The site might take months to dry out. There was the cost of replacement gear and compensation for loss of equipment. An utter disaster – and the prospects of getting government compensation were not high.

11.12 a.m.

Gavin watched the film crew drive away, listening to his personal stereo tape player: Bob Dylan, 'Watching The River Flow', *and as long as it does* . . . He had been as forceful as he could be in the interview because he was thinking of Lewis Summers in his hospital bed and of Carly, Susan and wee Kenny. That was what had made him angry, almost incoherently so.

6.00 p.m.

Grampian and STV used almost six minutes of the footage of the altercation at Errolbank in a big story: CONSTRUCTION WORK BLAMED FOR TAY FLOOD DAMAGE, which claimed that the developer, 'who made a visit to the site today', was being blamed for work which had altered – and weakened – the river bank. It cited some of the most damaging provisional conclusions of the Interim Report produced by Dr Marina Killick. It also allowed several ugly-looking locals to shout their mouths off, Kevin noticed, watching the programme at Daniel's house.

Next day, nearly all the qualities and tabloids used the story, most on their front pages, some with pictures grabbed from the TV. One face appeared prominently, that of the long-haired man called Cathro: the one he'd called 'Pict-features'. Some bloody papers also featured the story about the so-called near-disaster allegedly caused by one of his dredgers which had been anchored offshore at the site. Although one had sunk at anchor, the other had drifted downriver, beaching itself on the Naughton Bank just off Wormit. If it had continued, according to the reporter, it might have struck one of the bridges . . . He threw the papers straight into the bin.

Friday, 20 August, 2.00 p.m

But Kevin's troubles were only just beginning. The Hay Estates, owners of all the houses and farms in the Carse which had been destroyed or damaged by the flooding, were contemplating legal action against Loyal Homes and, sensing impending financial crisis, all of his debtors – bloody leeches – were trying to get in first.

4.00 p.m.

According to his accountants, it would be a week or two before they would know whether he could survive the crisis. He wasn't going to wait around. He ordered them to batten down all the hatches and, in the meantime, to transfer all his liquid assets to the holding company, Blue Water Ltd, in Jersey. While they prepared to take the flak in London, Kevin returned to his flat, left the engine running while he packed a small suitcase.

8.00 p.m

'Fuck thi lot o thum!' was Kevin's final remark to his brother from a payphone at Glasgow airport just before boarding the plane to Boston for his connecting flight to Antigua.

28

Daniel drove alone across the bridge, sunlight darting his eyes despite the smoked glass. The river was sullenly high, a muddy surge of sickish green, but plated down the middle and riveted with diamonds where the sun, oozing behind the Fife hills, blow-torched the water. The hull of the mud barge stuck awkwardly in the silt near the rocks off Wormit was silhouetted like a new Tay Whale. Tiny flashes showed where people on the shore were taking pictures. Not for the first time, Daniel regretted his lack of involvement in the detail of the project. Basic scientific advice should have prevented the foolhardy attempt to cut a permanent channel through the sandbank. A mad idea. Sandbanks were beyond human control. They built up, they disappeared, they returned elsewhere. What had Kevin been thinking of? He shaded his eyes from the glare as he exited the bridge and turned on to the roundabout. His eyes were deteriorating. That was the next thing. Spectacles. Nearly everyone he knew had been wearing specs for years, but his vanity had resisted the need to go for an eye test.

He parked the car and found his parents in the kitchen.

'Mon in, Danny,' his mother said, smiling. She was wearing a smart pink trouser suit with white court shoes. His father in his usual crumpled nylon shirt, head was slumped forward on his chest. She saw the direction of his gaze.

'Yir faithir's jist haein ane o eez wee naps, ken, afore eez tea.'

For the first time, Daniel saw the wheelchair. 'Wutziz? When did this happen?'

'Aw, well, son, see, eez bin under thi doaktirz fir a lang time, as yi ken,' his mother said. 'Eez bin aff thi legs fir a week, bit wuv eh bin wahntin thi wheelchair, ken. Ut wiz ordir'd, bit wuv hud ti wait months fir ane. Thirz a queue fir wheelchairs like, ken, the NHS. Nae enough t'gae roon. Fir abdee like.'

Daniel shook his head in disbelief. 'Uf yid tellt iz eh cud a got yi ane nae bathir. Ee looks awfy, diz ee no? Jist a wee ald mannie. Christ, eez no seevin'ay!'

'Shusht!' Betty said, holding her fingers to her lips. 'Come awa ben, an we kin hae a wee chat. Z' brah t' see yi, Danny.' His mother led him through the front hall to the back of the house and the cork-tiled conservatory with the view of the river and the hills to the north. Daniel had no trouble in locating the swamp of the building site. It looked like an enormous cowpat on a putting green.

'Yir faithir disna like this room at a,' his mother was saying. 'Bit eh think ut's brah. Eh come in here sometimes jist ti wahtch thi wattir, the birdies an that. Mind, ut gits awfy wahrum.'

'How no yase thi air-conditioners then?'

'Aw, eh canna go them, son. Naw, eh jist open thi windows . . . thi wutchumacallums . . . Frenchie doors . . . ti git mehsel a bittie breeze.'

They sat down in the cane armchairs. Daniel's seat was unaccountably lumpy. He removed a large teddy bear, which he threw into the corner. 'Lissen maw,' he began, 'young Kevin's kinda lost thi heid on this buhldin fiasco – eez buggir'd aff ti oor place in Antigua.'

'Aw, that's nice. Wee holiday is it?'

'Naw, wut eh mean iz – eez buggir'd aff oot o eez responsibilities. Eez left iz in thi shit, mithir.'

His mother glanced sharply at him. 'Za brah thing t' say aboot yir ane brithir! You laddies dinna lit iz inta yir comins and goins. Eh say ee musta hud eez ain reasons. Daniel . . .' she looked closely into his face . . . 'uts yirsel ehm mair bathir'd aboot. Yuv no yir troubles ti seek. How is Kylie?'

At the mention of the name, Daniel turned to look out the window. 'Shiz daein ahriyt at thi clinic – so ehm tellt.'

231

'Pair wee thing. Ehv nivir met ir, bit ehm stull sorry fir thi wee lass.'

Daniel pulled a face. 'Ehm sorry eh nivir brung ir ti see yiz, maw, bit mibbe, ut wiz a fir thi best. Shiz jist no riyt fir iz, maw. Shiz owir young. Thi hale ehdea wis bliddy wrang fae thi stert.'

'Eh did wonder, son, when yi tellt iz ir age . . .'

'Eh. Eh, well, ehm takin care o ut, ken, tidyin up meh ain mess eftir iz. Zat no wut yiz wir eh telln iz ti dae? So, ehm peyin fir thi detox an fir thi divorce.' He glanced at the neat figure of his mother sitting knees together on the edge of the seat gazing out at the broad line of brilliance rippling through the mighty river. 'Huz t'be done, maw.'

His mother made no signs to indicate disapproval. Finally, she sighed. 'Eh, riyt, son. Ut's a pi'y yi cudna mak a go o ut. Shiz number three.'

'Thirz a lot mair fish in thi sea. Z' thi wey ut iz wi iz. Big mistake.'

Betty attempted to change the subject. 'Eh hud a call fae Tracey thi ithir day. Shiz daein brah. Ir business is boomin despite the lehs printed beh thi pippers.'

Daniel closed his eyes and spoke quietly. 'Dinna even mention thi name t' iz, mithir, eh? Eh dinna wahnt t' talk aboot ir, see ir, ir even hear aboot ir. Eftir wut she done ti Kylie – thi bliddy hoor! She beh'ir keep oot meh road. Ehm telln yi!'

There was an embarrassed silence. Daniel coughed and wiped his nose. 'Anyway, maw, back ti Kevin. Eez no rung yi, no? See, ee didna tak eez mobile. Z' no easy trehin ti git in touch wi um. Thi bliddy thing o ut iz – thirz guid news. Eh, thi government ir gonna pay oot compensation fir the failure o the flood-warnin system, an ut wull cover oor investment an overheads.'

'Sorta insurance?' his mother queried.

'Wut? Naw, naw. Thirz nuthin comin fae thi insurers. That pert o thi deal wiz a wee bit dodgy.'

'Za above meh heid . . . this stuff . . . eh dinna ken . . .'

'See, the flood-warnin system is a statutory responsibility – ken, the government – so there's liability. That means compensation. We hud 45 per cent in thi company. Ut wull cover that jist brah.' He grinned for the first time since he'd arrived. 'O coors, thi ithir fowir investors wull git sumhin an a: thull git a leh'ir fae iz explainin thi insurance cock-up an how thir wull be nae pey-oot.'

'That disna seem fair.'

'Ehm a businessman, mithir,' Daniel protested. 'Aw eh, thull no be happy bit snoh meh fault thi renn fell. Thull probably sue iz anyway. Ut wull tak twa year ti come ti coort an ut wull get threw riyt oot. Thuv a signed the pippers, so thi dinna hae a leg ti stand on.'

'Ir yi hungry, son? Eh kid fix yi sumhin.'

'Cup a coffee wull dae iz, maw.'

'Eh wahnt ti check on Ron.'

While he was waiting for coffee, his mobile went off. He located it in the jacket pocket on the back of the chair and opened it out, stepping outside on to the patio. It was Kevin.

'Lo, bro . . .'

'Kev, mi man! Waur ir yi?'

Kevin laughed. 'Waur um ih? Yi dinna wahnt t'ken, Dan!' He laughed again. Daniel could hear music in the background. 'Lashings Bar,' Kevin told him. 'Yi ken thi ane, near Nelson's dockyaird. Eh took thi moh'ir an drove doon here.'

'Aw eh. Thi bar on thi beach?'

'Riyt bruv. Thi surf's jist twin'ay feet awa fae iz as eh speak. Lissen . . .'

Daniel listened. Watching the ugly green surge at Balmerino, he listened to azure waves warmly palming the beach in the sway of the busy bar, to the chink of glasses highly charged with the laughter and tears of happy music.

'Okay,' Daniel said. 'Z' brah, Kev, bit when ir yi comin hame?'

'Hame? Eh've only bin here a week.'

'Eh need yi here, man. See, thirz gonna be government dosh in compensation fir the failure o the flood-warnin systems. Eh've worktit oot. Wull cover wir losses.'

The line seemed to go dead. Then was reconnected to the Caribbean, distant waves . . . 'That's brah,' Kevin was saying. 'Ehm pleased fir yi. Bit ehm jist no bathir'd. Eh need a break. Yi kin sortit, eh've nae doots.'

'Aw dinna dae this t'iz, man! Yir crappin oot, iy?'

'Eh canna be ersed, ken wut ehm seyin?'

'Yi wee crapper! Yir forgettin ehm a bankrupt? Eh hae t'keep mehsel ahent thi scenes. Snoh easy fir me. Frontin ut wiz wut yi wir t'dae.'

Eh lik ut here, man. Z' dead brah. Sweemin in thi ocean, man, ut's, ut's, well, kinda meh natural terrain. Eh kin be mehsel. An eh'v met a cracker o a lassie . . .'

Daniel's impatience cut him short. 'Aw, noo wir cuttin t' thi chase!'

'Yir wrang, bruv – z' mair than rumpy. Here, man, here, thi wattirz is blue an wahrum an – mair important, man – thir on thi beach, no in yir hoose an halfway up thi fuckin golf course! Yi ken wut ehm seyin?'

'Yir funny! Zis yir last word?'

'Sure – eh'm keepin a rum punch waitin.'

'Well, gie ir ane fir me, yi bam. An gie iz a bell sometime. Ir eh'll send the Inland Revenue boys doon fir a holiday!'

A Seat for all Posterity

Green tiles and white tiles and large shiny white pedestals rising to shoulder height for concealment, privacy. Brass gleaming dully, tinkling of water. Mine, thinks Moray Neill, as it drizzles down into the substantial Victorian ducts of the Seabraes Gentlemen's Lavatory, at number 40, Perth Road. Spacious, gleaming. In the parlance of the *Scottish Source*, a superbog. Light coming in from the green thick glass panels overhead, the shadow of feet walking there. And under his own feet, mosaic tiles, Roman interlock. Alone, he thinks, as he shakes off odd drops. Après moi, le deluge, he thinks, becoming aware of a sudden and contrary urge to windward. He has to go into a cubicle. A shadow on the glass above looms into the temple, footsteps on the steps coming in. Haste in this matter of waste. Moray, unzipped, pushes a coin into the slot and turns the handle and without difficulty, enters and pulls the solid oak door behind him. Solid oak, built to withstand a siege from without. And to maintain rigid secrecy in the privy council. Thuds behind the arras. Bruits in the balkans.

234

Seated, Moray, considering, faking, the relief of Mafeking. Laid out in ink on news-sheets brought here by prosperous Victorians in lum-hats, tarred brims. Major colonialists. Founders of colonies overseas. Schemes of colonial irrigations. The white man's burden unburdened here. Schemes closer to home too. These sewers by Messrs Bateman; labyrinthine brick ovoids beneath the city of Dundee; his testing ground for construction of the sewers of Paris, a few years later. A watering hole for rough buffaloes. He could imagine the thud of solid workmen's boots on the steps, the unbuttoning of horn buttons, the unslinging of fobs, the preparatory loosening of waistcoats, the whole operation most rigorously conducted with the Victorian attention to time-and-motion efficiency. Gladstonian men, jaws clamped tightly between hedges of hair, intent on keeping up the rhythm. Men not lacking in fibre, sound men, men with voices of thunder and the crack of doom between their cheeks. Reliable men, men who'd still be behind you when the seas began to get choppy. Mighty men in imperial chambers. Men whose hands pulled together the links of the chains of empire over the waters. Men of devotion, bending in prayer, regular as clockwork. Men of strictures who never loosened their morals, who enshrined the rules in epithets for others:

White Papers will be issued at the Cabinet Office.

They probably had an entire library section devoted to the Scientific System of Loosening of the Human Bowel: *Methods and Practice*, by Dr A. P. Ure-Dollop. And other fundamental matters. Moray closed his eyes and listened to the silence. Almost meditating. He had grown tired of the slimy trade he had got himself into. The money was welcome, but his earlier fame seemed to have abandoned him. He had a couple of stories to chase up: the fall into debt of the local lottery winner, the victim of a botched sex-change operation, the rash of pregnancies of pre-teen girls, the soldier sacked from the Queen's Own for being a closet gay . . . and dozens more. Though whether he could sell any of them was now more dubious. It was as if his confidence had gone, since falling out with Sharkey.

At bottom, all was muck and brass. He made brass out of other

235

people's muck. Fundus del mondo. Arsch dei Welt. On that gloomy thought, it was, he knew, time to go. He heaved himself up, feeling the lethargy of his bones. Getting old. Papers, cold and rough. New editions required. A matter of supply and demand: he must telegram Rear Admiral Shanks-Armitage and the Colonial Under-Secretary. He pulled up his trousers and buckled up. Unlocked the door and revealed himself in the doorway, across tiled surfaces. Suddenly, Moray realised that no-one had come in at all. The footsteps heard had come to nothing. *Unused*. Moray ran water on his hands. No towels. Disused smell too.

Up the stairs. The fresh night air. A quick glimpse of the stars. All was in ordure. And so back to his base inglorious trade. Not so much a dealing in souls as in arseholes, in memorials familiar to colons, not carved in columns, epitaphs of turds not words. He mustn't complain. End or be. His calling was to be a spigot and faucet in Sir Philip de Cundy's great rum puncheon, supping and pishing amongst what passes for life among the lower echelons, the realms of waste and opportunities wasted. Sediment and sentiment. Life in the raw, life at its *Source*. Ironic it should end where it began, getting sedimental.

29

We walked down the steep brae to the quaint harbour where sunlight was reflecting brilliantly off painted surfaces and glass and metal. Several yachts were up on stocks on the north quay and a dozen colourful craft listed sideways over their hulls in the shelter of the harbour wall. Some boys, probably not local, cast orange floats from the harbour wall into the diminished water. Dark rocks stood head and shoulders in the shallows outside the harbour mouth. Across the river we could see large and prosperous houses ascending the treed hill, and, to the west, tall scaffolding towers of oil rigs ready for dismantling, with the city beyond. I was persisting with an obsession I had about sightlines, from a programme I had seen on TV.

'There is no such thing as a straight line. I mean nowhere . . . in the world . . . in the universe.'

'You'd better explain.' Marjorie said, laughing.

'Nothing to explain. It's a mathematical fact. Anything which might appear to be a straight line is only a fragment of the circumference of a circle. There's a very simple formula you can use to work out the radius of the circle if you know the length of the apparently straight line. Anyway, the point is . . .'

'Oh good, there is a point,' Marjorie giggled. 'No straight lines but there is a point.'

'Figuratively speaking.'

'Oh I see! *Figuratively*!'

'Don't get me started!' I said. 'There is no actual point in

237

mathematical terms. Everything is pointless. A point is only symbolic, theoretical, but you're making me digress. The idea is that in nature there are only circles and arcs; everything bends around the horizon, rotates upon itself. Everything is kind of in the process of being reversed, encircled. What goes around comes around. Everything comes to he who waits. Crewe Station will return to Einstein if he stands still long enough.'

She stopped and looked at me, with a startled expression. 'I won't even pretend that I know what you're going on about,' she said.

We had stopped to look into the shallow water of the dock near the slipway, water so clear we could see the sandy bottom. To our surprise we saw an enormous fish idling by.

'My God! look at the size of that!' I said.

'There's another,' Marjorie exclaimed. 'What are they, I wonder?'

'Pollack,' said an elderly man walking an enthusiastic Jack Russell. 'Wily fish. Those lads have no chance of catching them. No chance.'

We walked on a path that took us around the front of the new houses.

'Lucky beacon,' Marjorie said. 'Used to be lit by coal, then oil. A full-time job I should imagine, keeping the fires lit.'

'Lots of birds on the mudflat,' I noted. 'Look – turnstones, redshanks, dunlin, mallard, eiders. There's a pair of shelducks.'

'It's nice to be with someone who likes birds,' Marjorie said. 'No, really, you're very pleasant company.'

'Thank you, so are you. What are those?'

'I used to bring binoculars,' she said. 'Now, I see where you mean . . . could be purple sandpipers. I also see golden plovers, just there by that big puddle. It's great here at low tide. There's some lapwings and curlews. That bird flying low out there is a cormorant. So much to see.'

'The tide is very low. Fancy walking out to Lucky Scalp?'

Marjorie looked bemused. 'Can we walk out? I mean is it possible? It looks rather wet.'

'Well, we could take off our socks and shoes.'

238

It was quite muddy, but there is something exhilarating and bracing about walking in bare feet. The shingle scar of Lucky Scalp is about three-quarters of a mile out. It took us about twenty-five minutes. The mud was at its thickest just below the shingle beach, where a wide channel ran around the island. The island is small and shaped like an elongated 's' with a low stone-built shelter on its eastern end, which someone had tried to roof with logs and blue baling twine.

'It's ridiculous that I've never been out here before,' Marjorie said, as we stood in the strong breeze beside the shelter. 'Oh, that's a swan, I think,' she said, pointing towards Tentsmuir. 'In the bay.'

'Oh yes.'

'Isn't it great about Carly and Gavin moving back into their cottage?' she said. 'Best news I've had for ages. Not that I didn't enjoying having them with me, although it was a bit of a strain. Gavin's mum lives in Errolbank, you see, but she's in sheltered housing, couldn't put them up.'

'Yeah, and the new town plan being abandoned and the company going bankrupt. Serves them right.'

Looking east, we saw the prominent gasometers, the Law and Balgay humps, the four multi's standing high on the Hilltown, a few ships at harbour. A city with bridges, a city of aluminium and glass, concrete and steel, half-hidden behind a shifting mirage, reflecting sky in the wide waters, like the view of San Francisco from Alcatraz island. I thought of Uncle Ron, who had sailed for Fiddler's Green before he could swallow the anchor. I thought of Duncan Law on the seven seas. I heard inside my head, the thundering, threatening opening to Debussy's 'Dialogue du vent et de la mer'. It was in my blood, this place. I could not look on it objectively.

'Come on,' I said, swallowing the lump in my throat. I turned from Marjorie and began to tramp mud to the shore.

When I looked back, fifteen minutes later, Lucky Scalp and its curving shingle beach was almost indistinguishable, except for the spiky grass tufts. It had merged into the long curving scallops of mud. Everything was in abatement, empty, but I felt the opposite. I felt full of tears, swelling with remorse, or joy, I didn't know which.

I looked on the empty distant bay and it was as if the tide was fully in; I felt the effects of inundation, the surge and deluge and turgidity of some huge outpouring. I was washed up in some kind of catharsis, purified by some flood of emotion, some tumult in my blood stirred by this local lagoon. I stood and closed my eyes, and when I opened them again after several minutes, everything had an unexpected clarity. You know that sensation – when even the humblest thing has a magical significance, a tender glow – and detail is exhilaratingly perfect.

'That's Green Scalp,' Marjorie was saying at my elbow. 'That dark strip of seaweed and mud. It's full of mussels. That lovely golden sand there reaches right out into the huge shifting sandbank known as the Horseshoe. Because its shifting it's known as "foul ground". Are you alright?'

'Fine, fine.' And it was true. I felt full of joy.

We passed in front of a large iron sign post: GAS WARNING PIPELINE, which towered ten feet above us, before turning back along the seaweed-covered fence to the shore. With the pine trees backing the warm sand of the beach, it was, for long minutes at a time, like Corfu. There were the bleached stone blocks, like Trojan ruins, tumbled where time had tossed them, on the littoral.

I felt that year's first hint of cold air that afternoon, there by the river, the sun partly occluded by distant cloud, the sea-level the merest of smudges of felt-tip pen on the horizon. The detritus washed up, as in licked clean and given a new start. That's how I felt, renewed. Then I saw the seashell.

'It's a cowrie shell, is it?' she asked. 'Although I know nothing about seashells.'

'Don't know. Gastropod of some kind. Maybe it's a conch? So called because if you listen to it, you hear the murmur of your conscience.'

'Get away!'

I picked it up again, smooth alabaster of polished chitin. It was bone clean. I held it to my ear as I had done almost seven months before.

Marjorie watched me.

'I can hear nothing,' I said.

'Not possible,' she said.

'The sounds of silence. Wait – there's a sort of murmuring. I can almost make out . . . words . . . something that somebody said.'

'Echoes of the past?' Marjorie intoned in a mock-serious voice. 'More like you're making it up.'

I laughed. 'Yup. Seems a shame to leave this prehistoric telephone lying here . . .'

'Ha! That's a good one.'

'This shell is amazing. I mean, it must have come thousands of miles, from tropical seas, just to get here. And then, for me to find the very same shell again . . .'

'Let's see it,' Marjorie said, smilingly mystified. I handed it to her. 'It's big. Ah yes, that's a tropical shell alright. But just how do you think it got here?'

'It must have scuttled the floors of the seven seas. How do I know? It drifted . . .'

Once she stopped laughing she said: 'You have no idea, have you? I mean, the thing can't float and it's too delicate to travel far without being broken. No, someone has brought this here and dropped it. Or maybe someone coming back from a voyage dropped it over the side. It certainly hasn't come here under its own steam. What an incredible idea! You're an incurable romantic, I do believe!'

'Well, I am . . . I admit. Come on, let's walk out as far as we can go,' I said. 'The tide is way out. It's amazing out there.'

'Uh-huh. No way. I'm not going, nor should you. Too dangerous. What's the point? We can see from here.'

'The point? Does there have to be a point?' I asked, capering around her. 'Human life is tending towards pointlessness, towards absence of meaning. Or to such profusion of meanings that there is no single meaning. Maybe the point is there is no point?'

'That's awfy profound, professor! Anyway, shouldn't we fight such a tendency?'

'From birth to death – what could be more pointless? Survival of the species – the human duty to procreate – that used to be the point, but now we control our environment, manage our species, programme out our weak . . . so now, it's just a one-way trip, a relay race over a series of points. We exist at each of these points then we do not exist. But see, here, at the estuary, in a sense, everything comes back, returns, there is a circularity, a recycling of life. And the sense of it affects us. Must do.'

She stopped. I stopped. We were quite close, our elbows touching. She was looking out to the little dune hills that lead to Abertay Sands.

'How do you mean affects us?' she asked.

'Well . . . in some subconscious, psychic way. It's hard to explain. It's the sort of thing that only comes to you when you're talking about it. Sort of sudden realisation.' I began to warm to my theme. Funny how you can know what to say just as you're saying it, with no prior thought on the subject. 'Anyway, maybe this circularity is more obvious here, more visible, at an estuary I mean, and somehow, by some process I don't know, it seeps into our consciousness and gives us calm. I find that it does. Maybe you don't?'

'Hmn, I suppose so. It's a peaceful place.'

'Yeah, and your man Douglas Young put his finger on it, explained it all.'

Marjorie looked baffled. 'My man . . . Oh! Yes, Douglas Young. He was related to my husband. I'd forgotten I'd told you that.'

'Poet, pacifist, patriot, professor. Lanky, long-bearded galoot. Quite likely, by all accounts, to harangue you in a great gush of voluble and eloquent Greek. Which is ironic because it was a Greek, Hippocrates, who said that the best waters are those that flow from high places and earthy hills.'

I turned to wave vaguely at the Sidlaws. 'He commended especially waters whose flow breaks towards the rising sun. I rest my case. He had it all worked out. And Douglas Young was hugely interested in metaphysical tides too. Spent most of his life in the headwaters of national consciousness.'

'Pity I never actually met him,' Marjorie said. 'He was quite a guy. A very distant relative. Very distantly related to Derek.'

We had come to the ramparts of the dunes and gazed out on the long bleached sands that stretched out to infinity, to the faint white dot that was the Bellrock Lighthouse, studded with tiny dots of seals in the shimmering haze of the pale horizon.

'Doesn't it feel great to be here, poised between two contrary elements, the sky and the sea, and two opposing movements, the sun or moon and the tides? The variety of possibilities, the range of identities is so immense . . . it creates a quality of emotional recurrence which is life enhancing like nowhere else . . .'

Marjorie laughed. 'Hah!'

'Seriously, there's something about this place. I don't know exactly what it is, but it makes me feel as if I'm *somewhere*. As if I'm on the planet; no, that's not what I mean. As if it's a sort of destination, you know, in itself, a terminus, not a kind of place you're at on the way to somewhere else. That's mystical mumbo-jumbo, but I've always had this kind of feeling of needing to be at the centre ever since I was a child. The sort of centre, a sort of place that was somewhere. For a long time I thought that it was in the south of France, the Riviera, then in Minorca, and I've stayed in both these areas for a time, but they weren't complete. They turned out to be way-stations, nice enough in their own way but not *entire*. Not somewhere you could settle. Forever, like, without needing to go . . . to move on. This is nothing to do with geographical centres; it's more a sort of psychic resonance that would be in some way in accord with my – I don't know, maybe my – personality. And maybe, here, well . . . On the other hand, maybe my feelings are just a product of my living here for six weeks. Sentimental attachment just.'

'I know one place I don't belong is in the classroom,' Marjorie said, dolefully.

'I've never asked you about teaching.'

'Oh – death of the soul,' she said. 'If you're talking about increasing pointlessness, then teaching is it.'

That put a damper on the conversation. An oystercatcher's rippling *keveee, keveee* intruded distantly upon the whitewashed regression.

'I'd like to walk off the Point a bit,' I said, rising, 'out on the sands. Coming?'

'How far do you plan to go?' she asked uncertainly.

'To the Lighthouse,' I declaimed, then laughed. 'No, no, of course not. Just a mile or so. Just till I can feel myself at the brink.

243

The sort of point of tension between faith and no faith. I need to affirm. I want to run and jump and roll all over in the sand. Ideally, I – we – would take all our clothes off!'

'My goodness!'

'I want to just let go and . . . well . . .'

'I don't think we should go any further,' Marjorie said, hanging back.

'Come on!' I shouted. 'Let yourself go!' And I began to run along the sand and somehow I felt I was back at the beginning, or maybe it was the beginning the first time. I turned around and waved at the shoreline, the dense trees, the lonely figure of Marjorie standing there, casting a single shadow on the sand. 'Come on!' I heard myself shouting. 'You can get so far out you're almost off the edge.'